More Critical Praise for Anthony C. Winkler

"Winkler never glosses over Jamaican deprivation, prejudice, and violence, yet the love of language—and the language of love—somehow conquers all. It's almost as if P.G. Wodehouse had strolled into the world of Bob Marley . . . Or as if a more salacious Alexander McCall Smith tangled with the younger, funnier V.S. Naipaul. But, truth be told, Winkler sounds like no one but himself . . . A body of work to treasure and trumpet." —*The Independent* (UK)

"Every country (if she's lucky) gets the Mark Twain she deserves, and Winkler is ours, bristling with savage Jamaican wit, heart-stopping compassion, and jaw-dropping humor all at once."
—Marlon James, author of *The Book of Night Women*

"Hilarious, bawdy, vivid, and insightful . . . Winkler is unequivocally unafraid . . . Winkler can ask the big questions without becoming tiresome." —*Caribbean Review of Books*

Praise for *God Carlos*

"Readers are transported along to Jamaica, into Winkler's richly invented 16th century, where his flawless prose paints their slice of time, in turn both brutally graphic and lyrically gorgeous. Comic, tragic, bawdy, sad, and provocative, this is a thoroughly engaging adventure story from renowned Jamaican author Winkler, sure to enchant readers who treasure a fabulous tale exquisitely rendered." —*Library Journal*

"A gusty, boisterous, and entertaining slice of historical fiction . . . In scenes of a mixture of pride, madness, and comedy, Carlos plays out his role as deity among the naked islanders . . . living a fantasy that most readers will find believable, if horrific. Along with the horror, the book does offer some beautiful moments of discovery, as when, as Winkler narrates, the ship takes the Mona Passage to Jamaica . . . we hear of an Edenic island, green and aromatic, opened like a wildflower. For all of its scenes of braggadocio and brutality, th
like that vision." —Alan Cheuse,

"Darkly irreverent . . . With a sharp tongue, Winkler, a native of Jamaica, deftly imbues this blackly funny satire with an exposé of colonialism's avarice and futility."
—*Publishers Weekly*

"A tale of the frequently tragic—and also comic—clash of races and religions brought about by colonization . . . His narrative is rich in historical detail and without an agenda. It falls somewhere between the platitudes of James Michener's *South Pacific* and the immensity of Madison Smartt Bell's trilogy of novels about the Haitian slave rebellion . . . Anthony Winkler spins an enlightening parable, rich in historical detail and irony."
—*Shelf Awareness*

"With perceptive storytelling and bracing honesty, Mr. Winkler, author of a half-dozen well-reviewed books, has a lovely way of telling a good story and educating concurrently . . . *God Carlos* teaches history in a subtle but meaningful way. Too literary to be lumped in with typical historical fiction, and too historical to be lumped in with typical literary fiction, *God Carlos* defies categorization."
—*New York Journal of Books*

"Winkler is renowned in the West Indies for his comic genius. In *God Carlos,* he undertakes the formidable task of imagining the region's damaged history—unwritten and seemingly unreachable—with such ease and insight that we find ourselves transported to sixteenth-century Jamaica, as we watch the story unfold before our eyes."
—Robert Antoni, author of *Carnival*

"Set in the sixteenth century, Winkler's latest novel is something like *Heart of Darkness* meets *Animal Farm*. But what happens when Jamaica's most flamboyantly irreverent and fiercely contemporary novelist tackles the past? Why, the past becomes flamboyantly irreverent and fiercely contemporary. Winkler's achievement here is not that he remakes himself as a historical writer, but that he remakes history."
—Kei Miller, author of *The Last Warner Woman*

"A vivid and powerful account of the tragedy unleashed upon the native peoples of the Caribbean in the years following the arrival of Christopher Columbus."
—Jaime Manrique, author of *Cervantes Street*

Praise for *Dog War*

"Winkler applies his wicked sensibility to immigrant experience in Florida . . . He has a fine ear for patois and dialogue, and a love of language that makes bawdy jokes crackle." —*New Yorker*

"A family comedy par excellence, Winkler negotiates the fine line between laughing with and at a character with aplomb . . . Winkler's timing is well honed, and this comedy of cultural and generational clashes hits the right notes nearly every time . . . This is Winkler's first novel to be published in America, but his reputation as a comic novelist precedes him. With *Dog War*, he more than lives up to it." —*Time Out Chicago* (four stars)

"*Dog War* offers an amusing glance at America through an immigrant's eye, a breezy treat to keep you company on the beach at Montego Bay or, perhaps, your local dog park." —*Entertainment Weekly*

"*Dog War* has its laugh-out-loud moments, for it is sweetened by Jamaican-patois dialogue from Winkler's homeland and wry, tongue-in-cheek narration . . . [A] delicious comedy of manners." —*Booklist*

"When was the last time you laughed out loud at a book, and I mean the hold-your-sides, near-hysterical-with-joy kind of laughter? *Dog War* is a pitch-perfect and truly uplifting read, wonderfully written with a flourish and an art that is like the best conversation. Winkler is the Prozac of literature, the true feel-good factor we seek in Oprah and the likes. You want to help somebody? . . . Give them *Dog War*, they'll be forever in your debt." —Ken Bruen, author of *The Guards*

"*Dog War* is a delightful satire of Jamaican, and, especially, American life, as funny as a Donald E. Westlake crime caper and as outrageous as John Collier's *His Monkey Wife.*" —*Tampa Tribune*

"An acclaimed comic novelist in his native Jamaica, Winkler makes a long overdue American debut with this laugh riot . . . Winkler's wit, his ear for dialect, and the sublime creation that is Precious add up to one howlingly funny book." —*Publishers Weekly*

"Winkler paves every step with delicious laugh-out-loud prose that offers a wide-angled view of Jamaica's culture." —*Jamaica Gleaner*

Praise for *The Lunatic*

"By far the funniest book I've read in a decade, although its ribald atmosphere is sprayed with the pepper-gas of aggressive social satire."
—*Washington Post Book World*

"*The Lunatic* is a small masterpiece and should not be missed."
—*ForeWord*

"*The Lunatic* is beautiful and insane and unlike any other in its comedy of character and idea, landscape and language; a sensibility that jostles the senses."
—Benjamin Weissman, author of *Headless*

"*The Lunatic* is a brilliantly written and outrageous Jamaican fable."
—*Jamaica Gleaner*

Praise for *The Duppy*

"This book is laugh-out-loud, hold-your-side funny. You don't even realize the message in this poignant and philosophical story until you stop laughing . . . Winkler is a wonderful writer with a sharp pen and amazing pedagogy."
—*Today* (NBC), "Cover to Cover"

"Not many books come with a money-back guarantee, but publisher Akashic Books is so sure that readers of Anthony C. Winkler's *The Duppy* will laugh out loud, it will refund people's money if they do not. Luckily for Akashic, safer bets are hard to find."
—*Hipster Book Club*

"The comic and philosophical narrative is stimulating, and the critique of religion is brought to a clever and positive resolution. Recommended."
—*Library Journal*

"*The Duppy* is like Kurt Vonnegut Jr. stringing up Mitch Albom's *The Five People You Meet in Heaven* like a piñata and beating it with a stick."
—*Atlanta Journal-Constitution*

"*The Duppy* is the most laugh-out-loud funny novel I've read in years . . . The book blends postmodern metafiction with folklorist regionalism in a raucous contemporary satire of the wages of sin."
—*Stop Smiling*

The FAMILY MANSION

BY ANTHONY C. WINKLER

Published by Akashic Books

ISBN-13: 978-1-61775-166-0
Library of Congress Control Number: 2012954412

First printing

Akashic Books
PO Box 1456
New York, NY 10009
info@akashicbooks.com
www.akashicbooks.com

For Cathy, Becky, and Adam, with love

CHAPTER 1

The family mansion, a hulking presence of mortar and stone, squatted with the indifference of a concrete Buddha in the center of an enormous manicured lawn ornamented with flower beds, ivy hedges, topiary trees, and an army of neatly trimmed bushes. No one was in sight, and a vast sea of silence covered the land like a morning fog. The trees had shed their leaves in the cold, and the bushes looked stumpy and dowdy like old women at a funeral. Occasionally the morning stillness was broken by the startling sound of wild laughter that seemed to rattle from somewhere deep inside the house and that had a humorless herky-jerky lilt to it like the bleat of a disgruntled goat.

It was February 1805, the dark of night in a country borough in England, placid and seemingly deserted of all life. The only human forms to be seen were frozen statues of Artemis, the Greek goddess of hunting, caught in the middle of a chase with a leaping dog, also made of stone, bounding at her side, both of them posing in the petrifaction of sculpture next to an enormous yew tree. Nearby was another statue, this one of the god Pan gamboling beside a rosebush, which in the general dreariness had the squat appearance of a pygmy. Here and there in the dimness lurked similar figures made of stone, part of the garden statuary that had gradually accumulated over the years, acquiring the green tint of mildew or bad beef.

From the house came another peal of laughter, automatic and regular like the horn of a fogbound ship. Inside the house, in a chilly room flickering to a half-dead fire, an imposing gentleman, his cheeks bracketed by gaudy muttonchops, his face red and swollen from the cold, was peering intensely across a desk at the young man who sat before him laughing. Nothing funny had been done or said, and the older man occasionally wiggled his nose as if to signal his perplexity at the periodic salvos of laughter.

The room in which the two men sat was crammed with ornate plaques and paintings and figurines. Behind the older gentleman, some distance above his head, hung the stylized painting of a distant ancestor gazing out proprietarily at the world as if he were its owner. He stood against a backdrop of a fuzzy cloud bank or what some viewers might take to be a foggy mountain. (In portraits like this one the mountains were always made to look fuzzy and inconsequential so as not to upstage the gentleman or lady who was paying the artist.) On the head of this particular ancestor was an imposing and ridiculous-looking furrowed wig that draped down past his breastbone and might have been mistaken for the pelt of a full-grown Merino sheep. On one side of the ancestor in the painting was a stack of books no reasonable man could imagine such a puffed-up, pretty creature reading, and on the other a spyglass suitable to a pirate or a peeping Tom.

Books littered not only the painting, they were also scattered everywhere throughout the room: in a disciplined phalanx on the bookshelves; in small piles on the spacious desk like the rubble found on the grounds of a half-built brick building. Many of the books had the crisp-ness of unsoiled newly printed money. None of them had been read completely through. All of them, however, had been fondled over by the older gentleman. He liked being surrounded by books since he believed that they reflected well on him even when unread. His son, who sat across the desk and was at that age when he didn't care much about what the world thought of him, disliked books and made no bones about it.

The two gentlemen were members of the Fudges family, the older one being the paterfamilias, the younger man who laughed a lot being his unfortunate second son. They had been discussing the young man's future, about which the old gentleman was quite concerned. He had had high expectations that tonight his son would have announced his engagement to the widow Bentley, who was the best catch available in the entire district. But something had happened, something extraordinary that not only did not result in the engagement being announced, it sparked an announcement of just the opposite kind by the widow—namely, that there would be no marriage between Fudges and Bentley. What exactly had happened was known only to Fudges the younger, whose Christian name was Hartley, and it was this information that his father was trying his best to pry out of him. But all he had gotten for his efforts so far were the annoying mocking laughter of his son and the dismissal reply that everything was fine, nothing was wrong.

Fudges was a peculiar surname that was oddly plural even when it referred to a single family member. This was the deliberate design of the elder Fudges. Many years ago the name of the family was *Fudge*, but by the early seventeenth century that word had come to suggest shiftiness and hedging, to say nothing of a particular kind of confectionery. So the elder Fudges began spelling his name with an added "s," lessening the linkage between the family name and the namesake candy and confusing hostesses who didn't know whether it was singular or plural. If you meant one family member you said *Fudges*. But what did you write if you meant several family members—*Fudgeses* or *Fudges*? This sort of confusion was exactly what Fudges the elder calculated would cause his name to become memorable. A man liked his name to be enigmatic and mysterious, not circumstantial and ordinary.

The elder Fudges, as he faced his second son, was asking himself what could have possibly happened between his boy and the widow to upset all their hopes and carefully laid plans. Hartley Fudges, on the other hand, was being so tight-lipped and secretive that he conceded nothing and offered no explanation.

Hartley Fudges was twenty-three years old. He was neither particularly bright nor especially dumb, neither ugly nor good-looking. His facial features were a bit jumbled as if nature, with no theme in mind, had assembled them from various grab bags of miscellaneous noses, eyebrows, chins, and foreheads. If a man may be compared to an earthquake, Hartley Fudges was an imperceptible tremor that left no lingering aftershocks. He had been born the second son into a minor aristocratic family and had been his mother's favorite child—she had six children but only two survived to adulthood, Hartley and his older brother Alexander. Before she could thoroughly spoil Hartley, which she was devoutly trying to do, she herself was carried off by an outbreak of typhoid when she was only forty-two. In spite of this tragedy, Hartley was definitely born with a silver spoon in his mouth. He was as pampered as any young aristocrat child could be, raised by nannies and cosseted by a small company of servants and sent to both Eton and Oxford where he learned to talk like an aristocratic Englishman.

Every time an Englishman opens his mouth he tells the world to which social class he belongs. Upper-class Englishmen went to the finest schools where they were taught how to speak with a certain posh accent that would distinguish them from the man in the street. This accent is known as *received pronunciation* or, informally among academics, as RP.

Received pronunciation is a hideous style of speech that sounds as if the alphabet were being blown through the speaker's nose. It is so distinctive that its use immediately signifies that the speaker is from the upper classes. Why it was necessary to so publicly tell the classes apart is baffling to us who live in the twenty-first century. We can only guess that part of the perceived necessity may have been founded on the fact that dueling was an accepted albeit illegal custom among the upper class for resolving conflicts and settling differences, and without knowing it, if telltale accents did not exist, a bamboozled earl or duke or count might find himself trading shots at fifteen paces with his neighbor's gardener. That would never do. Only gentlemen who used received pronunciation as their main mode of speech were entitled to slaughter each other on the field of honor. Hartley Fudges, by this measure, was indubitably a gentleman. Every word he spoke came through his nose. He faithfully tacked an aspirant sound before any word beginning with "h." He committed no malapropisms. And if he swore, he uttered odd expressions such as "egad" and "zounds."

England of Hartley Fudges's day was a rigidly stratified society with horrendous and gaping differences between the classes. There were more lords and earls and dukes and counts and marquises than blackberries in summer. Lifestyle differences between the privileged and the poor were obscenely evident and indefensible even while a glib windbag such as Samuel Johnson (1709–1784) tried to justify the principle of subordination as necessary to the survival of England. By subordination he meant the shuffling of the population into layered classes where the few had much and the many had little. Belonging to the few who had much was Hartley Fudges, a man of twenty-three on whom an expensive education had been wasted, producing a jack-in-the-box who did not like to read but who spoke impeccably through the nose using only the purest received pronunciation.

The father of Hartley Fudges gazed at his second son with obvious fondness. Earlier he had glimpsed Hartley and the widow sitting in the corner of the drawing room talking animatedly while all around them revelers swirled in a kaleidoscope of bright colors and convivial chatter. He had not drawn close enough to overhear their conversation, but if he had, he would have noticed that the widow had gotten progressively drunker and drunker as the night passed. She began to slur her words and issue grand opinions about everything under the sun, from blasting that Gallic beast Napoleon to praising the wonder of Johann Ritter (1776–1810), the German electrochemist who claimed to have discovered some new properties of light.

Had Hartley Fudges heard about that discovery? Hartley Fudges had not. He was not a reader of magazines or books and found all their speculation about life, the arts, and science that was their lifeblood almost unbearable. He was in the middle of explaining his dislike of reading when the widow interrupted him and suggested they find someplace where they could talk in private. Excited at the prospect of being alone with his quarry—a recent widow who was said to have an income of over £10,000 a year—Hartley stood up and escorted her to a room that served as a makeshift library. It was tucked away off a hallway near the kitchen, as inconspicuously as an appendix off a colon, and was rarely used and dimly lit by a single candle, making it the perfect place for any one of the Fudges men to swive the occasional attractive young maidservant.

The lovers entered the room stealthily. Hartley closed the door carefully behind him, and drew close to his prospect of £10,000 and the freedom and luxuries such a fabulous income would buy. In the wavering candlelight his widow looked younger than her twenty-nine years, the dim light acting like a balm to mask the lines and wrinkles hinting of the facial shriveling that loomed ahead. She was six years older than Hartley, who had drawn near enough to sniff the muskiness of her body that came from once-a-week baths, and even though she smelled to him like a closet that had not been opened for months, in his imagination £10,000 pounds a year would perfume even a stinkpot with the aroma of fresh spring blossoms.

She shied away briefly from his attempt to kiss her and stared up at him with grave earnestness. "Mr. Fudges," she asked demurely, "you know that although I am a woman, I have a scientific bent. It is my nature. Do you mind if I make a crucial measurement?"

He had no idea what she meant, but her tone seemed to

call for a display of gallantry. "Of course not, my dear," he said magnanimously just as he felt her hand sliding down the front of his pants and grabbing a gentle hold of his private parts, which immediately became engorged to her touch. She tried to circle the shaft with her index finger and thumb but couldn't. Hartley endured this scientific groping with a stoical demeanor and a manly sigh. She was soon finished and gazing at him with a sad expression.

He chuckled. "Did I pass?"

She made a little birdlike noise and shook her head gloomily. "I'm sorry, Mr. Fudges," she said in a matter-of-fact voice, "but you're altogether too big for me. I simply couldn't manage you."

"But Madam," he protested, suddenly realizing that she was serious, "I've seen many naked men. In that regard I'm quite average, I assure you."

"If you are," she said crisply, "then nature is being very unkind to Englishwomen. I only know that you have a beast down there whose care and feeding I could not possibly undertake. I'm sorry. I want no more than six inches; indeed, five is my heart's desire."

She headed for the door. He stepped in front of her to beseech her not to be too hasty, and to rethink her decision. She glided nimbly around him and slipped into the hallway. A few minutes later, when the piano player took a break, she stood up and said to the assembled throng, "Ladies and gentlemen, I have an announcement to make. Mr. Fudges and I have decided that we are not suitable for each other, but will still remain dear friends. Thank you."

And then she sat down. The elder Fudges hurried to the side of his second son who was standing in a corner looking as if he were being punished.

"Damn!" the father cried under his breath. "What the devil was that all about?"

The second son laughed.

The dilemma facing Hartley Fudges was that he had been born the second son in a monarchical nation whose strict laws of succession mandated that the firstborn male inherit everything upon the death of the father. Nothing was left for the other sons except what the firstborn chose to provide through his generosity. Known as the law of primogeniture, this doctrine had its roots in a twelfth-century conflict between King John and his nephew Prince Arthur. For men like Hartley Fudges, it was a law that essentially dispossessed them of their homeland and cast them out into the cold. And although its prime justification was initially to ensure a smooth succession to the throne, the doctrine soon came to apply to all England, mainly to give it legitimacy. None of the other European countries practiced it, and the founding fathers of the American Revolution had specifically rejected the principle as undemocratic. Only England had clung to it for six centuries.

With the first son getting everything, the second son had few options. A military career was one possibility, except that in 1805 a Corsican half-pint by the name of Napoleon Bonaparte (1769–1821) was running rampant over Europe and sparking a succession of wars that greatly increased the risk of death in battle. Another option was to become a cleric and exercise spiritual leadership over a congregation of farmers and working-class families. One was unlikely to be killed in the line of duty if one chose this path, but early death from boredom was a distinct possibility.

The third alternative offered the greatest promise: marriage to a woman of wealth such as the widow. Widowed only recently, she was so fresh from the deathbed of her elderly husband that up to now she had drawn little attention from the hordes of wife-hunting second sons. But it was only a matter of time before she was spotted and overwhelmed with both suitors and offers.

The final alternative was to go abroad and make one's fortune in the colonies.

Wide-ranging and immense, the British colonial empire in 1805 included the subcontinent of India, Canada, Australia, to say nothing of its beachheads in Africa, Malaysia, and its possessions in the West Indies. At one time a quarter of the surface of the earth and the people living there were under the control of Great Britain. The manpower required to administer these far-flung holdings to a large part was provided by second sons such as Hartley Fudges.

Hartley's father was not unsympathetic to the plight of his second son. Himself a second son, the elder Fudges had at one point in his life been on the threshold of a similar dilemma when, through the mercy of God, his older brother, the first son, was struck dead by smallpox, which in those days killed four hundred thousand Europeans annually. Unfortunately, the first son had only recently gotten married and left behind a pregnant widow who spitefully gave birth to a son. This undeserving infant would have inherited it all, leaving the elder Fudges penniless, if God had not smote the pretender with a lethal dose of diphtheria. That was how the elder Fudges had escaped the fate of Hartley and become the first son and why he was outwardly such a pious man who always acknowledged the power and wisdom of God. It never occurred to him that with infant mortality hovering around 50 percent, what had happened to him was no more than the indifferent grinding of statistics and had nothing to do with the intervention of a homicidal deity.

If Hartley had been born to a fabulously wealthy family, he might have dabbled in some occupation or sideline as a gifted dilettante. He might even, for the fun of it, have tried his hand at running the family's business, if there was one. The problem was, however, that he was a gentleman of some means, but of not enough to make working an option. A gentleman of his day could work only if he didn't have to; if he worked because he had to, he was no gentleman. It was a fine line to walk and an ethic that put the second son in an impossible position.

Hartley Fudges thought he had a profound philosophical mind. But the truth was that he was as profound as a beanpole. He read a little but misunderstood a lot. What he shared with many Englishmen of his class was an expansive inner world populated by the mythological figures and events that had been beaten into him at Eton.

The public schools of England, then and now, stamped their graduates not only with the same way of speaking, but with a remarkably similar worldview. Many years after Hartley Fudges had come and gone, anthropologists studying ancient cultures would come to the hypothesis that language not only affected thinking, it also altered reality. This was indubitably true of the upper-class English mind-set and its art form, poetry. Both were pillars of the same exclusive country club—the upper-class point of view—to which intruders were not invited. When John

Keats (1795–1821), who had no upper-class credentials, began publishing his poetry, his work was derided by one brainless critic as "the Cockney school of poetry." Today, the dope who wrote that patronizing review is unknown for anything except that stupidly wrong opinion.

For Hartley Fudges, what mattered deeply was that the surface gestures and conventional symbols due to his rank be observed. Being a member of the aristocracy, he demanded that the courtesies due to him and his rank in society be respected and upheld no matter how scruffy the circumstances. He once flew into a snit because a whore he was screwing under a bridge in London refused to call him "My Lord" or "Earl" Fudges or any other honorific to which he was entitled. Instead of the proper nomenclature, she was calling him any vulgarity that sprang to her common mind as he held her pinned and wriggling against the damp roughness of the stone undergirding the bridge.

"Lord have mercy," she gasped in the crease of his neck as he pumped her vigorously.

"No mercy," he hissed.

"I'm not talking to you," she squealed. "I'm talking to God. Take that thing out of me or I'll scream for my pimp."

"Not until I'm finished," he panted without a pause.

She blasted a scream in his neck and within seconds Hartley could hear the footfalls of someone scrambling toward them.

"'ere, Milord!" a male voice said gruffly. "You're hurting 'er. Stop what you're doing or I'll hit you with this rock." And he raised his hand holding the rock high like a club.

With a sudden jerk, Hartley freed himself from the

woman, pulled up his pants, and stalked off from under the bridge.

"Thank you, Milord," the man called after him as Hartley disappeared into the night.

"*Milord* my ass," the woman spat bitterly.

Hartley Fudges considered himself a Platonist, a follower of the Greek philosopher. Not that he had mastered the thinking of Plato (427–347 BC). To tell the truth, he found every kind of philosophy a bit on the fuzzy side. He rather liked the idea of Plato's myth where the cave dwellers mistook shadows cast on the walls by a fire for reality. But, really, he could not say he actually understood what Plato was getting at. However, he also knew that a young gentleman needed a stand in philosophy—a point of view, as it were—that he could talk about in polite company. So when anyone asked him anything philosophical he was ready to answer as a Platonist and had memorized appropriate passages here and there of Plato that he could quote.

The problem with blinking philosophy was it was so vague and hazy that even when he got the surface impressions of an idea right, he often got its underlying meaning wrong. Ask him a question about anything and he had an answer. But his answers were without understanding. He knew many pretty facts and figures but they were stacked up in his head like stuffy books in a reference library that everyone quoted but no one ever read.

This much was plain to Hartley: Plato claimed that every object in the world had its perfect equivalent in another world. A comb in this world was a mere imitation of its ideal counterpart in the next. Every horse on earth was the imperfect copy of the ideal horse. It was the same with every stone, every plate, every cow, every dog, and every necklace. Somewhere in the other world was the perfect prototype of which the earthly model was an imperfect copy.

Exactly where this other world was Hartley did not know, but neither did Plato. Yet Hartley and his classmates liked knowing about the old Greek and his philosophy, even if they thought the whole business a bit dotty. But never mind, it was better if the upper class knew highbrow things that the lower classes did not; knowing a bit about Plato definitely helped make clear the difference between Milord and Milord's butler.

A damp morning was sponging down the windows of the mansion by the time the two men were ready to go to bed. They made their way through a cavernous ballroom which was being cleaned up by a number of weary servants under the watchful eye of a uniformed butler who bowed slightly as they walked past.

The elder Fudges was more openly fond of his second son than of his first, whose name was Alexander and was filled with his mother's pretensions. "Do you know, my boy, what I would do if I were in your shoes?" he said in a paternal voice. "I would go abroad and try my luck in the colonies."

Hartley responded with a raucous laugh.

"And where exactly would you go, dear Papa?"

"In a word, Jamaica."

They mounted the grand stairway and made their way up to the second floor, where they would sleep in ornate bedrooms. On the walls were paintings of more ancestors, all staring out from inside rectangular gold-gilded frames in the stilted poses and humorless expressions usually found in a rogues' gallery. Neither man took notice. They had seen them many times before and fully expected to one day take their places inside picture frames hung on the wall. The father, at least, was assured of his wall perch because the death of his older sibling and his older sibling's son had given him the benefits of primogeniture. Hartley, on the other hand, had only a faint chance of ever hanging on the wall.

"Jamaica, eh?" he murmured just as he reached his bedroom door. He was about to ask the old man why that colony but he decided he was too tired to listen to the long-winded explanation that was likely to ensue. So he simply said, "Good night, Papa," and slipped into his room, closing the door softly behind him.

Hartley changed into his pajamas and climbed into an enormous four-poster bed whose bulk and heft dominated the shadowy room like a sneer does a face. He did not wash or brush his teeth. This was 1805. Modern toothpastes would emerge later in the 1800s, and the oral custom of the day, practiced by some people but not by Hartley Fudges, was to keep the mouth clean through the use of chewing sticks much like a dog today with a bone. The dentifrice whose chalky and tangy taste we begin and end the day with would emerge in the mid-1850s, but the chewing stick had been in use as early as 3500 BC in fabled Babylon.

Moreover, for all its imposing size, the family mansion did not have indoor plumbing and Hartley did not feel like splashing himself with water in the pitcher and washbasin that a butler had left on a nearby table. The room was jerkily lit by a candelabra, which he blew out just before he crawled between the sheets with the grime of the night's revelry still clinging to his flesh.

Within ten minutes he was fast asleep.

CHAPTER 2

An aristocratic Englishman such as Hartley Fudges was both born and made. Nature had produced a rough draft, social engineering the final one. He had been raised by a series of grim nannies, who potty trained him, bathed him, and kept him clean enough to be turned over to his parents briefly each day so they could play with him like a newly bought dolly. He was characteristically dressed in lacy outfits decorated with flounces and embroidered hems, as was the custom of the day, and sent to public schools, which, in spite of the name, were really private, expensive, and exclusive, where he was grounded in both Greek and Latin mythology in the original languages. He would attend a university whose lectures were given in Latin. The big accomplishment would be to get in—for once in, getting out with a degree, barring commission of a felony, was virtually assured. His education would not be useful, but ornamental like an epaulet, and would help identify him as a member of the upper class.

That Hartley Fudges was now twenty-three was something of an accomplishment. It was not easy being a child in nineteenth-century England. Infant mortality was staggering and chances were good that you would not live to see your first birthday. Being a child made you smaller and weaker than adults but earned you no special treatment. If you stole anything and were caught, you were hanged in public just like any hardened adult criminal. The modern concept of childhood as a period of innocence did not exist in the eighteenth century or early nineteenth. It was written in the merciless scripture of the day that sin was sin regardless of who committed it, whether an old man or a young child. For example, in 1801 a twelve-year-old boy who stole a silver spoon was hanged. This was not an isolated incident, a case of justice running amok. Instead, it happened regularly. In 1816 a ten-year-old convicted of shoplifting died on the gallows. And in 1831 the same gruesome penalty was applied to a boy found guilty of arson.

To be born in nineteenth-century London was also to be a target for every random hoodlum living in the largest metropolitan pigsty on God's good earth. It was to step across the foyer of heaven and into the main chamber of hell. Every grubby germ, every nihilistic virus, every thuggish parasite, every microscopic blob of infection and disease was out to kill you. Typhoid, cholera, diphtheria, whooping cough, tuberculosis stalked your cradle without mercy. The medical profession was next to useless in protecting you. It didn't even believe in the existence of the microbial world or in the mechanism of infection, and its standard treatment for virtually every illness was to open a vein and bleed you. This was as useless as trying to stop the doomed *Titanic* from sinking by flushing one of its toilets.

Partly responsible for the prevalence of infection and disease was the chief method of locomotion throughout the sceptered isle of England, namely the horse.

The horse was an instrument of domesticity, entertainment, militarism, and everyday transportation, and its fecal imprint was evident in every major city and borough throughout the empire. In 1780 some sixty thousand horses clip-clopped daily through the streets of London. By the mid-1800s, eight million horses a year were annually crossing London Bridge. Raw waste poured into the River Thames, the source of drinking water for the city, from over sixty sewers. Side by side with housing areas existed slaughterhouses and hogpens where daily butchery was done openly. Drains commonly overflowed, plastering the ugly brown stains of sewage scum on the walls of houses and buildings. In some parts of the city, raw sewage was dumped from the windows of houses onto the streets below. You could hire a crier to precede you on the street ringing a bell and crying, "Hold your hand!" Over the entire city a noxious stench from this nastiness hung like a pestilential miasma. Paradoxically enough, the English feared what they desperately needed the most—fresh air and a bath.

Finished with his schooling, Hartley Fudges would face the world as an English gentleman and be identified as such by his elegant manners and his received pronunciation. His classical education concluded with the grand tour, where the young man was sent for a year or so to sample life in other European countries. (Europeans had a taste for periodically slaughtering each other, but between wars they also liked to visit the foreign battlegrounds of earlier bloodletting.)

Hartley had only just returned from his own grand tour. He had done the usual circuit of France, Germany, some of the Balkan countries, ending up in Amsterdam where he spent the final three months of his tour courting a rich young Dutch woman. His wooing was interrupted by a summons from his father, who forced him to come home by cutting off his supply of money, which was and is a time-honored way of curbing the self-indulgent wanderlust of young masters. Suddenly penniless, young Hartley had no choice but to return home.

One month after he arrived in England, his Dutch love sent him a Dear John letter announcing her engagement to a German. Hartley's response was to laugh and hurl her letter into a blazing fireplace. Since returning home, Hartley had spent most of his time wooing the widow Bentley. And now that she'd decided against him, he had no idea what he would do next.

Hartley woke up around noon, and the first thought that popped into his conscious mind was his rejection by the widow. He lay in bed for at least an hour, sloshing through the swamp of impressions from the night before. He tried his best to think of another approach he might yet use on the widow, but he could come up with nothing. His heart was heavy as he regarded the road ahead. His mind roamed over all the possibilities, and he even began to daydream about his brother becoming sick and dying, which would automatically elevate Hartley to the position of the first son. Since Alexander his brother had no children of his own yet, he had only to die for Hartley to have uncontested rights of primogeniture. If something like that could happen to his father, why couldn't it happen to him too?

Well, he didn't want to start the day with a pessimistic frame of mind, but he thought it highly unlikely that God would intervene on his behalf and strike down Alexander. Yet the prospect was so appealing that he lay in bed going over the grisly details. He ran the scenario lovingly through his imagination, heard his brother coughing one evening, watched as he became progressively worse, until finally he was forced into bed by a debilitating lung ailment. A doctor was summoned who pronounced his brother ill with a virulent pneumonia and bled him of two pints of blood. A day later, the poor fellow had the decency to die.

There was a funeral that Hartley attended in his imagination looking as grim as a starving vulture. Neighbors and friends of the family expressed their condolences to him, and he mingled among his guests appearing every bit the bereaved sibling and modestly muttering "Thank you's" to mournful comments directed his way. The next day, he would wake up the first son with every expectation of inheriting his father's property. It was that simple; it could happen that quickly.

But as things looked right now, it would not happen if it were left up to God. His brother would not be struck down. And no matter how badly Hartley desired it, there would be no lung ailment, no ornate funeral, no line of sympathizers, and no change in the order of succession.

Like a wet gray animal, the bleak winter day nuzzled the windows of the room in which Hartley had slept. The prospect was so gloomy and dreary that he began to daydream about giving God a hand by murdering Alexander himself. He lay with his hands folded under his head, stared at the canopy of the four-poster bed, and began fantasizing about the best way of murdering his brother.

As a second son who stood to most benefit from the crime, he would be the chief suspect. He would need an ironclad alibi, one that put him miles and miles away from the scene of the crime. While he lay in bed thinking about the murder, he saw that the plot was an impossibility, nothing more than a pipe dream. Feeling frustrated and stymied at every step, he rolled himself up in the sheets of the bed like a cocoon and tried to think. But he could not think, and thinking when he was in no mood to think only made him feel peevish and ill-used.

He rang for a servant to help him dress, and a few minutes later a middle-aged uniformed man rapped on the door and glided into the room smoothly with the oily unctuousness of someone steeped in long servitude.

"Good morning, sir," crooned the butler.

"Good morning, George," replied Hartley with a yawn. "Is the master at breakfast?"

"No, sir. He left early this morning."

"Where did he go?"

"I'm not sure, sir."

"Help me get dressed, will you, please?"

"Certainly, sir."

Hartley dressed, with the valet's help. The process took him nearly half an hour because his clothes were tight fitting and snug, as none of the modern convenient clothing fasteners had yet been invented. Chicago mechanical engineer Whitcomb L. Judson (1836–1909), for example, would not patent his invention of the zipper for another eighty-six years. So Hartley wore a simple gray outfit that had no fly or zipper and consisted of an ensemble of gray tight-fitting *pantaloons*—which had become a symbol of democracy since the French Revolution—a simple shirt, and a tailored coat.

Recently, the two revolutions—the American (1775–1783) and the French (1789–1799)—had contributed to the democratization of fashion reflected in the relative simplicity of Hartley's outfit. Before these two upheavals, so-called sumptuary laws had dictated rigorous standards of dress to differentiate between an aristocrat and a commoner. Distinctions between the classes were still being signaled in their respective styles of dress, but these differences had become more muted and existed not so much in design as in the use of particular fabrics. The clothing of an upper-class man, for example, was often trimmed in silk and lace, while the lower classes wore simple trousers known as *sans-culottes* (without breeches), made of homespun fabrics.

Having dressed, Hartley had breakfast by himself, sitting with a bemused air about him as if he hadn't quite decided who he was and what he was about to do. He was served by a man who was not particularly conscientious and whose attitude Hartley found annoying. Servants were notoriously sensitive to the power centers in a household and had a keen sense of whom to butter up and whom they could safely ignore. It was plain that the man had decided that Hartley was just another sponging second son.

Halfway through breakfast, Hartley beckoned to the servant to come to him. The man ambled casually across the room.

"Yes, sir," he muttered indifferently.

"Tell the stable boy to saddle my horse," Hartley said.

"And which horse is yours, sir?"

"The same one that was mine yesterday."

"Yesterday the stable boy asked me this same question, sir. Which is why I'm asking you."

Hartley said through gritted teeth, "Tell the boy to saddle up the horse I rode yesterday."

"Very good, sir," the man replied in a voice whose tone suggested that Hartley was something of a nuisance. Then he loped off toward the kitchen and disappeared.

A few minutes later Hartley was cantering the horse down a narrow bridle path that threaded through the woodlands of the property.

The English countryside, then as now, was a profuse garden of loveliness that rivaled the biblical splendors of Eden. Spring was still two months away, but by April a gaudy explosion of blossoms and flowers would ignite the land with a spectacular beauty that would make Englishmen scattered all over the globe yearn for their homeland and moan a variation of the plaintive words that would one day be written by the yet unborn poet, Robert Browning (1812–1889): "O, to be in England / now that April's there . . ."

It was too cold to be riding, and Hartley knew that the moment he mounted his horse and trotted down the bridle path. But he also knew that to turn around and go back would make him look ridiculous before the servants, which was the one thing in the world upper-class Englishmen most dreaded. So he rode on bravely, his nose leaking, the cold air stinging his lungs, and to take his mind off the wintry conditions, he began once again to rehearse last night's encounter with the widow.

The landscape around him looked like it had been shorn; everywhere sprouted the stubble of denuded trees and bushes and twiggy bramble. Now and again a blast of winter air would sweep over the bridle path, making the bare trees shudder as if spasming from the cold.

As he trotted his horse through the woods, Hartley,

with a little effort, might have glimpsed scraps of childhood memories dangling from the bushes and trees. All around him was the stage in which he had reveled during the best years of his childhood. As a boy, he used to ramble through these woodlands, his imagination seeding the dense foliage with fantasy dragons, prowling highway men, knights errant looking for trouble, and in this very spot he had left many a villain bleeding to death after a fierce and savage sword fight. His sword, which the unimaginative world thought was made of wood, to his mind's eye had been forged from the finest tempered steel, invisible to the probing eye of the intruding adult. But no adult living could have been in the place he was at that time, for then he had been adrift in that estuary of childhood where imagination and reality mingled like river and sea as they do only in the mind of the very young. Those years when he played alone and carefree in this world of make-believe had been the happiest of his life. And now that he looked back and could see the imaginary and playful splendor that was once his, he could no longer partake of it without feeling ridiculous—a certain and dismal sign of adulthood. Then he had been a lighthearted child; now he was a scheming man.

Hartley broke through the trees at a trot and saw the house towering majestically over the bare fields and felt a pang of regret. If he'd only been born some few years sooner, all of this would be his, and the thought of missed opportunity through blind fate galled him into a rage that shook him like a tremor. The horse, meanwhile, had also got a glimpse of the house and broke into a run for the stables. Hartley pulled brutally on the reins, not wanting to appear as if he were fleeing the cold, and in response, he felt the animal shiver and tremble under him as it slowed down reluctantly with a noticeable muscular spasm.

"That's a good girl," murmured Hartley, patting the horse on the neck and feeling the tendons and striated muscles stretching with the effort.

A few minutes later, horse and man cantered into the paddocks at a leisurely pace as though the bitter cold did not exist. The horse was emitting steam like an overheated engine, but the man sat on its back looking as if it were a beautiful spring day.

"A bit chilly, isn't it, sir?" the stable boy greeted him as Hartley dismounted.

"Is it?" Hartley responded as if he had no idea. Then without another word, he patted the horse on the withers and headed toward the main house, hoping with all his heart that he would find a brisk fire blazing in the drawing room.

In 1805 the physical world was something of a *terra incognito*, meaning that much about it was unknown and much of what was known was wrong. Of course, a hundred years from now people will no doubt say the same about us and what we presume to know. Yet there were measurable and major differences between the generation to which Hartley belonged and us.

Hartley and his contemporaries, for example, had no telephone, no electricity with all its conveniences, no airplanes, no mechanical means of transportation, no television, no computers, and no Internet. The year before, 1804, had seen the invention of the first steam locomotive by British engineer Richard Trevithick (1771–1833), who had demonstrated its practical uses for heavy hauling and the transporting of passengers.

Britain was in an expansive, almost boisterous mood as she acquired dominion over a substantial chunk of the globe. The world had weathered the puffed-up sterility of the eighteenth century, and its chief windbag, Samuel Johnson (1709–1784), had gone kicking and screaming into the salons of the afterlife where he could spend eternity hectoring and bullying the saints with his glib opinions on every issue under the sun. The poetry of the day was written in rhymed couplets that to the modern ear would sound like an advertising jingle.

Not that Hartley could tell a poem from the oink of a pig or cared in the least about either one. What he cared about was London, where he lived as one particle of the floating population in the most populous city on earth. Of London Dr. Johnson said in one of his more memorable apothegms, "When a man is tired of London, he is tired of life." Hartley Fudges was neither tired of London nor of life. The wonder was that neither was he tired of wallowing in an overcrowded wasteland of raw sewage, offal, and filth.

CHAPTER 3

A few days after his rejection by the widow, Hartley was taking a coach to London. There were some six passengers riding in the narrow cab of a horse-drawn carriage, and although they were crammed together uncomfortably close, four of them were treating each other with the cool indifference of riders in the yet uninvented elevator by staring off into space as though some fascinating show, visible only to them, was taking place just outside the window. Among the passengers were two middle-aged bankers, one bearded, one clean-shaven, on a business trip. Ordinarily, Englishmen thrown so close together in a public conveyance generally had little to say to one another because the enforced intimacy made every passenger an unwilling eavesdropper, but the two bankers were fortified with brandy that gave them an exhilarating chattiness and they were blithely exchanging opinions as if they were alone in a private drawing room.

They began their chitchat by discussing banking practices and making veiled references to unspecified sums of money invested in risky overseas operations, particularly India. Soon their conversation shifted to dueling—a topic that made Hartley Fudges perk up and listen attentively. The gentleman who had an unevenly trimmed beard was lamenting the death of Alexander Hamilton, who had been mortally wounded on July 11, 1804, in a duel with Aaron Burr.

"A brilliant chap, that Hamilton," opined the gentleman. "What a sorry waste."

"What was the duel about?" asked his beardless companion.

"Oh, some nonsense Hamilton said about Burr in a speech. But they've always been enemies. Goes back to the presidential election of 1800. Burr and Jefferson got the same number of electoral votes. Hamilton campaigned for Jefferson, who won."

"They ought to outlaw dueling," the beardless gentleman clucked.

"It's been outlawed in America for years just as it is here. Everybody knows where duels are usually fought in London, but the authorities still do nothing about blocking access to the grounds."

"Southampton Fields, isn't it?"

"Exactly. It's a ridiculous custom. Legalized murder, if you ask me. Point of honor, my foot! You want to kill a chap and take his wife, challenge him to a duel. Make up some nonsense about his insulting you and slap him in the face before witnesses. You present him with two choices, both equally bad. Either he fights you, which gives you the opportunity to kill him, or if he backs down, be branded a coward, in which case his wife will probably be so ashamed that she'll leave him. You've got him either way."

"Of course, he could kill you," pointed out the banker with no beard.

"Of course," the other replied gruffly.

The carriage rattled on with a herky-jerky motion,

slapping the rumps of the passengers against the thin cushions that barely covered the uncomfortable wooden seats. Most of the journey took the coach across rutted unpaved roads that meandered through picturesque villages and open pastures with the occasional plunge through a dark forest where the possibility of the odd highwaymen or footpad lurking behind a tree made the passengers uneasy. A highwayman committed his crime of robbery from the back of a horse, which he used to intercept the stagecoach by crying, "Stand and deliver!" or the even more popular threat, "Your money or your life!" The less glamorous footpad, using a similar phrasing, attempted the same wickedness on foot. Against this dual threat many of the passengers were armed and the coachman rode with a loaded blunderbuss—a primitive shotgun—under his seat. The police force was still in its infancy and regular patrols of the highway were rare or entirely absent.

Adding to a general sense of discomfort suffered by the passengers was a swaying, unpleasant ride which could make even the most hardened traveler sick. Sitting beside Hartley, for example, was a matronly looking woman who was turning as green as a freshly peeled avocado.

"Thank God nobody has ever challenged me to a duel," the clean-shaven gentleman said fervently.

"Oh, I had a debtor challenge me once. I knew right away what he was up to. Trying to escape having to repay his debt, that was his goal. He thought one way to do it was to murder me in a sham duel."

"What did you do?"

"I said to him, *Look here, you. That dueling nonsense is for gentlemen. I am not a gentleman. I'm a businessman. And if you slap me again, I'll knock you across the room.*"

"Really? What happened?"

"He slapped me again, and I knocked him clean across the room. He went so far as to have his second call on me. I had my men give the second a good thrashing. Of course, if I had been a gentleman, I would have been doomed to fight the duel with him. But as a businessman and a banker, I didn't have to go along with his stupid rules about honor."

This was too much for the green lady. She turned to the bearded banker and said sharply, "Sir, honor is not stupid, nor is not being a gentleman any occasion for boasting."

"You may say so, madame," the banker replied just as caustically, "because you are a female and no one will ever challenge you to a duel."

The woman stared out the window as if transfixed and began to turn green again. As Hartley Fudges listened intently to this exchange, an idea seized him like a cramp. For the rest of the journey he sat as still as a sunning turtle and stared out the window at the passing scenery while his brain hatched a plot to rid himself of his brother.

Dueling in 1805 was a vestige of medieval combat when knights in shining armor—whom one writer called "a terrible worm in an iron cocoon"—settled their disputes in hand-to-hand combat. The word *duel* is derived from the Latin word *duellum*, which is a blend of the word *bellum* and *duo*, meaning a war between two.

At the basis of the duel was a defense of one's honor; if the challenger chose to accept the apology of the one who offended him, the duelists would shake hands like gentlemen and leave the field without bloodshed. Indeed, many duelists strongly professed not to believe in dueling—Alexander Hamilton among them—but felt, when challenged, that they had no choice but to stand up for their honor or become social outcasts.

Like many revolting customs from ancient times, the duel was gussied up with a code of polite conduct and elaborate rituals. Among the requirements of the custom was that professional witnesses and informal umpires called *seconds* be present to ensure fair play between the combatants. In the event of unsporting conduct, the seconds would open fire on the violator who did not comply with the rules. But so unanimously understood were the ground rules of the duel that regulations independently drafted by the seconds of Burr and Alexander Hamilton were later found to be nearly identical.

There was, for example, the question of how far apart the combatants would stand—the distance varied but was usually ten paces apart, or about thirty feet—and of what weapons they would use. In earlier centuries the small thrusting sword was widely used, but by the nineteenth century the duel was usually fought with pistols. In the case of the Burr/Hamilton affair, .56-caliber dueling pistols were used from a range of about thirty feet. The pistols were loaded with a smooth oversized ball and fired from an unrifled barrel that made the weapon highly inaccurate. In an attempt to reduce the mortality of duels, the dueling code specifically prohibited the use of the rifled pistol which, from the typical range of thirty feet, would have been far deadlier.

As a code and practice that applied only to upper-class men, the custom of dueling had become something of a cottage industry by 1805. There were professional seconds available to stand in at duels, and there were reckless young duelists who were quick to issue a challenge at the drop of a hat over any imaginary snub to their honor. The periodic bloodshedding invariably occurred on the same popular dueling grounds. Hamilton, for example, fell in the same site near the village of Weehawken, New Jersey, where three years earlier his eldest son had been killed in a duel.

Whatever Hartley Fudges was scheming up, his reverie was interrupted by the coach pulling into its terminus, near the present Paddington Station, and the passengers, body sore and weary, clambering out into a swirling, noisy street whose background clatter and din was as perpetual as the roar of a waterfall. Hartley Fudges felt a pang of recognition: he was back in London. He was home.

London in 1805 was a crowded, dirty city exploding with industry and people. The streets were jammed with horse-drawn carriages, and the pedestrians swarming everywhere had the pallor and bustling, scurrying energy of constant motion that might be found in a population of hungry marsupials. Everywhere the eye looked it beheld smokestacks, grimy working men, sidewalk butchers, shrieking hawkers, and peddlers against a backdrop of persistent staccato hoof beats made by overworked horses harnessed to carriages, hackney cabs, carts, and drays.

Hartley Fudges loved London with the devotion of a foundling. The city teemed with people of every conceivable look, occupation, color, and background, and Hartley included in his acquaintances a wide assortment of characters ranging from old rumpots who spent their days in a babbling whirl of intoxication to a priggish widow woman who kept a boardinghouse during the day while leading marches of the temperance society at night. He knew prostitutes and gamblers and often patronized their services, and he was on nodding terms with many con men, usurious moneylenders, card sharks, pimps, opportunists, and dreamers.

That night found him in his favorite pub, the Fox and Hounds, where he drank port wine and had a bowlful of greasy stew and bread and butter for dinner. He was in a convivial temper, considering what was preying on his mind, and the hubbub and smokiness of the dingy pub seemed to add to his celebratory mood as he exchanged banter with other regulars. Yet he was obviously looking for someone, and frequently he would pause in the middle of a remark and peer around the crowded, noisy room. An hour later, he found his man among the maze of faces and went over to greet him. Then the two men huddled in a corner of the room to have a quiet but intense chat. The pub was candlelit, which intensified its atmospheric resemblance to a burrow and added a smudginess to every face, object, and piece of furniture in the room.

The man Hartley Fudges huddled with had the street name of Lord Hemmings. He was a small man who wore an air of inviolable dignity and moved with the energetic, scurrying gait of a rat. Like Hartley, who was also entitled to use the aristocratic title of Lord Fudges, Lord Hemmings was another poor dispossessed second son who was always broke. He had no obvious source of income and barely managed to eke by in the live-and-let-live amorality of nineteenth-century London. It was whispered that he had been a clergyman in the Church of England but had been dismissed from his post for having adulterous affairs with married ladies in his congregation. People, however, said about him that he knew everything and everyone abiding among the wilds of London. Through him adventurers and schemers had a pipeline into the hearts of sociopathic henchmen willing to do anything for money. His role in the world was to be a broker of darkness, to bring together willing, bloodstained hands with deranged minds that were bent on vengeance or other depravity.

After Hartley Fudges had explained what he was looking for, Lord Hemmings grimaced, leading the other to believe that he was racking his brains to find the right man for the job. In fact, his stomach was bothering him, and for the last day or two he had been breaking wind like a fiend. He was now fighting the impulse to fart, which he found disgusting, for like most upper-class Englishmen he despised the intestinal functions and would have rather been created without bowels.

"Now, let me see if I understand you," Lord Hemmings said carefully as he stealthily squeezed out his latest fart. "You are looking for someone to kill your brother in a duel?"

Hartley Fudges looked annoyed. "I wouldn't put it quite so bluntly," he groused, adding, "I'm the second son, for Christ's sake. He gets everything and I get nothing. How can that be fair? You've got to do something or you'll wind up in the poorhouse."

Lord Hemmings sighed and muttered, "I wish I'd thought this up myself before my older brother's wife had borne him three sons."

"Do you think you can arrange it?" Hartley asked, staring intently at his lordship, who was a short, drab man on whom even the latest fashions in clothing seemed frumpy.

"I have someone in mind," said his lordship. "There's

no better shot in Christendom, and he likes the excitement of dueling. He could also provoke St. Peter himself if he had to."

The men shared another drink and huddled together to discuss the financial arrangements. For arranging to hire a marksman who would provoke the older Fudges to a duel, for which his lordship would orchestrate all the details and act as a second to the shooter, his lordship would be paid the sum of £500, with £250 to be paid in advance of the deed regardless of its outcome and the other £250 to be due only if the older Fudges were killed. Naturally, his lordship was expected to pay his chosen assassin out of the £500.

"Five hundred pounds!" Hartley Fudges gasped.

"Exactly so," Lord Hemmings said coolly.

This was a considerable sum of money, roughly $50,000 in today's currency, and Hartley Fudges thought it an outrageous fee, but he said nothing except to groan and mutter something about being thrown by circumstances on the mercy of the moneylenders.

His lordship thought it infra dig to discuss monetary arrangements. His firm principle was never to haggle. If Hartley Fudges had said another protesting word, Hemmings would have gotten up out of his seat and abruptly walked away after saying, "You're beginning to bore me." Those who lived in this particular slice of England knew better than to bore his lordship. So Hartley Fudges stopped his moaning and ordered another drink from a flirtatious barmaid.

Hartley lapsed into a thoughtful silence. Then he began to squirm as if he were being overrun by biting ants and muttered in his beer that he would have the money before the end of the week. His lordship pointed out that once he had accepted the money and hired the duelist, the transaction would be a rung bell, adding that there would be no unringing it. Hartley Fudges chuckled at this witticism and the two men stared at each other appraisingly in the smoky confines of the pub before shaking hands tentatively like two distrustful horse thieves who had just made a crooked deal. After another drink, his lordship went away, squirming through the noisy throng and disappearing out the door while Hartley Fudges mingled here and there as if he were the pub's proprietor. He was good at mingling for he had a knack for superficial relationships and seemed quite the *bon vivant*.

No one could tell from his behavior that he just negotiated the murder of his brother.

For the next few days Hartley Fudges scoured the streets of London looking for a source of funds. He was already well known to most of the moneylenders, having transacted business with them in the past, and though chronically slow to pay, he had a reputation of one who would eventually repay a loan.

After checking with his usual sources and being turned down by five of the lenders he consulted, Hartley was able to secure a loan from a Viennese expatriate using as collateral the only property he owned in the world—ten acres of prime land on the banks of the River Thames, a bequest from a dead aunt. The paperwork was drawn up and furtively executed and within ten days the money traveled from the lender to Hartley to Lord Hemmings's pocket, and the bell was rung.

On the evening when the symbolic ringing of the bell

took place, Hartley and his lordship celebrated the occasion with a quiet drink in their favorite pub. Then they parted company, as without a squeak or a creak, the plot they had hatched between them was set into a silent and sinister motion.

The assassin handpicked by Lord Hemmings was an Etonian castoff whom everyone knew as Bottoms but whose formal title was the Earl of Bottoms. A burly young man with a disheveled hairdo and the distracted manner of an intellectual or a drug addict, Bottoms was another English second son who had not yet found his niche in life and whose calm and composed exterior suggested thwarted scholarship. One could quite easily imagine him tucked away in some fusty corner of a library poring over old papers on some esoteric topic, for he carried himself with the absentmindedness of an Oxford don that suggested tea and quiet evenings playing tiddledywinks. But, in fact, Bottoms was more of a ruffian than his appearance suggested, and he had already survived half a dozen duels, killing three men in the process, crippling one, and severely wounding two more. Two of these duels were fought over a woman, the other four over various social miscues, real or imagined, that required ritualistic bloodshed.

Hemmings and Bottoms met one Sunday morning in a park near Westminster Abbey. It was no coincidence that Lord Hemmings chose to meet his handpicked assassin on the Sabbath near an ancient and famous church with bells reverberating over the sleepy streets of London, or that his lordship laid out the proposition for murder as churchgoers rattled past in carriages and streamed by on foot. His lordship rather liked the contrast between the sanctity of the day and the foul plot he was proposing to Bottoms, for he wanted to make it starkly clear that evil was involved in what he needed done. He preferred a willing accomplice who would feel no squeamishness after the deed. Experience had taught him that where evil is concerned, it was better to be frank than to shilly-shally.

Bottoms and Lord Hemmings were of the same kettle of fish. Both were second sons who had been dispossessed by primogeniture. Both spoke the same precise received pronunciation and observed to the letter all the idolatries and idiotic grammatical practices of upper-crust speech. Both had had their heads crammed full of heroic stories and sagas from Greek and Roman mythology. Images and memorable lines of poetry littered the landscape of their consciousness like goose feathers on a golf course.

His lordship was the first to arrive at the park, looking forlorn and lonely sitting by himself on a bench in the gray and early-morning mist. A few moments later he was joined by Bottoms, and the two men began a leisurely stroll through the park.

"I've got an assignment for you, if you're interested," his lordship began, choosing his words very carefully.

"How much does it pay?" Bottoms wondered, sniffing the air as if something smelled bad.

"One hundred pounds," his lordship shot back. "Are you interested?"

Bottoms's brow crinkled in a spasm that indicated he was thinking. He was flat broke at the moment and £100 seemed like a bountiful godsend. "I am," he asserted.

His lordship summed up the situation tersely; for the money, Bottoms would have to challenge someone to a duel and kill him. He put the case in the starkest terms, making no attempt to palliate the deed or explain the motive of his client.

Their slow pace had covered no more than a furlong or two when Bottoms declared the assignment fun and said he would do it. "Fun" was the word that Bottoms always used to express a superlative.

"Good!" declared his lordship. "I knew you were my man."

Just then the bells of Westminster Abbey began a stately tolling, signaling the beginning of services, and the cheerless pealing made the misty morning air quiver with an echoing tonality that brought to mind the somberness of death, eternity, and gloom. Almost as if it were reflex, both men gave off a shiver of dread and desolation like children who had just heard a ghost story.

"What a life we live, eh?" his lordship said softly, sensing something grave and weighty in the moment.

"Yes," agreed the Earl of Bottoms inanely, "such fun."

CHAPTER 4

For the next two weeks, Bottoms and his lordship dogged the footsteps of Alexander Fudges through the maze that was nineteenth-century London, looking for an opportune time and place to stage a confrontation that would lead to a duel. It was not easy, following him in his daily treks, for London was a rough-and-tumble metropolis flooded with a crushing throng of humanity that frequently caused the narrow streets to spasm with gridlock, bringing all traffic to a standstill in a dense ganglia of vehicles and bodies. The polluted air rang with a constant clamor of business and industry as approximately 970,000 inhabitants along with some hundred thousand horses trod their way through narrow streets originally laid down by the Romans who founded the city on the River Thames in 45 AD. Added to the mix were hundreds of sedan chairs—single-passenger boxy compartments mounted on poles and carried by two men, one in front, the other in the back. These English rickshaws were first introduced in 1634 by Sir Saunders Duncombe and were still a popular means of getting around in 1805 London, weaving in and out of traffic with its bearers shouting, "Have care!" or, "By your leave, sir!"

The two stalkers discovered that Alexander Fudges was a chronic clubbie who spent many hours of the day socializing in private ritzy London clubs, one of which provided him with a furnished room. He frequently attended meetings of various agricultural societies, where he heard lectures given by speakers on the latest methods of producing crops and fostering animal husbandry. Lord Hemmings and the Earl of Bottoms played a game of cat-and-mouse unbeknownst to Alexander. Yet in spite of their attempt at stealth and their persistence, the tracking lords would often lose their quarry in the thick London traffic and have to give up the chase for the day.

Two lords following one lord through the streets of London in February 1805 was tedious and demeaning work—hardly a suitable occupation for a member of the peerage. Alexander, as the firstborn male Fudges, inherited all titles that had been conferred on his father, who was, in fact, a hereditary duke. The old man's formal title was the Duke of Fudges, which the family had had for generations. But since the oldest son was also entitled to use that name, it was a custom for the heir apparent to be given a courtesy title such as Lord Fudges. Sometimes, to avoid confusion, the heir to a dukedom would take a lesser rank such as marquis or earl until the death of the father, at which time the son would assume the father's name and formal title. In any event, under the protocol of English society, the cat-and-mouse game between his lordship, Bottoms, and Alexander was really "Lord Cat" and "the Marquis of Cat" trailing the "Duke of Mouse" and occasionally losing him in the vulgar crush of busy London.

After watching their prey and his movements for a couple of weeks, Lord Hemmings and Earl Bottoms decided that they would stage a scene at the weekly meeting of the book club, a hoity-toity setting usually with at least one author in attendance that was held at a private club near what was then known as the King's Mews—and had been since the reign of Edward I—but was later renamed Trafalgar Square. The Battle of Trafalgar would not be fought until October 21, 1805, when twenty-seven British ships of the line under the command of Admiral Lord Nelson would route a Franco-Spanish Armada of thirty-three warships off Cape Trafalgar. The Franco-Spanish fleet would lose twenty-two of its thirty-three ships. On the English side, not a single ship would go down to enemy fire, but in an incalculable loss, Admiral Lord Nelson, the brilliant maritime strategist whose tactics won the victory, would be gunned down by sharpshooters concealed in the mast of an enemy vessel.

On the appointed day, the two young lords showed up at the club wearing their Sunday best and looking every inch the ideal nineteenth-century gentlemen. They sat inconspicuously at a table by themselves near the entrance to the club where they could observe everyone who came and left. The book of the month was a geography of the Orkney Islands, which lie off the northern coast of Scotland, and was written by an earnest, burly Scotsman who lived there. During the course of the writer's talk, Alexander got up and headed for the bathroom, but to get there, he had to make his way past the table occupied by his lordship and Bottoms. His lordship nudged Bottoms and indicated the approaching Alexander with a jerk of his head. Timing his move just right, Bottoms, clutching a glass of wine, stood up as Alexander was passing the table occupied by the plotters, and the two men bumped into one another, the wine spilling all over the front of Alexander's shirt.

"Watch where you're going, sir!" Alexander exclaimed impulsively. In reply, Bottoms smacked Alexander's cheek with his open hand, hard enough to jerk the other's head violently back.

Friends of Alexander came rushing over to separate the two men. But it was enough. An insult had been given, and a blow had been struck that required satisfaction. A clutch of onlookers, mostly Alexander's fellow club members, began babbling with excitement about what had happened. Among them were a dozen dukes, a handful of marquises, a brace of counts, every jack man among them historically entitled to be formally known as Lord This or Lord That. Pretending to be nothing more than a friend of Lord Bottoms's, his lordship the Earl of Hemmings modestly introduced himself and volunteered to act as a second.

It was a squalid, frenzied scene, and the hangers-on who crowded the table vociferously discussing who was blameless and who to blame grew animated and excited like children romping at a garden party. One man, an older chap, tried to cool the hot-blooded spirits by saying, "Come, now, it was an accident. That's no reason to kill each other, is it?"

Alexander looked hopeful that this was an honorable way out, but Bottoms snarled, "I'll shake hands when I see his brains scattered on the grass at Southampton's Park."

"Now, sir," said the peacemaker hopefully, "if you knew the gentleman you intend to fight, you would like him, possibly even be his friend. Do you know him?"

"I know him to be a clumsy fool!" snapped Bottoms.

It was, summed up his lordship to the Earl of Bottoms as the two conspirators shouldered their way down a crowded sidewalk, almost too good to be true. Everything had occurred exactly as he had hoped. The duel would take place three days later at the crack of dawn.

"I'd practice my shooting between now and then, if I were you," his lordship suggested to the shambling, seemingly indifferent Bottoms who trotted at his side with a tipsy gait.

"I'll be ready, Hemmings," Bottoms said confidently. "I say, how about advancing me ten pounds? I'm a bit short this week."

"No advances," his lordship said sternly. "You'd only buy laudanum. Use the remaining time to practice your marksmanship."

Bottoms was protesting this decision and squabbling with his employer when he collided with a man trudging down the street in the other direction.

"Look where you're going, you fool!" the man snarled.

"Sorry," Bottoms said meekly. The man stood on the side of the road, glaring and shouting curses at them loud enough to draw the attention of onlookers. But he was a working man, and from his manner and dress, it was obvious that he came from the laboring class. To exchange insults or gunshots with such a man was unthinkable. So the two gentlemen burrowed through the throngs curdling the edges of the rutted roadway and ignored the insulting bellowing that sounded in their wake.

It wasn't a simple job being an English aristocrat in 1805.

On the morning of the duel the participants and their seconds woke up at five a.m. to prepare for their rendezvous with death. The duelists had nothing to eat because it was widely believed that food in the stomach made a belly shot especially deadly.

Lord Hemmings and the Earl of Bottoms walked together to the dueling grounds. They strolled past beggars curled up asleep on the side of the road looking like enormous insect grubs. The two men didn't say much. Hemmings at first tried the Earl with various topics designed to take the other's mind off what possibly lay ahead. Finally the Earl of Bottoms said rather sharply, "Look here, Hemmings, you're making me nervous with all your prattle."

"Sorry, old chap," his lordship murmured, "just trying to help."

"Well, it didn't help a bit. So do me a favor and keep quiet."

The two men walked in silence on streets so empty of life that their footsteps gave off a staccato clip-clop that made the foggy morning sound like a loudly ticking clock.

Soon they were walking on the grass of the park and headed toward the particular spot next to a grove of trees where duels were usually fought. They were nearing the grove when a sharp eruption of gunfire shattered the tranquility of the park. Two shots were followed immediately by a horrific groan and the sound of a body falling.

Daybreak was just upon them and the sunlight was too dim to cast shadows. In the gloom they came upon a duelist sprawled out prone on the ground with his desperate seconds on either side of him. The wounded man was bleeding from the neck, the blood gushing in a torrent with every heartbeat while his friends vainly tried to stanch the flow with a scarf. Nearby, the fallen man's adversary was putting on his coat, with the help of his seconds, and glancing with a mixture of curiosity and indifference at his victim.

"Sir," one of the seconds said to Hemmings as he and Bottoms drew near, "this is a private affair."

"These are public grounds," said Lord Hemmings, "and we also have business here."

Bottoms and Hemmings withdrew to the trunk of an old yew tree. Just then the figure crumpled on the ground made a noise like a boiling kettle and sagged limply into the arms of his friends.

"He's gone," one of the seconds whispered.

The other burst into tears.

"Help me with him," said the second who had made the death announcement, and the two men gently lifted the dead man by the arms and legs and disappeared into the park just as Alexander and his seconds materialized out of the gloom. One of the seconds was the older gentleman who had tried to patch things up at the club.

"Where are your seconds?" he asked.

"I am he," Lord Hemmings declared, stepping forward with a movement as genteel as his English.

"It is customary for two seconds to be present."

"It may be customary, but it is not required," Lord Hemmings snapped.

The second man turned his attention to Bottoms and tried his best to be conciliatory.

"Really, sir," he began, wiping his face which seemed to be sweating in the chilly morning breeze, "this is a trifle offense to fight over. One man accidentally bounces into another and it leads to this? Sir, I'm sure you're a reasonable man and that your intentions are honorable. My friend is prepared to accept an apology, even to acknowledge that the accident was partly his fault, if doing so will avoid bloodshed. There's no cause for anyone to be shot or killed here. No cause at all."

Bottoms swelled up like a bullfrog and said in a loud voice, "Is he a coward then? Does he intend to hide behind you, or will he face me like a man?"

There was no possibility, once those taunting words were spoken, for anything but bloodshed to follow, and the two men, shielded by their seconds, went through the courtesies of examining each other's pistols to ensure that they were standard unrifled dueling weapons. Each man took off his coat with an air of finality and gravity, handed it to his second, who in turn gave him the pistol, primed, loaded, and cocked. In the swirling fog, which made visibility difficult, the men stood back-to-back, holding their pistols at the ready against the chest, and began to pace off, with the exaggerated and ceremonial struts of warring roosters, the distance from which they would fire.

"One, two, three, four," the second chanted as the two men walked the required distance. "Do not move until both men have fired," the second warned Lord Hemmings.

At fifteen, the second stopped and declared loudly, "Turn and aim at my command. Do not fire until I say 'fire.' Any man who disobeys this rule will be shot down. Remember, you are gentlemen and must be prepared to die like gentlemen."

Backs to each other, separated by some thirty feet, the two gentlemen remained standing still, as if frozen there.

"Turn and aim!" bellowed the second.

With ceremony that went so smoothly the moves might have been rehearsed, the two men pivoted, faced their enemy sideways, one foot behind the other, their shoulder and arms extended, at the end of which the hand grasped and aimed the pistol. It was a pose that presented the smallest possible target to the field of fire. To hit a duelist in the heart who assumed this posture was next to impossible. To inflict a belly wound was likewise unlikely. More probable was that the shooter would be hit in the shoulder by a ball; it would be simply rotten luck if the ball struck him in the face or the throat.

The pistols of the era could be rigged with a hair trigger that fired with the slightest pressure of the finger. Bottoms had chosen to adjust his pistol to the maximum sensitivity of the hair trigger. As a seasoned duelist, he knew that a trigger that was hard to pull could cause a shooter to jerk just as he drew a bead on his target.

For a millisecond the two English lords were posed like mannequins in a shop window, their hands extended at each other and tipped with a loaded dueling pistol while personal eternity hung in the balance.

"Fire!" barked the second. A deafening shot blasted the morning, jolting Bottoms into a pirouette like a ballet dancer. For a fleeting moment he spun on his own axis, his eyes widened in horror and surprise. Then he toppled over and began to fall. His pistol discharged like a thunderclap as he tumbled to the ground, the ball knocking Hemmings off his feet and flat on his back. With the returning silence came the pungency of gunpowder and sudden death.

"Bottoms, you idiot," Lord Hemmings groaned from the ground, "you shot me!"

Bottoms lay dead on the ground, beyond caring about whom he had accidentally shot. There was a dark hole between his eyes where the ball had entered his skull, leaving behind a pulpy wound. Blood poured out of his forehead and festooned his face with a lurid red ribbon.

Hemmings, mortally wounded in the chest, lay writhing on the ground, sputtering with indignation. He tried to sit up but dropped helplessly on his back like an overturned beetle.

Alexander and his two seconds stood over the wounded lord.

"The idiot shot me!" Lord Hemmings cried, his voice sounding like it came from a dark, empty cavern.

Alexander, unscratched, strolled over to his fallen adversary and measured him with the glance of a hunter sizing up dying prey.

"I don't even know the chap's name," Alexander muttered.

Lord Hemmings groaned and felt a sudden spasm of spite and hate against Hartley Fudges who was probably somewhere enjoying breakfast while his lordship was bleeding helplessly to death.

"It's your brother, Hartley, who is behind this," his lordship whispered, for he was gasping for breath like a long-distance runner at the end of a marathon. "I'm dying and beg your forgiveness."

"I forgive you," Alexander murmured.

Hemmings smiled and went into a spasm of coughing, thick clots of dark blood pouring out of his chest wound. "I'm cold," he whispered, shivering.

Then he died.

The three men left the dueling grounds with the nonchalance of picnickers, talking over the events of the morning in hushed voices. They took a little-used path to avoid encountering other dueling parties that might later link them to the two corpses they left behind. Their luck held up. They met no one coming into the grounds. They were seen by no one as they departed.

Vagrants who sometimes slept out in the park stripped the two bodies clean, and to add confusion to the ensemble, they threw the naked corpses into the thick shrubbery where they lay unnoticed for at least a fortnight. When the bodies of the two dead lords were found, nature had been unrelentingly about her grisly business of digesting and transfiguring flesh, making identification difficult. By then it was nearly impossible to tell who they were, whether English or Egyptian, and what they had been in their lifetimes. Apparently no one missed them, because no one notified the authorities that they were gone. It was as if they never were.

After a brief inquiry, it was ruled that Lord Hemmings and the Earl of Bottoms had killed each other in a duel. The bodies of the two men were buried in Potter's Field. And the case was closed.

CHAPTER 5

Alexander Fudges, on any given day, was only a so-so shot. He could hit the side of a barn with a pistol from thirty feet away, but it was unlikely that from the same range he could hit the barn door. No one could have foreseen that he would kill the Earl of Bottoms with a single shot; that Bottoms, in the act of falling, would accidentally shoot Lord Hemmings in the heart; and that in his dying confession Lord Hemmings would implicate Alexander's own brother in the duel. Indeed, when Alexander had fired, his hand had been shaking so badly that the bead at the tip of the barrel of his pistol that served as its gunsight had been dancing in midair as jerkily as a moth bobbing near the flame of a candle. Yet the shot had been so uncannily accurate that Alexander left the dueling fields believing that God Himself had fired it.

Even though Alexander was a backsliding member of the Church of England, he had read the Bible all the way through at least once and had a good idea what God wanted of His English sheep. He believed the Almighty was a stickler for the Decalogue, expected regular church attendance and generosity when the collection bag was passed, and urged all of us to get along with our neighbors and be charitable to the poor. Alexander made up his mind to observe all these stipulations, and more, and fully intended to give a florin to the next mendicant he passed

#243 07-09-2013 1:34PM
Item(s) checked out to Parrish, Barbara.

TITLE: The family mansion
BRCD: 32244202066847
DUE DATE: 07-23-13

Deer Park Public Library
(631) 586-3000 www.deerparklibrary.org

who begged him for alms. A florin, which was two shillings, was certainly generous. However, the sidewalk beggars he passed that morning were still too sleepy to beg and consequently got nothing, for Alexander also believed that giving unbegged-for money encouraged idleness.

"I can't believe what happened," Alexander kept muttering as he and his two friends slogged through the morning mist on their way back from the bizarre duel.

"It was a miracle, if ever there were one," said one of his friends.

"Two miracles," gushed the peacemaker. "Three if you count the confession."

The three men trudged on grimly and speechless like a pod of turtles. When the peacemaking second suggested a celebratory glass of ale, Alexander declined and said that he would prefer simply to go home and have breakfast in peace. Shortly after that, he and his seconds parted company and Alexander retreated to his room at the club. So much was on his mind that he entered the club with the heavy tread of someone lugging an enormous, invisible burden.

For Hartley Fudges, the day of the duel crept past like an arthritic snake. Unlike his brother, Hartley did not usually have his own room unless he was entertaining a woman or had come into a windfall from the gaming table. For the most part, he slept in a chair in a common room of the Fox and Hounds along with a dozen or so other men. Most of the time he found the arrangement crude but tolerable. To a young man of twenty-three, haphazard lodgings were as much an adventure as an ordeal. The exception to this outlook was a time like now when he wished to be alone.

Then his only recourse was to rent a room for the night, if he could find one, or go and sit on the primitive pit toilet which reeked so noxiously that after a few minutes of exposure, one felt perilously close to suffocating.

He spent the whole day at the Fox and Hounds, starting when anyone walked in, expecting to see Lord Hemmings at any moment. By the time darkness had fallen and the Fox and Hounds was bubbling over with fellowship and good cheer, Hartley Fudges knew that something had gone ghastly wrong. As the evening progressed, he became more and more morose and unsociable until, abandoned to his funk by his usual flock of fair-weather drinking friends, he found himself marooned in a corner with only a tumbler of bitter ale for company. Eventually, in spite of the noisy roistering and laughter exploding like firecrackers all around him, he fell into a deep sleep and began a loud snoring.

He slept through the entire night and did not hear the pub close or the occasional loud arguments that sprang up among the drunken men but were quickly squashed by the landlord. Silence gradually descended over the room and those who had rented chairs settled in for the night, and all through this commotion and the dying hubbub, Hartley heard nothing.

He had a dream. It was a curious dream, not coherent and intact but disjointed and shattered like broken crockery, and in it something was poking him in the back. His eyes snapped open, and he beheld his brother Alexander standing over him, prodding him with a walking stick and looking very severe.

"You!" Hartley Fudges sputtered, rubbing his eyes as if to erase an annoying specter.

"Me," Alexander said simply.

Hartley looked around him, unsure of where he was or whether he was awake or dreaming. Scattered throughout the room—pleated, folded, crumpled, and twisted around chairs, sprawled on the floor, or propped up against a wall like casualties strewn on a battlefield—were a dozen slumbering, disheveled men, among them a marquis, an earl, a viscount, and a duke or two, all of whom gave off the effluvia of stale beer and dried sweat, and from whom came an unsynchronized rumbling, wheezing, and whistling.

"Good Lord," muttered Hartley groggily, "where am I?"

"In hell," his brother said.

In the dawn light, with the great heart of London merely fibrillating instead of pounding its customary robust daytime beat, the two brothers took a walk. At first Hartley balked at going but Alexander insisted, and after wrangling about it for five minutes, they stepped out into early-morning London. In another hour or so, the city would be teeming with grubby workmen, stylish ladies, cavalier gentlemen, messenger boys, butchers, horse-drawn carriages, hawkers and peddlers, pickpockets, beggars, streetwalkers, sedan chairs, and livestock, but in the morning mist its tangle of streets sprawled out damp and empty. Only the occasional horse-drawn taxi rattled past on the dirty arterial streets, while from the capillaries of lanes and mews dripped small clumps of workmen into the square. Wearing the deadpan, deliberate look to which aristocrats are bred, the two brothers strolled as if they were savoring the crisp morning air before it became befouled by the day's industry.

"Your paid assassin is dead," Alexander said evenly, "and I know the whole story, thanks to the confession of Hemmings. It's no use denying your involvement. I know everything."

"You do?"

"Yes, I do. Papa is in town, and I saw him last night. We are both agreed that you should leave England immediately."

"And go where?" Hartley asked.

"To Jamaica. He's written a letter introducing you to a schoolboy chum who manages an estate there. The man will give you a job that will keep you out of mischief. It's your chance to start anew and make your fortune."

"And if I refuse to go?"

"I'll press charges against you for attempted murder. I have sworn witnesses to your friend's confession before he died."

They walked on quietly for a few edgy moments.

"What happened to Hemmings?" Hartley asked.

"Both men are dead."

"How can they both be dead?"

"I killed the duelist. The other chap, the second, was accidentally shot by his friend. Their blood is on your hands."

Hartley stopped in his tracks to glare at his brother. The other stopped also and the two men scowled at each other.

"You get everything," Hartley groused. "I get nothing."

"I didn't invent primogeniture," Alexander snapped.

"You benefit from it."

"As would you if you were the firstborn. We must obey the rules of society whether we like them or not."

"I won't go," Hartley said firmly.

"Suit yourself," replied Alexander. "But if you're found guilty of attempted murder, you'll either be hanged or transported to Australia."

They walked a little farther, then turned around without talking and headed back in the direction in which they had come.

"What did you do with the bodies?" Hartley wondered.

"We left them where they had fallen," Alexander answered with a yawn.

They walked some more cloaked in silence.

"Do you know why your plot failed?" Alexander asked. "It failed because God watches over me and protects me and will not allow anyone to harm me."

"I wish your God would mind His own business," Hartley grumbled.

"He does. I am His business," Alexander said triumphantly.

When they arrived at the doorstep of the Fox and Hounds, they did not wish each other goodbye or shake hands or reminisce or exchange hugs as brothers might do. Instead, they stared into each other's eyes defiantly and probingly like enemies sizing each other up before the next battle.

"If you change your mind, you can send a message to my club. A ship called the *Mermaid* sails in seven days for Jamaica and Father and I have reserved a berth on it in your name. I advise you to be on her when she sails."

With that, Alexander turned on his heels and began to walk away. But he abruptly stopped and pivoted to make eye contact with his brother.

"By the way, I wouldn't try to murder me again, if I were you. I've already given the statement to the police implicating you. Should anything happen to me, you'll hang."

"It was nothing personal, Alexander," Hartley called after him. "It was just an idea I had to try."

"I assure you, my dear brother, that had you succeeded, I would have taken it very personally." Pausing, Alexander added, "Don't come back. There's nothing for you in England."

And then he was gone.

London was beginning to wake up in increments, its streets slowly coming alive with pedestrians and horses. Weak, waterish, and without warmth, the February winter sun peered blurrily down on the city like a nearsighted eye squinting through a dirty monocle.

In effect, Hartley was being sent into exile. Such was the commonplace fate of the second son. Between Alexander and Hartley had never existed any particularly strong ties, and whatever incipient love each might have felt for the other during the years in the nursery had long ago been blasted to smithereens by the harsh reality of primogeniture. Hartley felt that he was being dumped on Jamaica, an island he had never particularly wanted to visit. He knew it from his reading to be a quarrelsome, rebellious island with a large population of fractious slaves who were constantly in revolt. The mortality rate from yellow fever among new arrivals to the island was astonishing. Within three months after arrival, more than half the newcomers would be dead. The only good thing that could be said about the island was that it was the world's largest producer of sugar and a source of fabulous wealth. In 1750, for example, Jamaica produced half the sugar consumed in

Great Britain. So ostentatious was the wealth of its plantation owners that the saying "as rich as a Jamaican planter" was a simile commonly heard among the chic habitués of London's drawing rooms.

A few hours later found Hartley sitting bleary-eyed in his chair at the Fox and Hounds, trying to decide what to do about the ultimatum Alexander had given him. The truth was that there was no compelling reason for Hartley Fudges to remain in London. He had no job and intended to get one over his dead body. Now that the widow had rejected him, he had no prospects for marriage. His mother was dead and although he was near to his father, Hartley was too old for that kind of paternal closeness. He had a bushel of drinking friends and other acquaintances who might best be called fair-weather cronies. But he had no one close enough to him to be expected to weep over his grave. There was no good reason why he couldn't leave the city.

At one o'clock in the morning, he made up his mind. He would give up London and try his luck in Jamaica. A drinking friend of his appeared at his table for chitchat.

"I'm going to Jamaica," Hartley said softly.

"Oh, good show," the fellow chirped, finishing his tankard of ale. After reeling in place for a few moments, the man asked plaintively, "I say, where the devil is that anyway?"

To Hartley Fudges, London had been a tolerant, indulgent landlady, and taking his leave of her was a heart-wrenching experience. He took a coach back to the family mansion, where he supervised the packing of a chest with his clothes and personal effects. While there, he encountered his father, who was about to leave on a business trip to Edinburgh, and they had a heart-to-heart.

"Plotting to kill your bother in a sham duel so you can inherit my estate," his father chided. "Really, Hartley, you surprise me. You can't expect to profit from someone else's death."

"You did," Hartley shot back.

"The difference is, I didn't kill anyone or try to kill anyone."

"But someone did."

"Yes, of course. God did. But God can kill anyone He pleases. After all, He made everyone."

Hartley hung his head as if repentant and remonstrated very little in his own defense, and after a session of browbeating his son, the old man softened, handed him a letter of introduction to John Austin, an old school chum, and quietly gave him one hundred pounds. They took their leave of each other on the front steps of the family mansion which loomed behind them glittering with rows of mullioned windows and looking like an overdressed matron. They hugged briefly, ceremoniously, conscious that they may never see each other again.

Hartley made a last-minute call on the widow Bentley whom he had been courting, hoping against hope that she had changed her mind. It was still early in the morning and she saw him briefly in the dining room where she was taking breakfast. Her morning face, without her elaborate makeup, had a shriveling fleshiness that bespoke of the approach of hideousness. She was in a playful humor and while she munched on a croissant, they exchanged quips and witticisms.

"I've met your brother," she remarked, looking up at him impishly.

"I have no doubt," Hartley retorted, "that he'll fail your test."

"Oh, no," she giggled, "in fact, he's a perfect five inches. Exactly what I'm looking for."

"Madame," Hartley said irritably, "why would you want a Pekinese when you could have a wolfhound?"

"Because one nips while the other bites."

Hartley gave up: he'd had enough of this coded drawing room talk, a language he despised. He sprang to his feet abruptly, said a curt goodbye, and strolled decisively out of the room tracked by the amused gaze of the widow.

CHAPTER 6

The *Mermaid*, a brigantine, slipped her shore hawsers early one gray February morning and caught the outgoing tide to open sea. Dawn had not yet broken, and a cloying darkness hung over the estuary like an enormous cobweb. Even in the morning stillness the *Mermaid* flew a full but limp complement of canvas—three square-rigged sails on her foremast, a gaff-rigged mizzen on her aft mast, and three working jibs.

The *Mermaid* was in her early teens, nautical middle-age for a wooden boat, and showing signs of aging. She was the same pedigree as the Baltimore clippers, glorious sailing vessels that in 1805 were still hatching on the drawing boards of New England shipyards. But there was no glory left in the *Mermaid*. She had been roughly used most of her life as a beast of burden. Her sails, once white, were now the drab color of a drought-stricken lawn. Her rigging seemed to sag and be impossibly tangled; her ratlines dangled like loose suspenders. Yet she gave every sign of being a sprightly sailor, especially in the rakish tilt of her masts and the conspicuous sheen of her deck.

She had made the passage to Jamaica several times, usually hauling tools and provisions to the island and barrels of sugar and rum back to England. On this voyage she carried a crew of eighteen, thirty-two paying passengers, and fifteen shackled slaves who were crammed in the forward hold and whose presence, had it been widely known, would have been contentious. The House of Commons had already proposed legislation prohibiting any British ship from transporting slaves, but the measure had been bottled up in the House of Lords. On March 25, 1807, the proposal would finally become law, levying a fine of one hundred pounds for every contraband slave found aboard a British ship. Rather than pay such a steep fine, captains in danger of being boarded and searched by a British warship would resort to the brutal strategy of throwing chained slaves overboard.

The *Mermaid* drifted gently with the tide, her longboat, manned by six rowers, hovering protectively nearby in case of trouble, her deck swarming with a dozen crewmen who stood by in case they were needed. Below deck most of the passengers slept. The exception was Hartley Fudges, who stood on the poop deck looking at the city with the intensity of a departing lover. Matching his somber mood was a winter sky that daubed the color and sheen of a brown rat over the spires and steeples of London.

"Wind ahoy!" rang out from the crow's nest. Hartley felt a soft breeze caress his cheek and playfully tug at his sleeves. The sails of the *Mermaid* fluttered and partly filled and the ship spurted forward with a gentle motion, her bowsprit knitting the seam between the drab dawn sky and the ugly green sea.

In 1805, an ocean voyage between England and Jamaica was not for the fainthearted. Depending on the weather, the journey could take anywhere from four to eight weeks. Navigation techniques were still primitive, and the possibility of getting lost was very real. Charts on the New

World were notoriously inaccurate, and while many of the Indians were peaceful and welcoming, others were savagely territorial and would attack any vessel that ventured too close to their shores.

Calamitous weather aside, the most serious threat to a voyaging ship came from privateers. Little more than run-of-the-mill brigands, the privateer was a marauder supposedly authorized by a government to prey on enemy shipping—a sort of commissioned predator. But, in fact, the privateer did pretty much as he pleased and was not scrupulous about attacking only the enemies of the licensing government. Privateers prowled the shipping lanes of the West Indies preying on fat Spanish galleons and other vessels.

Privateers or not, the *Mermaid* would sail the route to Jamaica from England that was established by Columbus himself and took advantage of the prevailing winds and currents. She would steer for the Canary Islands and cruise southward parallel to the coast of West Africa, beginning her westerly run only after she had fetched up the Cape Verde Islands. Making landfall near Guadalupe, she would catch the strong trade winds that would send her scudding past the Leeward Islands on a heading for the Greater Antilles and Jamaica.

Aboard the *Mermaid* was the typical grab bag of European profiteers, adventurers, and plunderers. Jamaica has always bared her bosom to hard men who would use her without tenderness or love. The exception to this observation were the aboriginal Indians whose lifetime briefly overlapped the arrival of their exterminator, Columbus, and whose reverence for the land became apparent only after they had become extinct, leaving virtually no trace of their presence. The European replacements aboard the *Mermaid* consisted of dispossessed second sons like Hartley Fudges; landless Irish farmers; overseers and plantation functionaries; indentured servants; and, most wretched of all, shackled slaves gasping for breath in the sweltering, vaporous confines of the forward hold where they lay suffocating in the miasmic fumes of their own excrement.

The stark reality aboard a small vessel like the *Mermaid* was that every life hung on the soundness of the ship and the skill of the captain, a fact that tended to relax the class distinctions rigidly observed on land where everyone lived with the belief that he was in a separate boat. There would be some casual if cautious intermingling among different groups of passengers, except for the Irish and the English, between whom there had always been bad blood.

Most of the passengers were going to Jamaica for purely selfish reasons. The landless Irish, for example, were being lured by the government's offer of free arable land to white farmers who would cultivate it. By then the dwindling population of white people on the island was drowning in a tidal wave of black slaves. In 1805, there were approximately twenty-one thousand white people to three hundred thousand slaves. This imbalance was only exaggerated by the passing years. Whites simply did not thrive in the West Indies, particularly Jamaica, with colonizers suffering a mortality rate of over 50 percent within the first three months of their arrival. That kind of grim statistic was one reason some English writers of the day had begun calling Jamaica a "graveyard."

In addition to being risky, a voyage from England to Jamaica in 1805 was agonizingly slow and cumbersome. Passengers were thrown together in close physical contact that was anything but intimate. You saw the same faces every day but often did not know their stories. Greetings were exchanged daily with strangers whose names you did not know but who could not be ignored without being rude. But eventually, as the days dragged past, casual acquaintance was established among the passengers. Hartley, for example, as the weeks passed, found himself saying good morning to a middle-aged Irish gentleman at the same spot in the companionway that led to the deck, merely because every day they both happened to get up at the same time. Once on deck, Hartley would encounter the familiar crew faces and exchange small talk with other gentlemen and ladies whose daily orbit happened to correspond with his.

On this particular route that the *Mermaid* followed, the weather was temperate and mild, with a refreshing trade wind coming off the quarterdeck and a daily afternoon shower that cooled down the ship. But occasionally, a squally weather front would roll over the ocean and the *Mermaid* would toss and prance with a herky-jerky motion that would make some passengers seasick. The crew would quickly herd sick passengers to the lee side of the ship where their vomit would not be wind-borne all over the deck. Seamen would go swarming up the ratlines to take in sail, and for an hour or so the *Mermaid* would buck and roll frantically. But then the wind would ease and the rain would lift and the sea and the sky would blur in the twilight, and with the falling darkness the stars and constellations blazed with luminosity and brilliance that would enchant the stoniest heart.

One day, two weeks into the journey, Hartley and other passengers who happened to be on deck saw the hatch of the forward hold open and shackled slaves being brought up on deck for fresh air while the crew cleaned out their filthy habitation. During a lull in the transfer, a slave wearing leg irons that tethered him to another suddenly darted for the bowsprit, flung aside a crewman armed with a musket, and leapt overboard, taking his screaming fellow captive along in the suicide plunge. Weighted down with the irons, the two were immediately swallowed up by the bottomless blue, leaving behind a quick, shuddering ripple. Women screamed, men gasped, crewmen rushed to the deck rail. The *Mermaid* didn't even heave to for a perfunctory search—the unfortunate men were clearly lost. She simply kept her course while armed crewmen drove the other slaves away from the deck railing.

"That's a Coromantee for you," a burly Irishman muttered to Hartley. "Shackling him to an Ibo was pure stupidity."

"Why is that?" Hartley asked.

"Because they're very opposite people in temperament. The Ibo wants to stay alive. The Coromantee wants to cut your throat. They're like the Maroons."

"You seem to know a lot about both people."

"I should," the man chuckled, "I've managed them for twenty years in Jamaica."

"Where in Jamaica?"

"The Mount Pleasant plantation. I'm the head overseer there."

Hartley was startled. "That's where I'm going!" he cried. "I have a letter of introduction from my father to John Austin, the resident manager."

The burly Irishman looked stunned. "Austin is dead. He was murdered by a Coromantee slave six months ago.

I'm going to be the new resident manager."

"My name is Hartley Fudges," Hartley said, extending his hand.

The Irishman shook it vigorously. "Sinclair Meredith, at your service, sir. You've caught me in the place I hate the most—the ocean. I wish man would learn to fly. It'd make coming and going to Jamaica so much easier."

"Learn to fly!" Hartley grinned. "You mean, like a bird?"

"No, sir. I mean better than a bird. Faster and higher, making this ocean seem to us like a pond. And mark my word, sir, one day it will happen."

Hartley burst into a wild laughter. The Irishman looked at him and shook his head with an impish grin.

"I like a man who laughs," he said. "It gets lonely in the bush. But no one is ever lonely as long as he can laugh."

It was, Hartley would later admit, a providential encounter. And any sleuth who would go poking around into the cast of characters, as well as the tangled events that had to happen for him to meet Meredith, was certain to find God's fingerprints all over their meeting. That the Almighty would micromanage an individual's affairs was not an official teaching of the English church to which Hartley belonged, but it fell within the range of nineteenth-century Anglican beliefs. Nevertheless, whether or not God had anything to do with it, a friendship quickly emerged between Hartley and his godsend, Meredith. Over the next few days, the two men could be seen strolling the decks of the *Mermaid* talking about everything under the sun and the moon. It was quickly settled between them that Hartley would be given a position under Meredith, to whom he would report, and Hartley accepted this without quibble. Already he had found, what many of his like would find, that life abroad, away from the peering, judgmental eyes of other Englishmen, gave him considerable flexibility in his behavior and professed outlook. He hadn't even set foot on Jamaican soil but already was anticipating its liberating effect on him.

From Meredith, he also learned some interesting tidbits of information about the island that would soon become Hartley's home. The older man was a student of the country's history and had at his fingertips many facts about sugar production and skirmishes between England and Spain over possession of Jamaica. Nearly every morning he and Hartley would pace the forward deck, circling the foremast and chatting amiably within earshot of the occasional moaning that drifted out of the forward hold. Meredith's attitude toward the peculiar institution of slavery was both clear and morally ambiguous.

"Theoretically," he explained primly to Hartley, "I'm against slavery. It's a cruel, brutal business. But I've got a job to do, so I do it."

They trod the wooden deck of the *Mermaid* in a contemplative silence while Hartley digested this revelation.

"I'm not sure how I feel," Hartley said humbly. "I don't have enough experience to say one way or the other."

Circling the foremast and doing their best to keep away from the working crewmen, the two men exuded the academic air of master and student in a scholarly chat.

They discussed John Austin, the man whom Hartley's father had written to and whom Meredith was going to replace.

"His murder could have been avoided. If I had to give

you one piece of advice it would be this: try to show respect to everyone you meet."

"Surely not to the slaves."

"Especially to the slaves."

"Why?"

"Because they have nothing to lose. I warned Austin. But he wouldn't listen."

"What did Austin do?"

"He had a slave punished before his woman, their children, and everyone in his family. It was so unnecessary. I told Austin, 'You go too far. Whip him in private, the fellow is prepared to accept his punishment but not in front of the people who matter to him. He's a proud slave.'"

"How can a slave be proud?" Hartley scoffed.

"Pride is all they have left. It's the only consolation in a wretched life. Most slaves will put up with beatings. But they draw the line at humiliation and insult. Austin wouldn't listen to me. A week later, the man he punished hacked him to death with a machete. In front of English visitors too."

They strolled the decks in silence before Hartley asked, "You mentioned the Maroons. Who are the Maroons?"

"They're a mixed-blood people, the descendants of Indians, Spaniards, and African slaves. We've had two wars with them. The first was when we landed in 1655. The Maroons took to the hills and started a war. They slaughtered practically every patrol we sent among them. They were excellent at camouflage and would pick off our men at will. We started patrolling two men to a horse, one facing front, the other facing back. Even today, the area of the island where the Maroons settled is marked on the English maps as *The Land of Look Behind*. Finally, the government offered the Maroons 1,500 acres of land in the interior of the island where they could live as a separate people if they would agree to hunt down and return any escaped slaves who tried to hide among them."

"They agreed to hunt down their own people?"

"They didn't regard the plantation slaves as their people. That's what you have to remember about living in Jamaica. Your skin color may be the same as another man's but it doesn't automatically make him your ally."

They walked some more, following the roughly elliptical orbit of planets and skirting close to the forward hold where the slaves were packed.

"The second war," continued Meredith, "was because of something similar to what Austin did. Two Maroons were flogged in public for pig stealing. Many who witnessed their punishment were plantation slaves, who jeered them. So a war started. But how unnecessary a war! If the men had been privately punished, there would have been no war. I warned Captain Craskell, the superintendent, that there would be trouble if he insisted on the public humiliation of the Maroons. But he wouldn't listen. So we had a drawn-out war."

"That was long ago, though, wasn't it?"

"Ten years. Not so long. It was a very destructive war. At least three plantations were destroyed and all the white people on them murdered. The only thing that saved us were the dogs and the fact that only one group of Maroons, the Trelawneys, were involved. The other four Maroon tribes refused to fight."

"What dogs? What kind of dogs?"

"Bloodhounds. Big savage beasts. We brought one hundred of them from Cuba along with forty handlers.

A colonel by the name of Quarrell arranged the importation. Once the Maroons heard about the dogs, they surrendered. Most of them were shipped off to Africa."

"What happened to the slave who killed Austin?"

"He was burned to death alive. But before he died, he managed to free himself and fling a firebrand in the face of his executioner. I've never seen anything like it. But then, he was a Coromantee."

The two men continued their foremast circling in silence, before Meredith added, "Just remember, in Jamaica you can do more damage with your mouth than with your fist."

The man is a fool, thought Hartley to himself. But he said nothing.

The unthinking man asks, "What?" The thinking man asks, "Why?" This was not a truism known to Hartley Fudges since he himself was more unthinking than thinking. His tendency was to accept things as they were given and not ask why they were that way. This particular point of view was also paramount in Meredith's way of looking at life. He accepted everything and took his assigned place for granted in whatever apparatus, however evil, was prevailing.

One monotonous day at sea, Hartley and Meredith were talking about slavery and whether or not it was good or bad. Meredith was decisive in his opinion: it was neither good nor bad, but necessary. Without slavery, Meredith said, sugar production in the West Indies would be impossible.

"But why?" asked Hartley. "Why do people have to be enslaved to cut the cane and make the sugar?"

"Because it's tedious, backbreaking labor; no white man would want to do it. In fact, no black man wants to do it. But he has to."

"But why?"

"Why, what? . . . I'll give you a bit of advice," said Meredith with an avuncular air that he used often on Hartley, who was beginning to hate it, "don't ask why too often when you reach Jamaica. Some countries are why countries. Some are what countries. Jamaica is definitely a what country. And slavery is definitely not a why proposition. It's strictly what. What do you need in order to complete the harvest? I need twenty slaves. But if you ask a question as a why question, you're likely to get in trouble."

"With whom?"

"Well, with your conscience, to begin with. And with the feeling of being ridiculous."

"I don't understand," said Hartley.

"No, of course you don't. But you will."

"You're being cryptic."

"They outnumber us better than ten to one," said Meredith with a shiver. "And what we're doing with them is truly ridiculous. It is ridiculous to pretend that one man can own another like an animal. But we do it every day. The trick is to pretend that doing it is normal when it's really ridiculous."

"I still don't understand," protested Hartley.

"No, of course you don't. But you will."

Hartley was not satisfied. He felt as if the older man was being condescending and deliberately fuzzy with him. But Meredith was through talking about the subject and made it clear by strolling away, leaving the mystified Hartley standing near midship peering out at the encircling emptiness.

Three weeks passed slowly during which the friendship

between Meredith and Hartley Fudges grew and developed. At the beginning of the fourth week the cry of "Sail ahoy!" rang from the crow's nest and everyone on deck peered sharply at the horizon where a smudge of white indicated the presence of a vessel heading on an intercept course. The captain gave orders and seamen swarmed over the ratlines to set more sail. No one said anything to the passengers but Meredith muttered confidently to Hartley, "She's a privateer. The captain's going to try to outrun her."

Flying every sail she was rigged to carry, the *Mermaid* increased her speed in the steady trade wind. Darkness fell and a nail clip of a new moon hung from velvety black sky radiating a feeble glow. The captain ordered all lights out and under a mountain of darkness the *Mermaid* drove to a night breeze, trying to put distance between her and the intruder. Hartley and Meredith stood on deck watching this cat-and-mouse game being grimly played out. The pursuing vessel was trying to position herself between the *Mermaid* and the Lesser Antilles, forcing her quarry to change course and take an unfavorable tack in the trade winds. Around one o'clock in the morning, it was obvious to everyone on deck that the distance between the pursuing ship and the *Mermaid* was closing and that within a few hours, at the present rate, the two would be within range of cannon fire. The *Mermaid* was a shadowy presence plowing a dark trail through the night while her pursuer, arrogantly ablaze with lights, bore down unrelentingly on her. Every stitch of canvas she could carry, the brigantine was flying, and in the watery dawn light the two ships resembled coy dancers who were swaying to a synchronized rhythm only they could hear.

With the dawn, passengers gradually appeared on

deck to gather in groups at the railing of the *Mermaid* and ogle at the smudge of white on the horizon that marked the appearance of another ship. Word soon spread about what was really happening and a wave of anxiety swept over the passengers. Some women knelt down on the decks and prayed for deliverance. As the privateer closed on her, the *Mermaid* opened her gun ports, baring the teeth of four cannons she carried for self-defense. But even as the vessels inched nearer and nearer to one another, it was unclear whether the brigantine would be able to lose the privateer in her wake or whether the predator would come within range of delivering a crippling broadside. As the privateer drew closer, her lines and rigging became evident: she was a French-built frigate—a ship of war armed with twenty-four guns. She drew close enough to hail the *Mermaid* and order her to heave to or be fired upon.

The captain gave no reply but took the helm of the brigantine himself and sent the crew scurrying aloft to make little adjustments to the trim of her sails. The cat-and-mouse game lasted nearly two days. During that time the pursuer occasionally tacked as she tried to put herself between expected landfall and the *Mermaid*, but each time she did that maneuver, she lost ground to the brigantine who was driving for her first port that appeared in the distance fuzzy and dim like a pencil sketch.

On the third day when Hartley came on deck, he spotted the pursuing vessel coming about and heading for another set of sails on the horizon from which the *Mermaid* had come. A couple of hours later came the rumble of cannon fire and in the distance they could see the privateer had snared the other vessel with grappling irons and was pulling her close in a deadly embrace. On the deck, passengers watched impassively as the other ship was boarded to the occasional scream or report of musket fire. Hartley felt like he was watching a wolf devouring a lamb. The captain came on deck and a gentleman who wore a clerical collar hurried up to him and pointed to the carnage being enacted right in front of the *Mermaid*.

"Can't you help, Captain?" the man asked.

"We are not a warship, sir," the captain replied sternly.

"But what they must be doing to the poor ship," the chaplain sighed, "to those unfortunate people."

"I'm sorry," the captain said gruffly. "We can only be grateful that it's not us."

Driving in a quartering wind with a bone in her teeth, the brigantine scudded away until the strange frigate that in the distance looked as if she had engulfed the other ship was sinking lower and lower on the horizon. After that, the chase was over. By evening the frigate and her prey were once again a smudge of white canvas against the blurry horizon. Night fell and the *Mermaid*, her lights blazing, her crew and passengers infected with the jubilation of escape, mingled on the deck to starlight with a celebratory air.

The next morning dawned to an empty sea and speckles of land rising shiny and glittery like unburied treasures ahead of the brigantine's bowsprit.

It was the islands of the Lesser Antilles, all their unadorned beauty and splendor magically magnified to the crew and passengers whose eyes for the last five weeks had been scraping against the barren spectacle of waves and a horizon as plain and threadbare as a hangman's noose.

CHAPTER 7

After five weeks aboard the *Mermaid*, Hartley Fudges was sick of the sea. He was tired of its moods, of its never-ending changeableness. Many men grew to love its inconstancy with the longing of a child for a hardhearted mother. Hartley Fudges, however, had discovered that he was an unrepentant landlubber. The sight of the Leeward Islands sliding past the starboard of the *Mermaid* as the brigantine picked her way past the Lesser Antilles on course to Jamaica gave him a desire to feel the comforting contact of his feet with the unmovable earth. One morning he groaned to Meredith, "I'm sick and tired of being aboard a ship."

"Not much longer now," Meredith murmured. "In a couple of days you'll get your wish for land."

Hartley didn't really believe this, but within the next two days Jamaica loomed off the brigantine's port, emerging out of the sea in a diorama of vivid green mountains, shimmering pastures, and grinning white sand beaches. What struck Hartley most was the garish blend of blue and green hues as if a deranged artist had spilled dripping paint over every mountain and valley. It was this rich tapestry of color that had inspired Columbus to rhapsodize in his journal that Jamaica was "the fairest island that eyes have beheld."

The *Mermaid* skirted Jamaica, heading for her dorsal

side, and for hours the island bewitched the sea-weary passengers with a coquettish peep show of her contoured green valleys and swollen mountains. Hartley sat on the bow of the ship riveted to the spectacular unfolding of the island, wondering what lay ahead of him. It occurred to him that he could die there, but he shrugged off that possibility with a young man's cockiness. Meredith appeared at his side and pointed to a tangle of masts and spars that loomed above the shoreline and was almost hidden against the backdrop of green hills.

"Falmouth," he said. "Our destination."

Twenty-first-century Falmouth is a town in a stupor; nineteenth-century Falmouth was a bustling port that handled the export of sugar and rum and the importation of slaves. In 1805 when Hartley Fudges arrived, Falmouth was already thirty-six years old, having been established in 1769 by Thomas Reid, a plantation owner. It had been pressed into service as a port not because it made a good roadstead for oceangoing vessels but because it was conveniently located near some one hundred plantations worked by 106,000 slaves, who produced an avalanche of rum and sugar for the English.

The harbor was thick with ships swinging at anchor in an open unprotected bay, their rigging and masts and spars making a tangled cobweb against the skyline. Enormous big-bellied canoes called lighters crawled in a ragged line like giant ants to and from the ships, loading and unloading them. Sometimes the oarsmen and laborers broke into a chantey as they worked to unload the ships of tools, agricultural implements, and other manufactured goods, or formed a human chain to transfer barrels of sugar and rum to their gaping holds. Ashore, at the very edge of the sea, were rows of cut-stone warehouses and government buildings abuzz with scurrying overseers, slaves, dock-workers, shipwrights, carpenters, and hawkers and peddlers. On the day Hartley landed, the harbor was a thicket of masts and spars and stays and rigging from some thirty anchored ships.

The *Mermaid* was met by a pilot boat and escorted to her place of anchorage between two enormous barks whose masts and spars towered over her own. Dressed in their Sunday finery, passengers swarmed the brigantine's deck, everyone talking eagerly at once, their mood ranging from quiet joyfulness to open jubilation at finally and safely arriving. Never had land looked lovelier to the festive passengers, and the harbor rang with their excited chatter intermingled with the noises and cries from the lighters and anchored ships.

After an agonizing wait, the passengers of the *Mermaid* along with their luggage were ferried to shore by a lighter. They then milled around in a cavernous cut-stone warehouse, waiting to have their travel documents examined. An hour or so later, Hartley and Meredith found themselves in a crowded street swarming with slaves, laborers, and townspeople thrown together in an exotic, helter-skelter mix.

It was a hot, dry day with a February sun England felt only occasionally in August and the heat was so strong that it swept over the streets like a coarse broom. Everywhere Hartley looked were brown and black faces mixed in with a sprinkling of white, and in spite of the sapping heat, everyone seemed energetic, talkative, and vigorous. Hartley overheard snippets of talk coming from every side of him and realized with a shock that most of it was incomprehensible.

"What language are these people speaking?" he asked Meredith who seemed to have almost instantly blended into the surrounding sea of humanity.

"Jamaican," said Meredith, adding over his shoulder, "stick close to me and watch out for pickpockets."

While Meredith made arrangements to hire a wagon to transport them and their luggage to the plantation, bargaining with a burly brown man over price, Hartley was possessed by a feeling recently landed travelers often have of being in a dream. The whole colorfully chaotic scene seemed staged for his benefit, and he glanced from one strange sight to the next like a giddy theatergoer who had just blundered into the middle of a melodrama.

The most immediate danger to Hartley and other newcomers did not come from lurking pickpockets, but from a source that was barely visible: the mosquito.

Nineteenth-century Falmouth, for all its industry and wealth, was an unhealthy town wedged between swamplands that provided the perfect hatcheries for the yellow fever mosquito. In 1805, yellow fever was the scourge of Jamaica. It is spread by the bite of the *Aedes aegypti* mosquito, which flourished in the wetlands where humans lived. Magnified, the *Aedes aegypti* would be shown to be a loathsome monster, but its tiny size hides its gruesomeness. Little larger than a few specks of dirt, it has a shiny body wrapped in a chitinous shell that, under the microscope, makes it look armor-plated. Its legs are bent and strutted like the wings of a biplane, and its translucent abdomen bloats and turns red when the insect sucks blood from its victim. The mosquito is a killer but not an assassin. Its aim is not to kill the host, but to suck the blood it needs to survive. To do this, it injects its victim with an anticoagulant to enable the blood to flow freely—that is, when the virus is transferred.

Three to six days after being infected, the victim has symptoms that are flulike—body aches, a raging high fever, chills, headache, and vomiting. For many people, the indisposition ends a week or so later after a respite in bed. But many others, while appearing to briefly recover, develop a massive infection that shuts down the kidneys and liver, causing the jaundiced yellow complexion that gives the disease its name. The fatality rate in such cases, which number about one in six, is around 50 percent. Even today, there is no treatment for yellow fever beyond the usual preachments about bed rest and plenty of fluids.

Hartley Fudges, along with the other passengers of the *Mermaid*, was the proverbial "sitting duck."

Meredith said he knew of a boardinghouse where they could have a room for the night, and in the blazing heat the two men set off briskly toward it. The section of the town they passed through was laid out tidily with houses that crouched right on the edge of a rutted marl road that had no sidewalk, and every now and again the men would have to stop to allow a dray cart or carriage to squeeze past. Maidservants hanging clothes out to dry peered sullenly at them.

Soon they reached a white house that was practically indistinguishable from its neighbors except for a wooden fence protectively encircling a scruffy lawn whose bare spots bespoke a recent drought. Meredith knocked on the front door, and a black servant wearing a uniform opened it.

"Is your mistress at home?" Meredith asked.

The maid mumbled for them to wait here and they stood in the entrance of the front door from which perch Hartley examined the drawing room, which was furnished and trimmed in a style and with materials that belonged in an English cottage. The chairs and tables, along with the decorative touches, were of such strong English influence that the entire ensemble—from the porcelain figurines on display on a whatnot to the antimacassars on the stuffed chairs—might have been found in the house of a chartered accountant in London. Hartley was no expert but the small and tidy house struck him as vainly struggling to maintain the prissy decorum of a tea party among desolate and vulgar surroundings. Even as they stood in the foyer they could hear the noise of the waterfront like a distant boisterous drumbeat.

The landlady came and greeted Meredith like an old friend. They rented two rooms and had a quiet dinner. While they ate she stopped by their table and bluntly asked Meredith, "What's England going to do about that madman Napoleon?"

Meredith paused in his chewing and replied, "The king hasn't told me yet."

"Well, he better get up the gumption to do something. I know about those little Frenchmen. They're like cellar rats. Always spreading trouble."

Then she wandered off to make small talk at another table.

"What on earth did she mean?" Hartley asked.

"She's worried about Napoleon," Meredith said evenly.

"Here, in Jamaica, they worry about Napoleon?"

"They worry about everything that an Englishman in London might worry about."

"But why?"

"Because Jamaicans are worriers. And they think they are part of us."

After dinner, they went for a walk through the neighborhood of Georgian homes and took in the bracing sea air. They then returned to the house and went to bed early. Before he fell asleep, Hartley fed a swarm of *Aedes aegypti* mosquitoes. Lying in bed, he could hear them whining around his face and occasionally feel the piercing stab of a bite.

The next morning Hartley woke up early to a rooster outside his window trumpeting the daybreak, which came over the land with a startling suddenness. But as he lay in bed listening to the blaring rooster, Hartley heard someone moving in the house and decided that he'd better get up in case it was Meredith. He went downstairs and found his friend at breakfast. The two men ate, settled their bill, and stepped into the dawn which was already oppressive with the morning heat. They walked into the town square where the wagon loaded with their trunks was waiting for them, and with the night lingering in pockets of thinning coolness that brushed against their cheeks, they set off for the plantation with two black men—a middle-aged driver and a sideman of about twenty-three. The wagon was drawn by four mules, with Hartley and Meredith sitting beside the driver and the sideman slouched in the rear of the wagon bed.

They took the one primary road that led out of town

running east and west. It started out as a rutted path grooved by the wheels of numerous wagons and carriages, followed the seacoast with a steady stream of wagon traffic going in both directions, piercing through a swampy terrain thick with mangroves, and crossing the Martha Brae River that spilled brown water into the estuary. Along the way the driver was chatty with Meredith. Hartley only half understood what the men were saying, and it was only by carefully listening that he was able to catch a crude gist of their meaning.

At regular intervals the driver stopped to rest the mules. On one of the stops, Hartley struck up a conversation with the sideman and was haltingly talking to him when the driver ambled over and said in his best English, "You want buy him? Him for sale."

"You mean, he's a slave?"

"Yes, sah, and me selling him cheap."

The boy, who was ragged and barefoot, looked sullen. "Slavery days soon done, now," he mumbled defiantly.

"But you're a black man just like he," Hartley protested. "How can he belong to you?"

The driver scowled. He held out his arm beside the boy's and snapped, "Look how much lighter me skin is dan him. Him is a black man. At a certain time o' day, me favor a white one."

"You do what?"

"He says when the sun is just right, he looks like a white man," Meredith interjected.

"I didn't know black people could own slaves," Hartley said lamely.

"Who do you think sells blacks into slavery in Africa?" Meredith asked. "Other black people."

"If you see me at, say, six o'clock dis evening, you going think is one white man you looking at," the driver said boastfully.

"Him look like a white man because him stand so dat de sun dazzle you eyes and you can't tell horse from mule or mule from donkey," the sideman added tartly.

Without warning, the driver lunged and slapped him hard on the side of the head, nearly knocking him off his feet. The sideman rubbed his head and stared at him murderously.

"All right now," Meredith said, stepping between the two men, "enough of that. Let's be on our way."

For a tense moment, the two men were locked in a long, hard look of mutual hate.

"Try and sell me like me is a piece of yam," the sideman grumbled.

"You's my slave," the driver retorted. "Me own you like me own dem four mule."

"Slavery days over," muttered the sideman.

"Buy him, nuh, sah," the driver pleaded with Hartley. "A bargain. Only fifty pounds."

Hartley hesitated, pursing his lips as if trying to make up his mind. He looked around at the thickly overgrown hillside through which the road had been hewed and could scarcely glimpse a familiar tree. He would ordinarily have said a brisk "No," but being in a new country crammed with strange sights and oddities that almost seemed theatrical gave him the distinct feeling that anything was possible, even something so bizarre as owning another human being. Meredith looked at him with a troubled air.

"You can't just buy him and tie him to a tree like you

would a cow, you know," Meredith cautioned. "You have to feed him."

"Me don't eat," said the sideman tersely.

"He'll need a place to sleep."

"Me don't sleep."

With a sudden decisiveness, Hartley declared, "Done, for fifty pounds."

The driver gave a loud belly laugh and extended his hand for Hartley to shake. Hartley pumped it vigorously. Assuming a serious expression, the driver glanced at Meredith, gave Hartley a quick, measuring scan, and asked, "Him just reach Jamaica?"

Meredith nodded.

"First trip?"

Meredith nodded again.

"Dis must be cash money. We better settle up dis business when we reach de estate."

"Why?" Hartley wondered.

"Because you're alive now, but who knows about tomorrow. You don't season yet."

"What do you mean by *season*?"

"It means you're not yet accustomed to the island, its food, its atmosphere, its ways," Meredith said smoothly.

"Plenty man come here and dead," the driver said, chuckling. "You have to be strong to survive in Jamaica."

"I'm strong," Hartley said confidently, still unclear about what the man meant.

"Me not worth fifty pounds," the sideman interrupted sullenly. "Is thief him thief you."

"What'd he say?" Hartley asked Meredith.

"He says he's not worth fifty pounds, that the driver has robbed you."

"Shut up you mouth before I box you down," the driver threatened.

"You can't touch me. You don't own me anymore," the sideman gloated.

"Enough, I say," said Meredith sharply. "We've still got a long way to go."

The four men climbed back onto the wagon and resumed their journey.

The road scaled the hillside in crooked, lunging humps and soon became pitted and fissured like someone had bitten chunks out of it. All around them was a woodland so dense with trees that it loomed over the trail like a green wall and occasionally appeared impenetrable. The wagon rocked like a small boat in a choppy sea, and the road became so steep at times that the men had to get out and walk. The day wore on and the sun beat down on them pitilessly and in some particularly bad stretches of the road they all had to get behind the wagon and push to get it over a steep hump.

Left to his own thoughts, Hartley was intermittently regretting his impulsive purchase, but as the road got worse, the hill got steeper, and as the going got slower and more difficult, he didn't care if he had bought a hundred slaves, for his mind began to seem as reckless as their journey. The more cracked and wild the roadway got, the more sense buying his own slave seemed to make. Darkness fell, and the surrounding bushes and trees slowly became grotesqueries of night. As the darkness grew thicker and the road more difficult to see, they crested a hill and there below them in a valley glittered a handful of flickering lights.

"Mount Pleasant," Meredith breathed with relief.

The mood of the travelers brightened instantly. The sideman spontaneously began to sing.

"Shut up!" the driver barked over his shoulder.

"Oh, let him sing," Meredith said. "In fact, I feel like singing myself."

And he and the sideman started singing as the lights of the plantation puncturing the darkness drew comfortingly nearer and brighter.

CHAPTER 8

The plantation loomed like a monolith in what appeared to be an enormous area of desolation that might have been the dark ends of the earth. Yet among this vast, shrouded wilderness rose an imposing mansion boasting delicate gingerbread, impressive doors, mullioned windows, ornamented pediments, and Ionic pillars that combined, at first sight, to make the entire structure look out of place and ridiculous. There was a portico fit for welcoming the most elegant phaeton but was more likely there to shelter a grubby dray cart. The whole structure was encircled by a defensive wall punctured by gunports.

When the wagon rattled up to the main gate of the plantation, the mules blowing hard and a feeble light leaking from two dangling lanterns, the travelers were challenged and stopped by three night watchmen armed with pistols and machetes. After that, word quickly spread over the dark compound of the arrival of the backra. Candles flickered on throughout the main house and people poured out of the front door bubbling over with the welcome of homecoming.

The greeting party consisted of white faces mingling with a few brown and dark ones. Thoroughly confused about who was who, Hartley was soon shaking hands with a small circle of strangers whose names he was afraid he would not remember. So spontaneous and lively was the impromptu assembly that Hartley was reminded of a gathering at Christmas. Then he was sitting down at a large banquet table in a cavernous dining room and eating a hurriedly warmed-up meal among a babble of voices while dead ancestors peered down from stylized oil paintings on the wall. Outside, the driver and the sideman were served food that they ate sitting in the wagon.

During the height of the chatter, Hartley slipped outside to look at the night covering the earth with a thick velvet of darkness. It rang with the sounds of cicadas and crickets, and from deep within its dark unseen heart came a peculiar loud staccato noise of a hundred baby rattles. His new slave suddenly appeared at his elbow.

"What's that sound?" Hartley asked.

The boy listened for a moment or two before responding, "What sound, Massa?"

"It sounds as if someone's trying to clear his throat."

The boy cocked his head attentively before breaking into a wide grin. "Is croaking lizard, Massa."

"Why're you calling me that name?"

"Because dat's what slave in Jamaica call dem master."

Hartley thought about it, and then shrugged. "Where will you sleep tonight?"

"Don't worry 'bout dat," the boy replied. "Me will find a place."

The driver ambled over with a paper on which he had scribbled something.

"Here's you bill of sale, sah. You have de money?"

"You mean I can change my mind?" Hartley asked jokingly.

"We shake on de deal, sah," the driver said dourly,

"although I wouldn't blame you, now dat you get to see what a wretch dis boy is, if you have a change of heart."

Buying a slave and then changing his mind before he'd even paid for him would make Hartley look silly. Acting more decisive than he felt, he dug into his trunk, pulled out some pound notes, and carefully counted off fifty, which he handed to the driver. As the driver was walking off the boy hissed in a venomous voice, "One dark night, we'll buck up again."

The implied threat stopped the driver in his tracks, and he turned and approached the boy. Hartley jumped between the two of them.

"He's mine now," Hartley said sternly. "Leave my property alone."

The driver glared at the two of them for a long moment. Abruptly, he turned on his heels and walked over to his wagon.

"What's your name?" Hartley asked the boy.

"Cuffy," the boy mumbled.

"Cuffy? Who gave you that name?"

"Is de name of a slave, Massa. And me is slave."

"Stop saying that."

"If me must be a slave, me must be a proper slave."

Hartley chuckled as if the boy had told a joke.

A cool breeze fanned the dark trees, making them seem to whisper. Hartley ambled across the lawn, taking in the night, the expanse of fields, the dark patches of woodlands that surrounded the house, and the constellations and stars brightly glittering overhead. He thought he was alone, but when he turned he saw that Cuffy, almost invisible against the dark night, padded after him only a few feet away.

"Are you following me?" Hartley asked.

"Dere's something white man can do in Jamaica and something him shouldn't do. Him shouldn't walk 'bout at night alone," Cuffy said quietly, as if revealing a secret.

Hartley looked around him. He was in the back of the enormous house where no lights burned and where the shadows were thick and cloying and swaddled the whole yard in a cocoon of bottomless darkness.

"Why? Is it unsafe?" Hartley asked, glancing nervously around him.

"Jamaican night bring out thief," Cuffy said. "Is better white man walk in daylight."

Hartley, without replying, moved briskly toward the front door and disappeared into the dining room. The celebratory tone was now muted by fatigue, and yawns were breaking out among the six white faces that sat at the huge table. A few minutes later, the assembly wobbled to its feet and everyone went to bed.

His first night in the great house Hartley slept well. At daybreak he was blasted awake by a conch shell horn calling the slaves to work. He got out of bed and stumbled to the window, peering out into the dawn, and saw workmen and women streaming across the lawns and headed for the factory or the fields. Hartley dressed hurriedly, washed his face in a basin, threw open his door, and found the boy lying on the threshold, sound asleep. He stepped over him and was standing there wondering what he should do when the boy jumped up and rubbed his eyes frantically.

"Did you sleep there all night?" asked Hartley with perplexity.

"Yes, sah," the boy muttered sleepily.

"But why?"

"A slave must be ready to serve at all times," came the reply.

"It's a wonder you don't follow me into the toilet," Hartley rejoined sourly.

"Me is a slave," the boy said snippily. "Me is not out of order."

Hartley walked away, headed for the stairway, wanting to miss nothing on his first day at the plantation. Behind him he could hear the scurrying footsteps of the boy, hard on his heels.

Cuffy was a boy only in designation, not fact. In reality, he was the same age as Hartley Fudges. But because he was a young slave with no particular skill or training, everyone called him a boy. He was dark brown, of medium height, and had the fat-free chiseled physique of a greyhound. From a life of hard labor, he had developed a muscular body with thick arms and broad shoulders. He was slightly taller than Hartley Fudges and had an intensity to his personality that hinted of an explosive temper. His nature was to have things his way, which was an impossibility for someone who was enslaved, and his approach to life seemed combative and stubborn. Most striking were his eyes, which were the color of polished emeralds.

He was a creature of insupportable pride and was especially sensitive to any disrespect, slight, or flippancy directed at his person. It seemed to Hartley that he was always sniffing around for the appearance or hint of disparagement. Everything for him had to be proper. It had to be the ideal that the world expected. He did not want to be a slave, and his hatred of his slave masters ran deep. But since he had been born into slavery, he was maliciously determined to play the role to the letter that life had assigned him. So he slept protectively at Hartley's doorstep where he could raise an alarm in case anyone tried to break into his massa's room.

It was a perversity in his character that made him think this way, and it was one of his traits that had alienated him from his former owner, the dray cart driver. The boy had resented being the slave of a black man, for that was neither the ideal nor the norm. Now that he was owned by a white Englishman, he felt properly enslaved.

Most of this speculation was in Hartley's fevered imagination and based on snippets of opinion expressed by Cuffy. Hartley instinctively understood from his long acquaintance with servants that a line had to be drawn in the sand beyond which they dared not step. It didn't matter where the particular line was or what topics and behaviors it forbade; all that mattered was that the line was symbolically present and visible to the servant. Hartley thought he knew volumes about the servant mentality, and he intended to apply this knowledge to subdue his rambunctious slave.

Yet there was something sinister in Cuffy's manner. He was always sullen; his attitude was smoldering and defiant. Hartley had no doubt that if pushed far enough, Cuffy was capable of flying into a rage and killing someone.

Cuffy had not made any threatening movements toward his new English master. In fact, Hartley thought his slave was proud of having a master who was both white and genuinely English, rather than some cast-off Irishmen or Johnny-come-lately Scotchman or whimpering Welshman. Yet there was something about Cuffy that bore watching or caution. Hartley could not say what he felt or why he felt it. He only knew that there was something peculiar, something twisted inside Cuffy, something that could one day detonate and blow everyone nearby to smithereens.

Over the next few days, Hartley learned much about the plantation, Mount Pleasant. It was owned, he discovered, by a wealthy English family whom it supported on a grand scale but who were longtime absentee proprietors. The patriarch of the family had visited some years ago, but he didn't linger too long, claiming that the climate was too hot for his constitution.

The plantation had evolved throughout the years into a self-sufficient community. It had its own source of water, produced its own food, provided its own medical treatment through a clinic staffed by a doctor and two nurses. It raised its own livestock and did its own butchering. Its own system of aqueducts harnessed the flow of water to drive the mill that extracted the sugar from the cane stalks. Its own minister of religion resided on the plantation and tended to the spiritual needs of the slaves and freemen alike. However, this particular minister had serious doubts as to whether blacks had souls. He was not alone in this perplexity. Many ministers of religion turned their backs on the slaves and saw no point in trying to introduce them to Christianity and Jesus. One might as well try to convert the donkey in a manger or a wild beast of the field.

Its population, reflecting the racial breakdown in Jamaica, consisted of eight white men counting Hartley and Meredith, but no white women; 960 slaves; and 210 free black and brown people who held various jobs on the estate. This scarcity made white people stand out conspicuously, and wherever he went in public, Hartley had the feeling of being constantly stared at like an exotic migratory bird.

The buildings on the estate consisted of the main house, called the great house; a sprawling slave quarters; a storage structure where various tools and agricultural implements were kept; the mill where the cane was converted into sugar, molasses, and rum; a boiling house, a curing house, and the paddocks and stables where the horses were kept. There was also a butchering shed and an outbuilding where hogsheads of sugar and rum awaiting transshipment were stored. Every facility was relatively close together to make transportation from one to the other easy.

The plantation consisted of 1,500 acres cultivated mainly in sugarcane. Experience had taught the planters over the years that sugarcane, unless grown on a large scale, was not a profitable crop. Even on a large estate, growing cane was capital-intensive, requiring a huge labor force and expensive boiling and milling equipment, and it was only by large-scale manufacturing that the plantation was able to survive. Over the island's history the consolidation of estates became an inexorable necessity, and at one point flyspeck Jamaica—all 4,411 square miles of it—had more jumbo estates in production than did the entire continental US.

Hartley had been in Jamaica about two weeks when he fell sick. The sickness began with a feeling of fatigue, which at first he blamed on a visit to the boiling house and its hellish temperatures that often reached 140° Fahrenheit. But by evening he was feverish and wracked with chills that the people around him quickly recognized as the onset of yellow fever. Meredith, on being informed of his companion's illness, ordered him immediately to bed. Hartley needed no prompting and in the dim room, he crawled into bed under a sheet and a bedspread, chilled and trembling. Cuffy brought him a pitcher of lemonade and hung around his bedside, looking anguished and doing his best to be useful. Hartley was hardly aware of him for his mind was in that place of fragmented dreams and delirium that the feverish inhabit. When he was awake, which was seldom, he would hardly be aware of his surroundings, his consciousness flickering like a windblown candle.

He began to vomit. Since his confinement he had eaten no solid food but had taken in only liquids. The cook for the great house sent up a succession of broths with Cuffy, who sat on the edge of Hartley's bed and tried to spoon the oily liquid down his master's throat. For several days Hartley lay suffering in soundless agony—day passing into night, morning turning into afternoon—feeling more wretched than ever before in his life. Every white person in the great house sympathized with his suffering, for every one of them had either experienced it themselves or seen other newcomers ravaged by the sickness. Most of the people who were around him did not think that he would survive. On one visit Meredith said to Cuffy as they passed in the doorway, "You better make a coffin for your master."

But by the fifth day, Hartley was stronger and apparently getting better. His fever abated, and he stopped vomiting altogether. What was an even better sign was his restiveness at being cooped up in the bedroom. Meredith and others in the great house observed these signs with alarm rather than hope, for they knew that he had now come to the crossroads where his sickness would either leave him or it would relentlessly return with a renewed virulence. Hartley, not understanding the nature of his illness, was eager to get to work and one morning appeared at the breakfast table, keen on beginning a full day, only to be excused from work and told to return to bed.

"But I tell you," Hartley insisted, "I'm all well again. I feel almost up to my full strength."

An Irish overseer by the name of Yates cautioned him gravely: "It's the fever you had, and it is known to come back just when you think you're getting over it. And the second time, it's much worse."

"That's what I'm trying to tell you," Meredith said with exasperation. "It just *seems* to be over. But it isn't over."

"How do you know when it is over?" Hartley asked.

The cook, an old Ashanti woman named Delilah who rode roughshod over the Irish overseers, snapped, "It over when we tell you it over."

For the next few days, the people around him watched Hartley closely for symptoms of the second stage of the disease to appear, making him feel like he was passing through the perilous strait between life and death. He felt more helpless than he ever had in his life as he awaited either a blow or a reprieve. What made it worse was his awareness of his condition and his recognition that nothing he thought or did or said or chanted would affect the outcome. So he reluctantly did as he was told and remained in bed long after he felt it necessary. Meredith lent him a copy of Edward Long's *The History of Jamaica* and having nothing better to do, he began to read about the island.

He learned that history credits the start of the sugar industry to Sir Thomas Modyford, governor general of Jamaica from 1664 to 1670, who arrived from Barbados in 1664 accompanied by seven hundred planters and their slaves. In the years to follow, other groups of planter families and their slaves came from the Leeward Islands and Suriname. Jamaica, which the English took from Spain in 1655, initially struggled to survive and actually suffered a decline in population. The census of 1661, taken by the Spanish, showed a population of 2,956 (2,458 men, 454 women, and forty-four children).

In the early years of English colonization, Jamaica was a bigger producer of cocoa than of sugar. But in the summer of 1670 a cocoa blight hit the island, destroying all the trees. Jamaica turned to sugar, and the industry grew rapidly, from fifty-seven sugar mills in 1670 to 1,061 in 1786. St. Ann, Trelawney, and St. James became the mecca of growth with some fifteen new sugar estates being established between 1792 and 1799. With the growth of new estates came the flood of slaves from Africa until by 1805 they outnumbered whites by more than ten to one. And all this industry and effort was producing profits that immediately left the island and ended up in the pockets of unseen and often unknown absentee proprietors.

All this, and more, Hartley Fudges discovered during the week when he seemed to be getting better from the yellow fever. But then the second wave of the disease struck and overnight he was languishing on his deathbed, and there was nothing anyone or any science or any folk magic of 1805 could do to save him.

A healthy young man only rarely sees himself as part of a social pattern. If anything, he imagines himself and his individual destiny to be utterly unique. But the sick man is always trying to spot the cause and patterns behind his sickness, if only to take refuge from the belief that nature has singled him out for some special horrible death or infirmity. So as Hartley Fudges slipped into the delirium of his fever, he began to inspect the life patterns that had brought him to this sorry pass. He began to see himself as one of many migratory English men forced to leave their homes and risk their lives on some foreign shore where they were likely to die among strangers.

Oddly enough, he began to see the little stub of life he had so far lived as funny and irrepressibly comical. As he was enveloped and consumed by his fever and sickness, he would occasionally remember some episode from his earlier years and laugh uproariously over it. The people in the great house thought he was deranged from his sickness and expected him to die anytime now.

"Poor fellow," muttered Meredith at Hartley's bedside. "I thought he would fit right in." He headed for the door. "Tell me when he's passed," he added over his shoulder to Cuffy.

"Me massa not goin' dead," Cuffy retorted in a voice that snapped like an overseer's whip.

"Whatever you say," Meredith said, wrinkling his nose at the reeking stench of sickness and death that wafted from the bed.

Hartley broke into another insane laugh.

CHAPTER 9

Hartley Fudges traveled to, and came back from, the doorstep of death. He turned yellow and stopped passing water and should have succumbed to either liver or kidney failure. But he did not. At the last minute he had a surge of strength; his fever abated; the ghastly yellow that his sickness had painted him with was gradually replaced by the more natural buff and reddish complexion of a white man in the tropics. He was laughing deliriously on and off for at least ten days, and on the eleventh he opened his eyes and looked at the world like a traveler returning home from a long voyage. He had survived the fever.

During his weeks of recuperation, Hartley Fudges spent long hours with only Cuffy for company. They were about the same age, which gave them something in common, and when Hartley was not sleeping off the ravages of his disease, he and Cuffy exchanged stories about growing up in the last decades of the eighteenth century in London and West Africa. Hartley felt deep inside himself that he was superior to Cuffy in virtually every way—given the monumental differences between the playing fields of Eton and the jungles of West Africa—but the sickness of yellow fever which the Englishman had suffered laid bare between them a relationship of dependence that almost leveled the looming barriers of class and race.

In telling Cuffy about his life in London, Hartley made the city sound better than it really had been. Homesick and recovering from a serious illness made him idealize his days there, forgetting such important details as the perpetual stench of the city, its suffocating crowds of laborers, hawkers and peddlers, pickpockets and cutthroats mingling daily among bustling shoppers, to say nothing of the insufferable conceit of Londoners with their smug conviction that theirs was the best of all possible worlds.

In return, Cuffy told stories about the hunting adventures his tribe required of boys entering their fourteenth year as proof of their passage into manhood. One of the requirements was for boys to organize themselves into small hunting groups and stalk and kill a warthog. This feat was not easily accomplished because a warthog is armed with sharp tusks and is a fearless foe that will hurl itself at any hunting party, slashing at bare feet and naked legs. Cuffy told the story of a boy who was lazy and sluggish and reacted too slowly to a charging warthog. Both tendons of his ankles were severed, making him a cripple for the rest of his life. So killing a warthog was no easy task, especially since the animals had a habit of digging burrows into the soft earth and covering themselves with dirt, which made them nearly impossible to see until the hunter was almost on top of them, when they would explode out of the ground in a ferocious rage.

Until they had killed a warthog and brought the body for the elders to inspect and approve, said Cuffy, the boys were not allowed to return to the village. During this time, the boys had to fend for themselves, living off the harsh ungiving land. Some hunting parties did not return and were never found. Whether they were themselves the victim of predators or of starvation or of slave hunters no one ever found out; all the tribe knew was that some boys were always lost. So it was essential that the hunting groups contain at least one boy who could track game and kill it.

Here Cuffy's voice grew boastful as he declared that in all of his village, no one was better at throwing the spear with more deadly accuracy than he was and that all the other boys begged him to join their party and become their leader. He did eventually join a group, and on the third day of the hunt, they came across a family of warthogs living in a burrow they had dug in a dry riverbed. He deployed the boys in a circle so that the animals would be trapped. Then one boy began to beat a small drum until, unable to stand the noise, the boar exploded out of its burrow, shook itself off, and aimed its tusks at the drummer. But in that brief pause, before the boar could charge, Cuffy's spear whipped through the air and buried its point deep into the chest of the animal, drawing from it a frantic squeal of agony as it collapsed on the ground in a ghastly death spasm.

When Cuffy was finished with his story, Hartley felt a little overmatched, having no English warthog whose ferocity he could exaggerate. He countered with a fox and a story about hunting it. As Cuffy listened with an expression of rapture on his face, Hartley described the rugged countryside over which the hunters chased their game to the baying of hounds.

But that was not the same thing, objected Cuffy. Riding a horse after some dogs chasing a fox was not as perilous as facing a warthog with only a spear for a weapon. Hartley jumped to the defense of his warthog-less English countryside.

"You have no idea how rough a fox hunt can be. The horse has to jump over obstacles, some man-made, some natural. People fall off all the time and hurt themselves badly. Why, there was a man in a nearby village who fell off his horse and died."

"Killing a warthog makes a young man strong and fearless. It gives the tribe meat. It is better than riding after a fox."

"I hardly need to point out to you," said Hartley sarcastically, "who's the slave and who the master."

"Dat don't matter," the boy snapped. "You're not de massa because you hunt de fox. Me not de slave because me kill a warthog."

"Then why aren't you the master and I not the slave?"

"Cuffy don't know," said the boy looking around the room gloomily. "But somebody know."

It was to combat this perception of the English countryside as a worthless and sissified hunting ground that caused Hartley to play the only trump card he felt he had in his deck.

"Of course," he said casually, "in London we have dueling."

"Dueling? What dat?" asked Cuffy innocently.

Hartley himself had never fought a duel. He had never even come close enough to actually show up on the dueling fields. However, his illness had left him feeling vulnerable and weak, and under the intense gaze of his slave who was hanging onto his every word while trumping him with his African warthog, he began to picture himself in a more heroic light than was true. Without meaning to, he was soon telling the story of the duel between Bottoms and Alexander, putting himself in Alexander's shoes.

He told the story that Bottoms had insulted him in public, which resulted in Hartley slapping his face in reproof.

"How you do that?" Cuffy wanted to know. Hartley stepped over to where Cuffy was sitting and demonstrated by giving him an effete, almost effeminate slap on the side of the head. Cuffy stood up to copy the gesture.

"Careful now," he warned Cuffy, who looked as if he were muscling up to deliver a haymaker.

Cuffy, with an expression of concentration, delivered a light whiffing blow to Hartley's head. "Like dis?" he asked.

"Yes, quite like that."

Then came other embellishments. Hartley added details about the rituals of the duel, the naming of seconds, the choice of weapons, the selection of a dueling field, and other inventions of his imagination. Cuffy was duly impressed; this was so much better than the warthog.

"But why you fight dis man named Bottoms?" Cuffy wondered.

"Over a principle," Hartley said, immediately regretting his use of that word.

"What a principle?"

"It's something that matters. But it may seem not to matter, which is why it matters."

"I don't understand."

"No, of course you don't. You're too busy hunting hogs to grasp the important points in life such as a principle."

"What was de principle?"

Hartley sighed, conscious of being dragged deeper and deeper into the murk.

"We bet a farthing on a horse race. My horse won, but Bottoms didn't pay his wager."

"Why not?"

"Because it was only for a farthing. He thought the amount was so small that it didn't matter. But that was exactly why it mattered. It was the principle of the thing."

"Den what happened?"

"I asked him for my farthing and he said I was cheap. People overheard. I slapped him and challenged him to a duel."

"Which you won?"

"Quite so."

"Over a farthing, a quarter of a penny?"

"No. Over a principle."

"What principle?"

"That every bet, no matter how small, must be paid."

Cuffy sighed with longing. As for Hartley, he was quite pleased with himself and imagined that the warthog had been driven squealing out of the room.

"I want to fight a duel too," whined Cuffy.

"Only gentlemen fight duels," Hartley replied crisply.

"Then Cuffy will become gentleman."

Hartley laughed. The boy's face darkened with a shadow of anger.

"You laugh at Cuffy?" he hissed. "You no laugh at Cuffy."

And for a tense minute, Hartley thought the boy would strike him. "I'll laugh at anyone I please," he said sharply. "Now get out."

"Why I not become a gentleman?" the boy persisted, not moving a hair.

"Because you don't talk like one."

"So if I learn to talk like you, I become gentleman too."

"Not bloody likely. Plus, you could never talk like I do. Now get out of here and let me sleep."

Cuffy looked around the room, which was disheveled and littered like a recent battlefield.

"Dat not fair," Cuffy said in the doorway, his face twisted in a look of disappointment.

"I said get out!" Hartley screamed.

During his recovery, Hartley also tried to explain the teachings of Plato to Cuffy. But the trouble was that he himself did not completely understand Plato. He merely accepted him and his teachings because he felt as a matter of principle that every aristocrat in England should subscribe to some philosophy or another. It was one more way of distinguishing himself from the rabble.

Hartley began by explaining to Cuffy that there once was this great thinker who lived hundreds of years ago and whose philosophy was based on the belief that for every object or life-form on this earth there was a perfect version of it in the next world of which the earthbound one was a mere imitation. Cuffy had great difficulty at first with the idea of imitation, and particular difficulty with imitation over such a large scale that included all of the earth and everything contained in it. He found it hard to believe that everything here was a copy of the perfect thing there, and like the Aristotelian critics, he kept asking where the original perfect thing was stored. How did the imitation of it manage to find its way on earth?

But Hartley somehow overcame this objection the same way Plato had, by simply insisting that this was how it was. After a turbulent start, Cuffy began to see some advantages in thinking that everything on earth was an imperfect copy of everything perfect in heaven. He was particularly excited at the idea that there was a perfect version of him somewhere in the great beyond. And it gave him an idea: why not make the imperfect version of him that he was into the perfect version of which it was a copy?

He explained the idea to Hartley, who was unmoved by it.

"But if dere is a perfect me, why can't I be it?" he grilled Hartley.

"Don't be ridiculous. This is philosophy. You can't simply wake up one day and say, *From today, I shall be the perfect me*. Philosophy doesn't work that way."

"Why not?" Cuffy rejoined. "Just because I'm de first person to think it up don't mean it can't be done."

"You're not the first person to ever think that," protested Hartley.

"Name de man who think of dis before me!"

Hartley was beginning to sputter. "Now, look here, Cuffy. I don't know the name of any specific person who's thought of this before, but there must be somebody. Plato lived from 428 to 347 BC. That's a thousand years or more ago. You mean to tell me that no one in all that time has ever thought of being the perfect person he's supposed to be?"

Cuffy wasn't sure what year this was and Hartley decided that to explain to him the meaning of 428 BC would be a nightmare. So he held his peace, hoping that Cuffy would forget about the discussion and move on. But throughout the days that followed, Cuffy continued to say, "I'm going to be de perfect slave," until Hartley told him to shut up, which he did without an argument just as a perfect slave would. And at the end of the day, Cuffy said to Hartley, "Massa, wasn't I de perfect slave today?" to which Hartley replied pompously, "From what I've been able to observe, you seem to have been."

"From now on," vowed Cuffy, "dat is what me'll be: de perfect slave."

Hartley did not hear this last remark. Or if he heard it, he didn't believe Cuffy. What could he possibly mean that he'd be the perfect slave? There was no such thing. And if there were, why would Cuffy or anyone else want to be the perfect slave?

It was obvious that trying to grapple with the deep thinking of Plato had maddened up the African's brain.

All this drama was being played out in the great house—the dominant structure of the entire plantation. Built on the edge of a dense and impenetrable woodland, it differed from other houses in that it was enormous and surrounded by a grim cut-stone wall capped with pointed iron bars and interspersed with gun ports.

There were six white people living in the great house—four Irish overseers and Meredith and Hartley. There was a Mahoney, an O'Hara, a Yates, and a Fitzgerald who had been with the plantation for years. They were typically short, sinewy men, on the scrawny side, fair complexioned, and with green or blue eyes.

Yet in spite of these backras, the plantation could not exist without the labor of the slaves, who did everything. They cleared the land and dug holes for planting; harvested the mature cane, binding the stalks into movable bales; transported the bales to the mill, which ground up the stalks so that the cane juice flowed through lead-lined sluices into the boiling house. Slaves boiled the juice in a series of cast-iron "coppers," skimming off impurities and adding lime as a catalyst to help it crystallize. It was a slave who supervised the boiling in the room where the temperature could reach 140°F. When the juice was ready to crystallize, slaves transferred it to vats that used constantly circulating water to cool down the slurry and help it precipitate. The entire process of making, storing, and shipping sugar was handled completely by slaves.

All this industry involving 1,297 acres of land and 480 slaves produced 258 hogsheads of sugar and 170 puncheons of rum, making an annual net profit of £5,000—around $1,500,000 in today's dollars—for an absentee owner who had been to the plantation once in twenty-five years and whose children had never seen the property that put food in their mouths and clothes on their backs. To put this profit in perspective, consider that the highest-paid person on the plantation was Meredith, the general manager, who earned the lavish sum of £300 per year, more than any other overseer on any of the other five-thousand-plus sugar-producing properties in Jamaica. Hartley Fudges, the newest backra, earned half that.

Backra, linguists believe, is a word of African origin that comes from the Ibo or Efik language where its original meaning was one who governed or was in charge. In an 1805 sugar plantation in the West Indies, the backra was a human flag that symbolized ownership by the English. Some of the more experienced backras knew how to make sugar and supervised the process in its various stages. But a new backra like Hartley was as much a trainee as a new slave, except that being white he was presumed able to more easily master the intricacies of sugar manufacturing than could a slave. The backra hovered over everything and everyone, embodying in his person life, death, and favoritism. His every judgment carried the finality of eternity.

One morning Yates was showing Hartley around the boiling house when a couple drivers appeared with a captured runaway slave in custody. The drivers stopped Yates and asked what should be done with the man, who was a chronic escapee.

Yates ordered that the man be bound fast and his mouth wired shut after it was stuffed with cow dung, or, if the drivers preferred, with human or horse feces. The drivers were grinning with delight, for the escapee had caused them a lot of trouble over the past few months.

"How long we leave him tie up wid him mouth full of cow shit, Massa?" one of the drivers asked.

"Overnight," said Yates blithely.

The two backras rode off while the man screamed at them, "You can't put cow shit inna man mouth, slave or no slave! Massa, come back!"

"I say," said Hartley, "aren't you being a bit harsh?"

"It's harvesting season," Yates snapped, "and I've got five days to bring in five hundred acres of sugarcane before it begins to rot. He needs to be made an example of, to be taught a lesson."

"Well," said Hartley not wishing to make an enemy of the Irishman, "I'd say he should learn something from that punishment. Ugh! How did you think of that?"

"I just had an inspiration," Yates chuckled.

The slave women were a hardened bunch, and while generally not as muscular or as strong as the men, they still had to take their place on the cutting line during a harvest. Pregnancy was no excuse to not work, and many women had dropped a new baby in the grass and gotten up to immediately resume cutting the sugarcane. Women were punished as severely as men and encouraged to breed and multiply but not to form families. In fact, children were separated from their mothers at an early age, usually six, often by being sold to other planters. Some mothers, in turn, committed infanticide rather than have their children grow up to become slaves.

Toward the backras many slave women were openly flirtatious since having a child for a white man would give them a hold, however tenuous, on him. Sex between master and slave was often spontaneous and immediate with no foreplay except the most rudimentary and crude kind necessary for workmanlike lubrication. Kissing under such circumstances was a rarity; copulation occurred typically outdoors on the ground.

Once Meredith and Hartley were riding across a field about to be harvested when a shapely young woman suddenly appeared out of the cane and waved at Meredith.

"Excuse me, my young friend," Meredith said hastily, "but I have some old business to take care of."

Meredith rode over to the woman, got off his horse, and disappeared with her into the cane thicket. Hartley was left sitting on his horse, looking on with bewilderment.

The sun beat down on his head like a fist and his horse drifted toward a tree that provided some shade. Hartley stood in the stirrups and spotted Meredith mounted atop the woman, her dress furled up to her waist, his breeches drawn down to his knees, his exposed buttocks puffy and white as freshly kneaded bread dough, pumping her furiously. Hartley discreetly withdrew.

A couple of minutes later Meredith reappeared,

climbed on his horse, exclaiming, "I feel like a new man!" As the two backras rode away, the woman slipped out of the cane piece, gave a saucy wave, and continued on her way. "One of the advantages of being the backra," Meredith added with a grin.

The whole episode had taken perhaps a minute or two, about the time it took for a bee to pollinate a flower.

Hartley Fudges adapted quickly to plantation life. He was no saint, but a young man with a young man's hot blood. He was daily surrounded by a sea of black women, and aside from the magnetic draw of his superior position over them, he was not a bad-looking man. He had been on the estate for over three months before he took his first woman. He encountered her on the road leading from a field being prepared for planting. As he rode past, she called out to him, "Hi, Massa, beg you a ride, nuh, sah."

At first he didn't understand what she said, but he gathered her meaning from her gestures. He helped her up on the saddle behind him. Once she was settled, instead of wrapping her hands around his waist, she encircled his hips so that both her hands were resting playfully against his cock. Hartley, who had not been with a woman in months, was instantly aroused.

"Lawd Jesus," the woman moaned, feeling a huge tumescent muscle swelling in his pants, "what is dis?"

They were riding past a hedge of shrubs shaded by a towering mango tree whose thick trunk provided a shield from the road. Hartley rode the horse behind the tree and dismounted, helping the woman off and lowering her to the ground. She lay on the grass, and in a blink he had his pants down and was climbing on top of her. She wore no panties.

"Easy now, Massa," she squirmed as he prepared to penetrate her.

But he was not easy with her. Her sudden fearfulness goaded him on and made him swell with an intoxicating surge of power. He plunged into her with a savage thrust of his hips. She received him with a shriek and a gasp, digging her fingernails into his back as he drove deeper and deeper inside her until she was so filled with him that she felt sure that she would be ruptured.

"Sweet Jesus!" she bawled, undulating her hips in an attempt to expel or behead the thick monstrous serpent that burrowed into her belly.

With a final explosive thrust, he impaled himself as deep as he could get inside her and hung there shuddering. She felt the head of the serpent pulsating as it spat its seed into her womb. Hartley slumped against her with a feral grunt, and they were joined in a brief moment of intimacy.

Then he remembered himself, and springing up, he pulled up his pants, jumped on the horse, and galloped away.

"Where you a go?" she yelled after him. "Where you get dat big donkey cock from?"

But he was long gone, leaving behind a plume of dust.

Not all the slave women were willing playthings to the white overseers. Some said no and refused to be used sexually. In that event, the white man could enforce his will on her without worrying about legal retribution. A slave woman could no more say no to a backra than a cow refuse to give milk.

The first time Hartley saw an overseer racing after an

unwilling woman he was reminded of a scene from Greek and Roman mythology where an eager Pan would chase a nymph through the fields of Arcadia, eventually catching her and dragging her back to his lair to party. But Pan and his bucolic antics were so far removed from the grounds of the Mount Pleasant plantation in Jamaica that it took an act of lunacy for anyone to confuse them.

Hartley himself forced several women to open their legs for him. He did not physically strike them but he wrestled them to the ground and held them securely while he finished the deed.

In one particularly ugly episode, Hartley Fudges was on his way back to the great house when he came across a slim black slave girl walking toward the slave quarters with a basket on her head. Hartley trotted toward her, which made her stop and glare at him. He gave a halfhearted salute of greeting which she made no effort to return.

"I know what you're after, Massa," she sniped, "but you come to the wrong woman. Me don't want no donkey hood."

"You're very impertinent," Hartley said, enchanted in spite of himself. "Stop and talk to me."

She stopped and raked him up and down with a hostile glower.

"Massa, you can ride me down and catch me and hold me down and get what you want from me. But me going fight you all de way so it going feel like work instead o' enjoyment."

Hartley got off his horse and approached the woman. She put down the basket she'd been carrying, bent over, and picked up a hefty rock which she brandished as a weapon. Hartley hesitated, for she appeared deadly serious in her intent to use it. He turned as if to remount his horse, then spun and hurled himself at her, knocking her flat on the ground where he pinned her under his body weight. She began to scream—not an ordinary scream, but a shriek that was ear-splitting and haunting like the wail of an animal being devoured. Hartley tried to put his hand over her mouth, but she bit him savagely on the palm. Meantime, her deafening shrieking brought two slaves scampering over to see what was wrong. They found Hartley and the woman writhing on the grass.

"Me no want no donkey hood!" the woman bawled.

"She don't want no donkey hood, Massa," scolded one of the intervening slaves.

"Donkey hood?" Hartley sputtered, feeling suddenly ridiculous.

"Donkey cock, Massa. She say you big like a donkey, and she don't want it."

Hartley was about to deny that he had a donkey cock when an ignominious feeling of being utterly debased swept over him.

"Why don't you mind your business," Hartley snapped, getting off the girl and standing up. The woman staggered to her feet.

"You do have a donkey hood," she muttered waspishly. "Dat's what everybody call you behind you back."

"Shhh," hushed one of the men. "You chat too much."

"I could have all three of you whipped," Hartley growled, mounting his horse and trying his best to save face.

"You'd still have a donkey hood," the woman snapped.

"Hi, Phibba," one of the men said, "you only going make him mad."

Hartley rode off feeling very small and absurd. He

could kick himself for making such as scene where he was not only wrong but belittled.

That was the only time he tried to take a woman against her will. He decided that there was too much risk of making a spectacle of himself, that casual roadside rape was neither sporting or dignified.

And it definitely wasn't cricket.

CHAPTER 10

There was nothing to do in the remote Jamaican countryside where the plantation was located: there were no elegant dinners to attend, no lively dances that dragged on until dawn, no brilliant glittery parties. The property was bounded on all sides by dour forested mountains or densely wooded undeveloped acreage known locally as government land. It was land like this that the founder of the plantation had hijacked through patents many years ago when Jamaica was just captured by the English. There were no towns nearby, not even villages, and beyond the reach of the overgrown land unfurled the ever-present, empty sea. Days were frenzied with work on the production of sugar, but nights were lazy and empty except during the harvest when the factory operated around the clock. The white men kept to themselves and, without white woman to entertain them and keep them presentable, soon became disheveled and grimy. Blacks and browns did not mix outside of their own groups. Yet it was the plantation that gave focus and meaning to the lives of those who worked on it. The plantation was like an aged relative whose children did not love her but took care of her out of duty.

Feelings differed widely among the various groups about Jamaica. The blacks resented the island as a prison to which they had been abducted and stranded. The browns felt that they did not belong in Jamaica but had been marooned there by miscegenation. To the whites, Jamaica was a stray animal they would opportunistically milk but did not love. Without love for the work there was no meaning to the lives of those who labored on the plantation. The continual cycle of planting, harvesting, boiling, and cooling became an endless, futile, and repetitive exercise that was done mechanically and dutifully for abstruse reasons that made life itself seem ridiculous. And all this madcap expense of energy was performed to keep some unknown Englishman rich and well fed.

The Irish overseers were practical men to whom abstract reasoning about purpose and meaning was a useless exercise in self-provocation like picking on an aching tooth that is temporarily quiet. Many Irishmen were romantic and poetic, but not these O'Haras and Mahoneys and Yateses and Fitzgeralds. Men of the soil, they did not trouble themselves over what they could not see or touch or hold. The chatter among them during mealtimes was about this animal or that Negro or this upsetting incident. It was unspeculative and grubby talk like the chitchat of merchants or fishmongers. They did not concern themselves with why but only with what and whom. Absurdity did not trouble them, for it was the substance and grain of their lives.

So the days fluttered past in this setting of picturesque loveliness that no one particularly cared for. Among the inhabitants, few, if any, would call themselves Jamaicans. These Irishmen and Englishmen and tribal Africans and other assorted Europeans occupied the island as a fiefdom of emptiness they did not even pretend to like, to say nothing of love.

* * *

Hartley Fudges, like all newcomer whites, was soon bored to death by the isolation and social primitiveness. He received just one letter from his father, informing him that Alexander had married the widow Bentley and settled down quite nicely in her home where they seemed to be happy. Once again, Hartley thought bitterly, fate had given to his brother what was rightfully his own. For days after he received this letter, Hartley moped around feeling glum and ill-used. None of his pub friends wrote him, for he had left London so suddenly that most of them did not even know where he had gone. He felt himself to be in miserable exile, yet he also felt the pressure of having to set an example before the vast horde of blacks among whom he was living.

It was a paradoxical state of affairs, but now that Hartley was in Jamaica and being gawked at from every quarter by black and brown faces, he found himself exaggerating those traits that were stereotypically regarded abroad as English. His accent became exaggerated and proper. He dressed for dinner every night and observed traditional teatime as often as he could. He wracked his brain trying to see exactly what made him seem English to others, and he decided that to be English was to be well mannered, distant, grammatically correct, and to carry oneself with an imperturbable sense of dignity. Whenever he appeared in public, he did his best to reflect these signature characteristics with an icy demeanor. But mainly he remained aloof from everyone except Meredith. It seemed that the farther away he was from England, the more ridiculously English he became.

He was not unaware of what was happening to him

but he was powerless to prevent the transformation. Being the backra had made his life theatrical, and not a day passed when he did not feel that he was onstage and playing to a fickle audience.

He suffered some setbacks as would be expected for a young man living in such rough-and-ready circumstances. The worst was that he came down with gonorrhea. It was perhaps inevitable, given the fact that he indiscriminately lay with scores of slave women who themselves had lain with umpteen other men—backras and slaves alike—making an ideal daisy chain for transmitting the bacteria *Neisseria gonorrhoeae*. In 1805 there was not only no cure, there was no effective treatment for it.

Nevertheless, ever hopeful of some relief, Hartley Fudges went to see MacDonald, the plantation doctor, a gruff Scottish man who had scraped his way through medical school, boning up on the medical mythologies of the day and absorbing a lot of nonsense that passed in 1805 for science. The doctor prescribed the preferred medical dosage of mercury salts applied as a paste, which did absolutely no good, and told Hartley that if his condition did not improve, he would treat him next with doses of sandalwood oil, and if that was not effective, he would try a dosage of zinc salts. To ease the discomfort Hartley was suffering, the doctor gave him opium and instructions about how to use it.

"If I were you," the doctor advised Hartley, "I wouldn't fornicate with anyone until you're no longer discharging. We don't know how, but we think you're just passing on the disease by doing that."

That very night Hartley spitefully lay with a slave woman on the ground behind the mill, telling himself grimly that someone had given the disease to him and he was therefore jolly well entitled to pass it on. A couple of weeks later, when the woman began to show symptoms, she blamed the infection on the too-cold river in which she had taken a bath one night against the advice of a girlfriend. Slave lore of the day knew no more about causation than did medical science.

Without intending to, Hartley began to populate the island with his seed. All his indiscriminate coupling would soon bear unwanted fruit. He was not the only one accused of breeding the slave women—all the overseers were similarly guilty—and it seemed that every second child born in the slave quarters was fairer than its dark-skinned mother. In 1805, no way of proving paternity existed other than specious claims of a resemblance between the child and the supposed father, and Hartley had quickly absorbed enough of the uncaring mentality of the backra to simply walk away chuckling. By the end of his first year, he had fathered over twenty children to as many women. Many of the infants died in the first months of life and were buried in unmarked graves. Others were taken away from their mothers and sold in slave auctions. Hartley made no attempt to get to know any of the surviving children. He felt no paternal affection for any of them and made it clear through his neglect that he cared no more about them than he did for the farrow of the plantation's sows.

In the initial weeks Hartley had had trouble with the language spoken by the slaves. It was a patois dialect based on an amalgam of English and various African tongues such as Ashanti and Swahili. Spoken very rapidly and in a singsong lilt, it was the *lingua franca* of the island and the linguistic bridge between the races. Hartley never learned to speak it, and in fact held it and its speakers in contempt. But after a few months of hearing it spoken around him everywhere he went, he acquired a basic understanding of its meaning, enough for him to communicate. But he never even made an attempt to speak it. Clinging to his received pronunciation, he persisted always in expressing himself crisply and exactly like a good Etonian.

But there were events that occurred on the plantation that brought out in him, if not Eton, then certainly his Anglicanism that lay buried under the rubble of a life lived primarily by secular principles. Like most members of his generation, Hartley was neither religious nor irreligious. He rather liked the pomp and circumstance of the High Mass, and when it came time to bury, he readily conceded that no ceremony could match the ponderous gloom of a church funeral with its tolling bell and promise of the resurrection. Death, sudden and unexpected, worked its black capricious magic all around him.

One night Hartley was in the mill checking on the particular gang of slaves working as feeders. Feeding stalks of cane through the rollers of the mill was dangerous work. The slave who worked as a feeder guided several stalks of cane between enormous rollers that were propelled by water flowing through an aqueduct. The force of this water turned the vertical rollers that crushed the cane and extracted the juice which, boiled, cooled, and particulated, would become sugar. To stop this grinding action, the water flowing through the aqueduct had to be diverted or stopped up, which was not easy to do.

When Hartley entered, the noisy mill was badly lit by a

greasy flicker of light thrown off by oil lamps. At two a.m. everyone was weary of the constant rumbling of the giant rollers that dominated the badly lit room and made hearing another's voice difficult. The feeders were pushing the stalks between the rollers when one man said something to another, distracting him. The distracted man was trying to listen to his companion while feeding stalks of cane into the grinder when his fingertips were caught between the rollers. He tried to snatch his hand free, but it was too late. His fingers were being pulverized, popped open like pulpy cherry tomatoes. The man began to scream for his hand was disappearing between the grinding wheels, pulling him into the mechanism. From out of nowhere came a slave wielding a razor-sharp hatchet, and with one blow he cut off the man's arm just below the elbow. The severed arm, bone and all, was crushed flat by the grinder and disappeared with an off-key crunch into the mouth of the rollers. Writhing in a pool of blood on the floor, the man was shrieking at an unnatural pitch, his agony ringing above the constant rumble of the mill.

The slave who had cut off the hand knelt down and pressed a rag against the stump through which bone jutted and tried to calm the injured man down.

"Did you have to cut off his hand?" Hartley asked peevishly.

"Yes, Massa. If me don't do dat, him grind up like porridge and de mill must shut down because o' all de blood," the slave said. "Is de third hand me cut off dis harvest."

"Get him to the doctor," Hartley ordered.

"Is too late fe doctor, sah," the man mumbled. "Him is a dead man. Plus, de doctor not going come outta him bed dis time o' night to treat slave."

Yates, who was supervising the boiling house next door, came into the mill to see what was happening and took control. He ordered three of the gawking slaves to carry the wounded man outside, directed two others to clean up the blood on the floor and the onlookers to get back to work. For the rest of the night, the slaves were sullen and lethargic and went through the motions of working while muttering among themselves.

Hartley stepped out of the noisy mill and found the injured man lying on the ground while nearby a slave who had been ordered to stay with him lay sleeping. The severed arm was still bleeding and lying grotesquely atop the man's chest, which was heaving as he drifted deeper and deeper into shock. When he saw Hartley approaching, the wounded man tried to raise himself up but didn't have the strength. Collapsing in the dirt, he began to jabber at Hartley in some unknown tongue.

Hartley kicked the sleeping slave. "Wake up!" he snarled. "What's he saying?" he then demanded.

The other slave, now awake, listened for a few seconds before saying, "He calling on his ancestors to help him die bravely."

"Ancestors!" Hartley said scornfully. "Tell him to call on Jesus."

Thinking the backra was making a sick joke, the watchman yawned widely and stretched out his limbs as if preparing to once again sleep.

"Tell him!"

"Massa, he is Ashanti. He calls out to the god of Bosumtwi because dat is his god. He no understand Jesus."

"Tell him he's making a mistake! There is only one god, and that is the god Jesus. If he calls on Jesus, even at this late hour, he will be saved." Without realizing it, Hartley had raised his voice into an almost hysterical pitch.

"Massa," the man said with another yawn, "is him dying, not you. He knows which god he wants to call to."

"Do as I say," grated Hartley furiously.

The watchman was swelling up to deliver another argument when the injured man gargled the rattle of death, shuddered, and fell still. Hartley lost his temper and gave the watchman a swift kick to his rump, nearly toppling him over.

"Massa!" the man squealed, spinning around confrontationally. Hartley, who was armed with a pistol tucked in his pants, glared at the man, hoping he would attack. The idea flitted across the man's face like the shadow of a passing moth but quickly disappeared.

"Kick Samson, Massa?" the man blubbered abjectly. "Why you kick Samson? Me only do what you say."

And looking suddenly like someone broken, he limped back into the mill and disappeared. Not five feet away from where Hartley Fudges stood, the dead man lay staring at the night sky, the severed stump still seeping blood over the splintered bone.

During the first year of his stay at Mount Pleasant plantation, Hartley was accompanied practically everywhere he went to by Cuffy. Sometimes the boy was useful in keeping Hartley looking as resplendent as possible under crude living circumstances by tending to his master's laundry or keeping the shine on his shoes or making sure that his clothes were properly ironed. But as time passed the boy was turning into a nuisance. He became particularly aggravating by his constant complaints that Hartley was not treating him like a proper slave and was therefore causing him to lose face among his own people.

The first time Hartley heard this complaint, he crossly said to the boy, "What do you want me to do? Beat you?"

A light went on in Cuffy's eyes. "Yes, sah! Beat me and leave mark. People respect a slave with whip mark on him back. When me tek off me shirt, people will say, *Yes, sah! Dis is a proper slave*."

Hartley stared at him with disbelief. "I'm not going to beat you," he said crisply.

"So I must walk round de grounds wid no respect," Cuffy said bitterly.

"As a matter of fact, I've been thinking about freeing you," Hartley said.

"Freeing me! Freeing me, sah? Wha' me do dat make you want treat me so bad?"

"Most slaves want to be free. Why wouldn't you?"

"Free, sah? Free fe do what?"

"Do anything you like. That's what being free means."

"Free to be you slave?"

"Don't be absurd. Being a slave and being free are opposites. You can't be both. That's trying to have your cake and eat it too."

"What? What cake me have fe eat?"

"It's just a manner of speaking. It means if you eat something, you no longer have it. And if you have it, you haven't eaten it."

"Eat what, sah? Wha' me eat?"

"Never mind. Just leave me alone."

That conversation, or a variation of it, took place repeatedly over the next few days and provoked Hartley to the point that he very nearly succumbed and gave the boy a whipping. But he hardened his heart like a biblical pharaoh and would not give Cuffy a fashionable beating. Who was the master and who the slave, anyway? Hartley was determined not to let his own servant bully him into acting conventionally. So the subject came up again and again like sprouting overnight mushrooms but Hartley would not budge no matter how Cuffy pleaded.

One evening a weary and begrimed Hartley rode in from the fields where he'd spent the day supervising a galley of cutters. He was on his way to the great house after turning in his horse to the care of the slaves in the stable when he heard the sound of someone being whipped. There was no mistaking the rhythmic slash of the cat-o'-nine-tails or the ripping noise it made as its tongs cut into flesh. Accompanying this were grunts from the person being flogged. Curiosity got the better of Hartley and he followed the sounds until he came to a tree to whose trunk Cuffy was tied, his back crisscrossed with the welts.

"Enough now?" the beater asked, panting for breath because he was an older man who no longer did any physical labor.

"How it look?" Cuffy asked, craning his head to see the ugly marks the whip had deposited on his skin.

"It look good, man," the old man said, nodding his approval like a craftsman proud of his own handiwork.

"You bring de looking glass?"

"Yes, man," the old man said agreeably, taking a small mirror out of his pants pocket and holding it up to give the boy a glimpse of his torn back.

Hartley slipped away without being seen. Cuffy was paying the old man to beat him! That way he could brag about being the perfect slave and have whip marks on his back to authenticate it. Behind that deception lay a twisted and deranged way of thinking that stunned Hartley and brought home to him a somber truth: he simply did not understand Cuffy or his warped mentality. Hartley sneaked away like one who had blundered into an obscene private ceremony.

That very night at dinner he asked Meredith, "How do you free a slave?"

"You give him his freedom paper, signed and witnessed," Meredith said.

The two men were silent as they chewed their food.

Finally, Meredith asked, "Tired of owning Cuffy?"

"Sick of it," Hartley said sourly.

"I thought it strange the way you bought him."

"It was an impulse," Hartley said.

"I tell you what, I'll buy him from you for the estate. He's clever. He'd make a good feeder."

Hartley thought about it for long moment before shaking his head. "I'll just set him free."

"That's throwing away fifty pounds."

"There's nowhere to spend the money anyway," Hartley replied.

After breakfast that morning, Hartley accompanied Meredith to his makeshift office in the great house. Meredith drew up the bill of freedom and Hartley signed it with a flourish.

Hartley picked his spot carefully for the announcement of Cuffy's manumission. He knew that the slave quarters were a hotbed of rumor and gossip, that in the drabness of their daily life of servitude the slaves were constantly swapping speculation and hearsay about the backra and his goings-on. So he waited until dusk when most of the slaves were gathering for the evening meal, sitting in clumps joshing with each other. In the middle of this chatter, Hartley rode up asking for Cuffy, causing a sudden and unnerving silence to settle over the company. Everyone denied seeing Cuffy; a couple of men who had the same name stood up as he were asking for them.

"Why you want Cuffy, Massa?" one old man dared to ask.

"Him want beat him again," muttered someone furtively.

Hartley was about to leave when Cuffy, unaware that his massa was looking for him, came striding boldly into the slave quarters. He was wearing no shirt, and the welts on his back were plainly visible. By the time he realized that the man on the horse was Hartley, it was too late for him to run away or to pretend not to see him. He looked around nervously at the onlookers.

"Ah, Cuffy," Hartley declared loud enough for everyone to hear, "I'm glad I found you. I brought your free paper for you. As of now, you're no longer a slave, but a freeman."

And Hartley handed him the free paper. The other slaves surged forward to peer at the document, to touch it reverently, and to ask Cuffy if it was real or just for show.

Hartley turned around and cantered off toward the great house without looking back. He was thinking to himself that not only was Cuffy free, but so was he.

Yet the boy was not happy, and he trailed Hartley to the great house.

"You shame me before me brethren," he hissed venomously when he caught up with the backra at the main entrance of the great house.

"You have your freedom!" Hartley snapped. "What else do you want?"

"Respect," the boy said. "You take dat away from me."

"Would you rather have respect than freedom?" Hartley asked.

"Without respect, dere is no freedom," the boy said bitterly.

"Rubbish," Hartley shot back, riding away and leaving the boy standing forlornly in the shadows of the slave quarters.

But that night, as Hartley lay down to sleep, he heard the discreet noise of a body settling against the door of his bedroom. He listened intently and then called out, "Cuffy? Is that you?"

No sooner had he asked that question when he was swamped by an overwhelming sense of absurdity. The boy was free, surely he wouldn't continue sleeping in the doorway of his former master.

And on that disquieting note, Hartley Fudges fell into a fitful sleep.

CHAPTER 11

One morning Hartley woke up to a chilling outcry about a vicious murder at a plantation some twenty miles away. From the somber gabble at breakfast he learned the fragmentary story. The victims were a white overseer from Dublin and a slave woman who had shared his bed for the past five years. As was usually the case, the details were hazy and kept changing with every retelling of the gruesome tale. In the bloodiest version, the great house had been set afire, the overseer and his woman killed along with three white overseas visitors. It appeared to be the work of renegade slaves hoping that their grisly example would spark an islandwide uprising against the white man.

"I wish I could take off this bloody skin and walk about Jamaica like a free man," Yates muttered in his coffee cup.

"What do you mean?" Hartley asked. "You're a free man now."

"Free!" Yates said scornfully. "How can you be free when every black man on the island is trying to kill you?"

"Isn't that a bit overstated?" scoffed Hartley. "I mean, not every black man wants to kill us. If that were the case, we'd be dead by now."

Meredith, who was sitting nearby listening to the clamor, intervened suddenly. "This is hardly breakfast fare. It's too depressing." That was Meredith's usual attitude. Life in Jamaica was difficult enough; talking about it only made things worse. If you must talk about anything, talk about the rainbow you saw yesterday, not about the murder that happened last night.

So the two backras, the young English one and the middle-aged Irishman—both of whom had no opinions on rainbows—lapsed into a gloomy silence.

The next morning Hartley found Cuffy curled up against the closed door of his bedroom. Startled awake, the boy rubbed his eyes and looked around him as if he were lost. Seeing his former owner looming above him, Cuffy jumped to his feet.

"What are you doing here?" Hartley asked curtly.

"Sleeping, sah."

"Don't sleep in front of my door anymore," Hartley snapped. "You're a free man. You're no longer a slave."

A look of stubbornness jelled over the boy's features. "Cuffy don't wanna be free, Massa. Cuffy only want to be a perfect slave."

"Now, see here, Cuffy," Hartley said sharply, "I'm beginning to think that you're out of your mind. I've turned you free. Your whole life is ahead of you."

"When Massa was sick, who tek care of him? Cuffy. Who wash and iron Massa's clothes? Cuffy. Who shine Massa's shoes and boots? Cuffy." The boy was raising his voice as he became more and more agitated about his unappreciated services. Embarrassed by the outburst, Hartley strolled past the boy and headed for the breakfast room, Cuffy trotting stubbornly in his wake with a doggish air. At the doorway that opened up on the dining room where the backras were already at breakfast, Hartley stopped and turned to face his former slave who also abruptly came to a halt.

"Stop following me around or so help me God, I'll punch you in the nose," Hartley glowered, making a menacing fist.

The boy did not flinch. Instead, he tilted his head as if to present his face for the expected blow. When it did not come his expression once again turned sullen and resentful and he began to taunt Hartley loud enough for the breakfasting Irish inside the dining room to overhear.

"Massa full of mouth and nothing else. All him do is talk 'bout how him going lick down Cuffy. But is pure mouth him have 'cause him don't do nothing."

Hartley reddened and turned on his heels and strode into the dining room where he knew Cuffy would not be allowed to enter. A house slave scampered out the door and shooed Cuffy away. Hartley heaved a sigh of relief and mumbled good morning to everyone.

"You should not allow your slave to talk to you that way," Yates, who sat across the table from Hartley, scolded quietly. "You set a bad example that will affect the rest of us."

A murmur of agreement and nodding rippled over the eating men.

"He's no longer my slave. I freed him."

Yates looked surprised. "So why is he following you around?"

"He doesn't want to be free. He wants to be perfect."

Yates chewed his food for a long pensive moment. "What do you mean *perfect*?"

"Just that: he wants to be the perfect slave."

"Is he mad?"

"I think so," Hartley mumbled. "It's really uncanny. It's almost like he has read Plato."

"Who's Plato?"

"You don't know? He was a philosopher. I'm surprised you never heard of him."

"We've got plenty philosophers in Ireland. What we need are more carpenters. Send your slave away."

"I tell you, he's not my slave."

"If he's free, he doesn't belong here on the plantation. Send him away. If you won't do it, I'll do it myself. Why did you buy him in the first place?"

"It was an impulse. I'd just landed after being at sea for nearly two months. The boy was having trouble with his owner, who offered to sell him to me. So I bought him."

"Now that you no longer own him, tell him he can't stay on the plantation."

"I've told him that a dozen times," Hartley said sourly. "He doesn't obey."

"Better if you'd bought a dog or a horse," commented Mahoney.

Hartley was bitterly stewing to himself about the obnoxious behavior of Cuffy and was preparing a broadside on the evils of primogeniture, that unfair law that had driven him from his homeland and deposited him in this island wilderness, but was restrained when the group of Irishmen started on a new topic—a sultry slave woman they suspected of giving all five of them a virulent strain of gonorrhea.

"If she did it deliberately," Yates said savagely, "one of us should cut her throat."

"I don't think she even knew she had it. She's pretty ignorant, you know," Mahoney said.

"I really don't know her," Fitzgerald admitted. "I don't believe I ever talked to her."

"But didn't you fuck her at least once?"

Fitzgerald, who had the old-fashioned Catholic squeamishness about sex, turned red-faced. "Yes, I did. But who talks to them at a time like that or afterward?"

The men sniggered, their mouths twisting into furtive, conspiratorial grins like a cabal of plotters sharing a lewd private joke.

After finishing breakfast, Hartley rode around the perimeter of the sugarcane fields, looking for malingerers and trespassers. Armed with two pistols and a dagger, he was soon bored to death. It was Meredith's orders, however, that the backras make their presence felt by these horseback patrols, which were rotated among them. He trotted past a field that was being harvested, stopped under a shady mahoe tree, and watched as the cane cutters, slashing right and left with their machetes, reduced the stalks to stubble and piled up the cut cane into mounds that other slaves loaded into carts yoked to Brahman bulls and hauled away to the mill. The sun was scorching the land and ripples of heat shimmered in the air. When it was this hot the island wilted and all creatures sought respite in the scrap of shadows, but not the slaves, and especially not during harvest time. The cane cutters advanced steadily through the fields flattening the rows with their machetes. Every now and again the crack of a driver's whip sounded like the snap of breaking bone.

Hartley was looking idly on when out of the corner of his eye, he noticed someone flitting behind a nearby tree. He rode over to it and found Cuffy trying to hide behind a bush.

"What are you doing here? Have you been following me?" Hartley asked testily.

"A good slave stay with him massa."

"I'm not your blasted master! You're free. And you're no longer allowed on the plantation premises. Now go away."

"Cuffy don't want no damn free. You can't just dash 'way Cuffy like old shoe."

Hartley stared at the boy, who he thought must obviously have gone mad. A few yards away in the cane field a driver, looking bored and hot, was snapping his whip for practice.

"You there!" Hartley called out, beckoning to the driver to come to him.

The man ambled over, still playing with his whip. Cuffy shrank away behind a bush.

"You see this man?" Hartley asked, pointing to Cuffy. "He doesn't belong on the plantation. He's no longer a slave. He's free. If you see him anywhere around, run him off the grounds."

The driver broke into an evil grin and flexed his whip. "Hey, boy!" he snarled. "Off de grounds."

"Massa treat Cuffy bad," the boy blubbered, backing up with his eyes fixed to the snapping whip. He back stepped to the cut-stone wall bordering the thick woods that encircled the grounds of the plantation with a scruffy collar of thick bush.

"Massa," the boy shrieked, "don't send Cuffy away!"

This plea was followed by the crack of the whip and the sound of scurrying footfalls. A few minutes later, the driver reappeared. "Him gone, Massa," the man grunted.

"Good riddance!" said Hartley.

The backra nodded curtly and rode away, leaving the driver looking disappointed as if he expected some special favor in return. The man shambled back to the field being harvested, still snapping his whip for practice, making a sound like gunshots that bounced off the mountains with an ominous echo.

When he first landed in Jamaica, Hartley Fudges thought the island exotic and beguiling. The sight of a rugged mountain gorge being carved open by the rippling blade of a river flashing in the sunlight would occasionally elate his spirits and give him a glimpse of something inexpressibly majestic, making him feel like an intruder accidentally witnessing a master artist toiling away in solitude. But as time dripped past and with beauty so promiscuously scattered everywhere around him, he was soon struck only by a vast and incomprehensible emptiness, and no matter how picturesque or sublime the land appeared, he still felt that he was bleeding away the days and weeks of his passing life.

As the empty nights and dreary days passed, the strange story of Cuffy and his expulsion from slavery swept over the plantation. It was almost impossible to keep such a secret from circulating among members of this bizarre society, slaves or freemen. It was a preposterous enough tale to entice everyone, and against the gray sameness of hard labor and cruelty that was replicated day after wearying day in this isolated corner of Jamaica, the idea of a slave demanding harsher treatment and refusing freedom struck the regimented population of blacks, whites, and free colored as funny and drew from nearly everyone either speculation or a wry chuckling.

It was a curious place, the plantation, a world unto itself that was populated by black men and women in bondage who lived in dirt-floor hovels and were herded like animals through various menial jobs by a handful of white men who slept fitfully in a palatial mansion, its existence as ridiculously intrusive as an Egyptian pyramid. Paradoxically, the year Hartley Fudges landed as a dispossessed second son would turn out to be the most productive year for sugar in the history of Jamaica. That signal year the island produced 101,600 tons of sugar, the most of any country in the world. And Hartley was a small part of this record year. He didn't know it, and if he had, that knowledge would have meant nothing to him. But he was part of it.

Among the backras in this troublesome time, opinion ran stormily against Hartley Fudges. And it seemed like every new sighting of Cuffy trespassing on plantation property brought renewed and boisterous arguments among the backras. One windless night, much to the irritation of Hartley Fudges, the subject of this bizarre behavior by his slave became the topic of dinner table conversation. It was the sort of unconventional subject that the Irish chatterboxes worried like a dog with a bone. Mahoney, a wiry baldheaded man, thought that Hartley had badly mishandled the whole affair.

"You should have flogged him when he asked you to," Mahoney chided the young Englishman.

"So who is in charge, in that case?" wondered Yates. "If we allow slaves to tell us what to do to them and how to treat them, where does that leave us? It puts us on a ship where the crew gives orders to the captain."

Hartley, who'd had too much rum with his dinner, was reeling over the table like he was aboard a ship in a tossing sea. When he was drunk, his normal baritone voice changed to the shrill level of a soprano. He was also likely to erupt in chuckling, guffawing, and cackling that, tinged with his drunken soprano inflection, sounded ugly and sarcastic.

"I think he's off his head," Hartley Fudges muttered. Then he laughed.

"What nonsense!" Mahoney blurted out. "The boy wasn't asking for anything special. He just wanted to put on a decent show for his family and fellow slaves."

"So let him take his show elsewhere," Yates said. "A plantation is no place for amateur theatrics."

"None of you seem to understand how perilous our place in Jamaica has become," said Fitzgerald, a man who was generally subdued and quiet and only rarely expressed an opinion. "It's not because we're stronger than the Negroes that we're able to enslave them. It's because they believe we are. If they ever find out the truth, they'll slaughter us for certain."

"That's why we shouldn't treat them like anything else but slaves," Mahoney said firmly. "Or they might find out our secrets and weaknesses and rise up against us. We want them to look at us with respect and fear."

"Quite so," seconded Fitzgerald. "If we tell them all our secrets, we'll look ridiculous."

And every eye turned to look accusingly at Hartley.

What does it mean to look ridiculous, and why was the slave master so fearful of this? The reason is not complex: what the European was doing to Jamaica and other countries was outright brigandage. But his shadow self went to a good deal of trouble to project not only an outcome of inevitability but the conviction that usurping the minds and hearts of alien peoples was righteous and proper. It was not. To have the opposite exposed was to be found out and shown to be something else than the pretense. It is the same lesson taught in the fable "The Emperor's New Clothes." His nakedness is not what brings down the emperor and subjects him to public ignominy. It is the fact that he believes he is properly clothed. A naked emperor is nothing more than a naked man, and all men, in the beginning and the end, are naked. But the emperor who mistakes nakedness for clothing is not only naked, he is deluded. What is worse is that he is wrong, but thinks himself right. This stark exposure of wrong pretending to be right is what creates the cruel impression of ridiculousness.

If keeping secrets from the slaves was really the aim of the overseers, they were living in the wrong abode. In the great house, keeping secrets from the slave staff was difficult if not impossible. The problem was that most great houses traditionally had too many slaves. Some had as many as thirty slaves to serve only five or six residents. The great house that Hartley slept in, for example, had nineteen female slaves and six males but only six white residents. To keep that many slaves around was to implant idle eyes and ears in every bedroom, toilet, and hallway, making secret-keeping a vain hope. But a great house with many servants had by 1805 become a traditional symbol of a plantation's prosperity. Throughout the length and breadth of Jamaica it continued to be a time-honored symbol, until the collapse of sugar production after the slaves were set free in 1834. With the slaves gone, the houses were padlocked and abandoned, and these once majestic mansions were left to endure the fondling of obsequious vines and parasitic creepers.

Centuries later, the stone foundations of these great houses are scattered throughout the countryside of Jamaica like the bones of Paleolithic beasts rotting in a merciless eternity.

There were no more argumentative people on the face of the earth than the Irish: as Christmas approached in 1805, Hartley came to this conclusion. The Irish overseers argued over everything, with passion and style. No matter what topic might come up, one of them would take the pro side, another would adopt the con side, and a clamorous exchange filled with similes and metaphors and noisy declamations would swell from the wraparound verandah of the great house and blow over the darkened fields where the cane stalks grew in disciplined rows like a military formation. These quarrels usually took place at night and were loud enough to be heard in the slave quarters some hundred or so yards away. Often, bewildered slaves trying to sleep in dimly lit hovels would hear the uproar coming from the great house like the sounds of snarling dogs.

It seemed to Hartley that not only were they argumentative, the Irish overseers were also nervous and fearful about their situation in Jamaica. The position of the white man, to even a casual observer, seemed perilous. So the Irish overseers fulminated among themselves about their unhappy predicament, cursing the day they'd first laid eyes on this island.

Here, among the stumps of Jamaican history, was being hatched an attitude toward the land that persists even to this day. It is an attitude that blames every human misstep and calamity on the innocent land, as if the island was not merely the indifferent stage of human misconduct, but its cause. Continents, however, do not come in for this anthropomorphic abuse, only islands. People do not walk around muttering curses at the continent of South America because they were robbed in Peru. But because they are so small, islands are often scapegoats for human wrongs.

Centuries later, long after Hartley Fudges's footprints had been erased from the land, the descendents of the men and women of the nineteenth century would continue the tradition of blaming poor Jamaica for the stupidity of its people.

CHAPTER 12

Jamaica in 1805 was a nervous, fretful colony. Almost no trace of Spanish occupation, which ended 150 years earlier, was left on the island except the merest whiff that lingered in such names as Rio Bueno and Ocho Rios. But by 1805 an avalanche of typical English place names such as Fair Prospect and Williamsfield had effectively buried what little remained of the ancient conquistadors. Stewardship of the island was now in the hands of English and African descendents of a hardy and rugged group of men.

Typifying the breed of Jamaican planters in 1805 was Simon Taylor, the richest planter on the island. Born in the eastern parish of St. Thomas in 1740, Taylor was a rash, stubborn man who was described by General Nugent, a former governor of Jamaica, as being "in strong opposition to government at present and violent in his language against the King's ministers for their conduct toward Jamaica." The portrait of Simon Taylor is softened by the ex-governor's remarks that he "has had an excellent education [he went to Eton], is well informed and is a warm friend to those he takes by the hand."

Living in Jamaica as he did made Taylor the exception rather than the rule among plantation owners. Most of the plantations were under absentee ownership, the day-to-day running entrusted to local managers and overseers.

One consideration that kept the owners and their families away from Jamaica was the high mortality rate of white people, including their own sons and daughters. One Jamaican planter had eighteen grandchildren born on the island, fifteen of whom died at an average age of 23.9 years.

During these bad old days, life in Jamaica was tumultuous and unpredictable. By 1805 Jamaica had a disproportionately strong voice for its size in British parliamentary government. Its lobbyists were influential and cunning, and they fought hard to keep the present system of slavery. But the antislavery movement was a moral juggernaut that was impossible to stop. Many of the churches, the Baptists and Moravians particularly, were categorically against slavery and had sent missionaries to Jamaica to help in the fight for its abolition. Some of these missionaries preached openly against slavery and took the rabble-rousing position that not only did black slaves have souls, they would also end up in the same heaven as was in store for white men.

Shifting alliances and allegiances among England, France, and Spain remained a problem as well as a fact of life in the eighteenth and nineteenth centuries. In the Caribbean this rivalry was particularly intense as the big European powers, seeking to expand their West Indian holdings, probed the defenses of different islands. Guadeloupe, for example, was annexed by the French in 1674, captured by the English in 1759, and occupied until 1763 when it again passed on to France. The British took over the island in 1794 and again in 1810, the second occupation lasting six years. Some islands even ended up under dual ownership. St. Martin would eventually be half French and half Dutch; the island of Hispaniola, half Spanish and half French.

By now the English were beginning to realize that no island was more important to their interests than Jamaica. During the Anglo-French War, the British secretary of war declared that "the loss of Jamaica would be complete ruin to our credit," and that fifteen thousand French troops landing in Jamaica would be a greater disaster than if they landed in England. Before the abolition of slavery, Jamaica generated astounding wealth that made it more important to the English than all their combined possessions in Canada.

Hartley Fudges lived the little picture, his hours consumed every day with his duties as an overseer, having only a vague idea of the part he played in the big scheme of things. With every passing day and week, he found himself sinking deeper and deeper into an ugly, unsociable frame of mind that made him avoid the Irishmen and their constant bickering and pedantic arguments over nothing. Weekends were especially difficult for him because unless the plantation was in the middle of a harvest, there was little for all the overseers to do. Many of the slaves spent their Saturdays cultivating their small plots of land and Sundays lugging their surplus ground produce to sell in the market.

This curious custom of slaves growing their own food was mandated by law as early as 1678. Saturday was the one day of the week when slaves were permitted to cultivate their own gardens, keeping and selling whatever produce they grew but could not consume. It was also the practice to occasionally give slaves a free weekend or Sunday to travel to nearby markets where they could sell their surplus goods. This temporary ticket to freedom was issued by an overseer who wrote down the particulars on a piece of paper that slaves had to surrender on their return to the plantation at the end of the free period. As the returning slave looked on, the overseer would then burn the expired pass, a custom memorialized in Jamaica today in the quaint idiom, "Your freepaper burn," meaning your holiday is up.

Granting the slaves an occasional respite from the merciless grind of hard labor they were expected to perform, however, also had at its bottom very practical economic reasons. Slaves were relied on as the main source of manual labor on the plantation; moreover, hungry or underfed slaves did not have the strength or energy to work hard.

Yet feeding such a robust labor source meant a huge additional expense to the plantation. Various attempts to find a cheap source of carbohydrates for the slaves had come to naught, sometimes through sheer bad luck. The infamous mutiny on the HMS *Bounty* in 1789, for example, had taken place as the vessel made its way to Jamaica with a cargo of breadfruit shoots meant to feed the slaves.

It was particularly hard on weekends when the fields were mainly empty of hands and only the occasional worker idling about the property on some unknown errand could be seen. Then the heaviness of time and the persistent feelings of wasting his life gnawed at Hartley with the virulence of physical illness. Everything he saw around him seem pointless and empty. The furled hills combed in pleats of green that poised in the sky all the way to the ocean held no appeal. Everything he saw was plain and humdrum and tawdry; day or night, nothing struck him as beautiful—not the uncut jewels of starlight scattered across the night sky like spilled treasures, not the Milky Way leaking luminescent stardust. On his days off he went nowhere but wandered around the property either on foot or on horseback. For the land he felt neither love nor respect. Everywhere he looked he saw the same opulent luxuriance of the tropics that he found cloying and overdone, and nearly every day he muttered under his breath the same bitter verdict about the surrounding landscape, "Too rich. Too rich."

If he had been a poet or had the heart of a poet he might have scribbled rhapsodies of appreciation to the beauty everywhere, and every day he would have had a different slice of loveliness to tantalize his imagination and send molten words and images bubbling out of his pen. But his heart had no poetry in it, and his imagination was a stark empty cupboard.

Every now and again the plantation would have a scare, which came mainly from the sea. Many Jamaicans saw the sea as the enemy. It was the sea that had brought marauding Europeans to Jamaica's doorstep. It was the sea that had deposited shiploads of black slaves onto Jamaica's shore and left them there like chattel to be bought and sold. And it was the sea that piped the clamor and confusion of distant foreign wars to Jamaica, unnerving the already jittery population. When manumission finally came, it was no wonder that many of the slaves fled into the interior of the island where they established townships and villages as far away from the sea as they could get.

With Spain and France and England constantly jockeying for power in the Caribbean, the sight of any sail on the horizon was almost always cause for alarm. From the veranda of the Mount Pleasant great house the arc of the horizon was plainly visible, and anyone watching—with or without a telescope—could plainly see the occasional ship passing under full sail. With a telescope the flag of a vessel might even be glimpsed if the ship was not too far out. Because the plantation was up on a hill and miles away from the ocean, there was little danger of bombardment that some of the coastal plantations had suffered. Occasionally a ship would attack an island belonging to an adversary nation and burn its plantations to the ground. But Mount Pleasant was too high up on the hill and too hard to get to for any marauders to pillage.

Yet once in a while there would be a flurry of excitement caused by passing ships. One day, for example, three ships were sighted sailing near to the coast, headed toward Montego Bay. They flew French flags and appeared to be men-of-war. The lead ship had her gun ports open, and the small armada sailing parallel to the coastline of Jamaica had numerous telescopes silently trained on them from the shore. But eventually the three sailing ships struck out a course for deep sea that took them away from the island. Whatever their intent was, whether to probe the defenses of the colony or to spread the disquiet and uneasiness of a distant war to Jamaicans, no one could say. But everyone was grateful to see the three interlopers disappear below the horizon as if they had sailed off the edge of the world as mariners once feared would happen when the world was flat.

Christmas came and went. Christmas Day was declared a day of rest and free passes issued to those slaves who wished to visit their ground produce gardens or to take their surplus crops to sell in the market. In 1805 Christmas was a quiet holiday, not the climactic revel the writer Charles John Huffam Dickens (1812–1870) would later depict and glorify. On this one occasion the slaves were allowed to disport themselves in their own way. Suspended was a prohibition against street dancing and many slaves, some dressed up in traditional homemade costumes, others carrying and beating drums, took to the streets in a John Canoe parade.

Dancing in the streets at Christmastime was an ancient custom whose origin was shrouded in mystery. All throughout the plantation was heard the intoxicating throbbing of the drums as the revelries began at dusk and continued until darkness had fallen. The earliest reference to this custom—variously called Jonkanno, John Connu, and John Canoe—occurred in 1725, although the performers were not given a specific name until 1774 when historian Edward Long referred to the celebrants as John Canoe dancers. Costumes worn by the dancers were festive and colorful and consisted of some well-known John Cannu figures such as Horsehead, which referred to a dancer whose costume was capped with a movable jaw resembling a horse's and whose zinc teeth, manipulated by the concealed dancer, made a hideous clacking sound. Cowhead was a similar grotesquerie but one whose handmade head, complete with real horns, was fashioned to resemble a cow's. The sight of these two writhing, prancing figures, both of whom would shriek "John Canoe!" at intervals before exploding to the rhythms of the pounding drums, would cause children to cry and run screaming to their mothers. Also included among the costumed characters was Pitchy Patchy, a funny-looking figure clad in glued-together scraps of cloth and strips of paper who would whirl around in a blur as he gyrated to the hypnotic drumming.

Parading through the slave quarters, followed by a semidrunken celebrating crowd, the procession eddied at the gates of the great house in a cataract of swirling bodies while the drums throbbed with the mesmerizing rhythm. Several of the backras strolled onto the veranda and peered out at the crowd that was in a boisterous, ecstatic mood as the revelers danced and stomped their feet joyfully.

"This night would almost make you believe that there's no slavery," Hartley said wryly.

"Right now there is no slavery," Meredith replied.

"Who was John Cannu?" Hartley asked.

"No one knows for certain," Meredith said. "I read somewhere that he was a *cabocero* or village head on the Guinea coast, a brave and faithful warrior. The Prussians left him in command of a village and he held out against a superior Dutch force for a long time."

The two men peered at the festive crowd that shimmered with cat paws of movement like the placid face of a lake crinkling to the breeze.

"This is what happens to people who can't read or write," Meredith muttered sadly. "They can only dance to celebrate life. There's no other way to memorialize anyone or any event."

Hartley was thinking, as he scanned the shadows and the teeming throng, that somewhere in Plato's ether was a perfect dance of which this one was a pale imitation. If he allowed his imagination to run riot, he would have had to consider that the ensemble of the moment, in Plato's world, would also include him and Meredith as perfect forms, which would make him an imperfect copy of himself. Since he was presently the only inhabitant of his body, he couldn't understand who was in the perfect body that existed only in Plato's world. It was a frivolous thought and one he quickly dismissed. But such abstract Platonic nonsense seemed to pop up in his consciousness with frightful regularity that would distress a weaker mind.

The crowd wore itself out as the evening dragged on, and soon the drumbeat became erratic then sporadic, and finally with a flurry it died out altogether and the crowd crumbled into clumps and bunches that broke off from the main body and drifted listlessly to the slave quarters. Meredith came over to Hartley and told him to find the driver known as Watkins and collect from him the drums that had been used in the John Cannu dancing. There were six drums and Hartley was charged with getting every one of them and personally turning them over to Meredith.

"Why?" wondered Hartley.

"Drums are banned among slaves in Jamaica," explained Meredith. "In Africa, people say that some tribes communicate by drumming. In the event of an islandwide revolt, we don't want the slaves communicating with each other."

Early the next morning, Hartley wandered into the slave quarters looking for Watkins, whom he found sleeping under a tree. The shacks that slumped all around like a growth of wild mushrooms seemed even dirtier and more desolate than usual and a palpable sense of dissipation and waste hung over the huddled buildings. The air was sticky and damp, and every breath Hartley drew smelled as if infected with the exhalations of a sick bed. Aside from the man sleeping under a tree, no one else was in sight, not even a child. Next to the ragged sleeper were drums arranged in two clumps of three and two. Oblivious to where he was or to Hartley who stood over him, Watkins was snoring loudly and gave off the smell of old rum. Unsure of what to do, Hartley was about to rouse the man when he heard a soft female voice whisper, "What you want, donkey hood?"

He turned and saw the slave girl he knew as Phibba looking him over saucily from the shadowy doorway of a nearby hovel.

"Don't call me that name," Hartley said sharply. "I was about to wake him up and get him to help me carry the drums to the great house."

"I'll help you," she said. "Make him sleep."

"There are supposed to be six drums. There are only five."

She went over to the sleeping man and, using her fingers, calculated that there were indeed only five drums, not six.

"Are you related to this man?" Hartley asked.

"He's my father," she replied, walking away. "I'll check the house."

Hartley wanted to ask, *How can that man possibly be your father? You're not the same color. Is your mother white?* but he stopped himself when he realized that the mother must have been impregnated by a white man who, if he were even aware that he had fathered a child with a slave, had probably renounced paternity. He thought back to at least four women who had made the same accusation against him and how he had dismissed them.

Well, he didn't invent the system. He didn't own a plantation. True, he was promiscuous with the slave women, but so were all the other overseers, Meredith included. And when you got right down to it, many of the women who he had screwed since he arrived in Jamaica had asked for it. He was no one extraordinary or exceptional. He was just a young man sowing his oats. Every day he had to run the gauntlet of lovely dark-skinned women. What was he supposed to do when a woman got up on his horse and then put her arms around his waist so she could feel him up and arouse him? There was only so much temptation a man could resist. He went over these rationalizations like a shopkeeper taking inventory of unsold goods.

He was going on in this key in his thoughts when Phibba emerged out of the dark shack with the missing drum. Each of them carrying three drums, Hartley and the woman walked toward the great house.

"Massa, you like de John Cannu yesterday?" Phibba asked.

"Rather a noisy affair, wasn't it?" Hartley answered offhandedly.

"De drumbeat never catch you?"

"No, I can't say that it did anything except give me a headache."

"You tek everything so serious. So de white man stay. Everything serious. Nothing fun. Everything plan out ahead o' time."

"I don't suppose you've ever heard of Plato?"

"We have a few Plato on de property. Which Plato you mean?"

"The Plato of books."

"Phibba can't read books, Massa. Phibba can't write except one word. You want see how Phibba write dat one word?"

"Oh, all right," Hartley sighed.

They lay the drums on the grass and Phibba picked up a stick and walked over to a patch of clay in the roadbed. Bending down, she scratched *Stop* on the makeshift slate with the intense concentration of one who had repeatedly rehearsed doing so.

When she was finished, she looked up at Hartley and asked proudly, "You know what dat say?"

Hartley almost forgot himself and blurted out, *Now, see here, woman. I went to Eton*. But he remembered where he was and replied, "It says *Stop*." Then, because his answer seemed to him to be so lame, he added, "I went to Eton."

Phibba looked up at him quizzically. "What name Eton?"

"It's a famous school that produces gentlemen."

"What is a gentleman?"

"I am."

"Oh, I see. Now I understand."

Hartley was not at all sure from her tone that she understood. "You do? What is a gentleman?"

"A man like you."

"What is a man like me like?"

"Him have a donkey hood. And him know how to read and write."

"He has nothing of the kind!" Hartley snapped.

She recoiled as if she had been punched. "So what is him den?"

Hartley suspected that he was being mocked, but her expression was so serious and attentive that he believed she didn't understand.

"A gentleman is a man who has good manners, speaks the King's English, treats everyone with respect, reads and writes several languages, and overall is a good fellow."

"And him have a donkey hood."

"Stop saying that!"

"You see what my word say?" she asked waspishly. "You nuh see is a word you use in prayer."

"*Stop*? A word you use in prayer?"

"De man who teach me to write dat word teach me what it mean too."

"What does it mean?"

"*Stop* mean to cease and desist, to come to a halt," she recited like a schoolchild rattling off a lesson. "Bet you never know dat me know so much word," she said proudly.

Hartley was at a loss for words. He heaved a sigh and asked the only question he could think of: "Why would you use a word like *stop* in prayer?"

"Because is what you say to God when you pray."

"Why on earth would you say that in a prayer?"

"You say, *God, stop de rain, too much rain fall*. Or you say, *Lawd, stop de wickedness of de foe*. Or you say, *You, God! Stop wid de sun hot! Beg you, stop de king o' England from mashing up we life*."

They picked up the drums and trudged up the cart track that connected the great house to the denuded stretch of yard where the dilapidated slave hovels were scattered like bones of a picked-clean corpse.

"Who taught you that prayer?" asked Hartley as they approached the stone wall that banded the great house.

"Why you want to know, Massa?"

"It's almost seditious," Hartley grumbled.

"What dat mean, Massa?"

"It's nothing good, I promise you. It's something very bad, indeed."

Phibba didn't speak for a long moment. Finally, she

said, “Nobody teach me, donkey hood. Is learn me learn it on me own.”

“If you call me that loathsome name again,” Hartley threatened, “I swear I’ll have you flogged.”

“Donkey hood, donkey hood, donkey hood,” she chanted with malice, her face twisted in a reckless grin.

Hartley set down the three drums he was carrying and grabbed her by the shoulders and threw her to the ground. In a blink he was on top of her as she struggled and squirmed underneath his body weight.

“Get offa me, donkey hood,” she gasped, “or me goin’ scream bloody murder.”

He settled on top of her with his face buried deep against her neck. From a subterranean part of her body lifted a natural musk of rising sexual excitement that almost made him giddy. Glancing around, Hartley was feeling ridiculous and was about to stand up when he felt one of her hands squeezing him in a delicate spot and the other pulling down his pantaloons until his naked bottom was brushing against the coolness of the morning sky.

“Make me feel dat donkey hood,” she gasped, fumbling with his clothes.

And when she felt it, she shivered and cracked open her legs wide to receive him with a loud moan that reverberated throughout her body like a shudder of joyful welcome.

CHAPTER 13

Donkey hood, known in England as the Marquis of Fudges, and the slave girl Phibba had become lovers. No more unlikely pairing seemed possible, and in the beginning their relationship made them the butt of jokes and after-dinner chat. Among the slaves the union was considered an out-and-out victory for Phibba. In the popular analogy that likens a romancing twosome to a fish and a fisherman, onlookers had no doubt about who had caught whom. Phibba was a fisher of men; Hartley Fudges was the landed fish. Yet in her own way, Phibba had been hooked too. She was drawn to Hartley with an extraordinary passion that made her long for him by day and hunger for him by night.

They made an awkward pair, not because one was black and one white, one a slave and one a master, but mostly because a plantation in nineteenth-century Jamaica had no physical stage where lovers could meet and do their private whispering. The surrounding district had no bars or restaurants for socializing or dining out. The lovers could only furtively meet in the fields or in the commons—two very public places that fueled gossip. Every meeting of the two became a spectacle much talked about by gawking onlookers.

From the beginning, it was obvious that this was no ordinary affair of the flesh between a black woman and white man on the plantation, with all the lopsidedness of a relationship between master and slave. It was obvious because the lovers did not hit and run, did not jump up in postcoital embarrassment and flee the scene of lovemaking. Instead, they lingered in each other's arms, talking quietly. And afterward, civility and playfulness existed between them as they walked away holding hands like they were bonded together with ties of domesticity.

For an overseer and a slave to have a love affair was neither rare nor unusual. But what was different about Hartley and Phibba was the incandescence of their relationship. As absurd as it may seem, the two of them carried on as though this intimacy were perfectly normal in spite of the gross differences between them, both physical and social. Hartley became the protector of his new love and used his influence as a backra to get her easy work assignments for the week.

One evening when they were together Hartley noticed an ugly welt on her shoulders made, Phibba said, by the driver's whip. That night Hartley went over to the driver's cabin, woke the man up out of his sound sleep, and warned him never to strike Phibba again or he would be shot down like a dog. After that, word got out among the other drivers that Phibba was under the protection of the newest overseer.

It hit like a thunderbolt, this love affair, and took everyone by surprise, including Hartley himself. But there was a wild freshness about Phibba that intoxicated the Englishman. Her dark skin felt to his touch as cool as a rose petal and as smooth as a river stone. She seemed to Hartley almost an ethereal presence, and he could not imagine for a second that in Plato's attic of perfect forms there could exist a prototype of Phibba that was better than the copy he loved.

Practically everyone was against this particular affair, and many gloomy prophecies were muttered about its prospects. Aware of the consternation he was causing, Hartley tried his best to remain nonchalant when he was around Phibba in public, but it was a vain attempt because the gleam in his eye belied his feigned indifference. If Hartley had been one of the Irish overseers, he would have come in for some good-natured teasing. But being a young Englishman, he kindled the national antagonism between the English and the Irish, the spectacle of his dalliance with Phibba worsening an already troubled situation. Hartley walked the plantation dragging behind him an air of self-consciousness as if he expected to be upbraided at any moment by his Irish critics.

Mahoney in particular took vocal exception to what Hartley was doing. If the Englishman had been indiscriminately screwing the odd slave girl, nothing would have been said because nothing would have seemed amiss. But this ridiculous mooning over one slave girl by an Etonian Englishman seemed at best impious and at worst indecent. Why couldn't Hartley be satisfied with picking off a woman or two from the plantation stock even if he used one more regularly than the others?

When a colonial Englishman becomes aware that his behavior has been indecorous, his tendency is to be superciliously civil, to pepper the air with "I beg your pardons," and other elocutionary flourishes he hopes will elevate him above his offense. Hartley began to behave with cold, unwavering courtesy toward everyone around him as if holding hands in the late afternoon when he and Phibba were out for a walk was perfectly acceptable behavior for a backra with a slave lover. The rest of his strategy was to pretend that disapproval of him and his behavior did not exist, as if when he entered the dining room the normal bantering did not immediately stop and the chilling silence of a church service not descend over everyone like a privacy curtain.

Over the next few months the affair between Hartley and Phibba grew even hotter and more blatant. Phibba had no past other than the jumbled memories of a childhood spent in Africa. She had been captured when she was twelve and put on a ship bound for the West Indies. The journey from the West Coast of Africa to Barbados was a nightmare so excruciating that it lingered in her personality more like a wound than a memory. Chained to strangers in the dark, stifling hold of a ship, sometimes sitting in her neighbor's excrement, she saw people die every day. The stench surrounding her was so overpowering that months after the voyage, she could smell the foul odor of decomposition on her skin like the universal stink of corruption. She had survived by focusing all her might on the weekly airing out of the compartment in which she lay and savoring to the full the few hours of respite she took from being allowed on deck, albeit chained. She had struggled hard to stay alive because she simply could not believe that it was her destiny to be a lifelong slave. Within her heart burned the fevered conviction that her slavery was only a temporary setback from which she was soon recover.

One of the things the lovers liked to do was to go swimming in the river that crisscrossed the plantation and provided it with the motive power for its mill. They knew several spots where the river coiled like a placid snake and the surface of the water was a languid green that shimmered with an inviting iridescence. One particular stretch of the river on whose banks many years ago rebellious slaves had been slaughtered by the white militia became their favorite swimming hole. Most people kept away from this part of the river because local legends said that it was haunted by ghosts of the massacred slaves. Here Hartley and Phibba went skinny-dipping at least twice a week in the evenings when the sun no longer beat down on the earth like the hammer of an enraged blacksmith. Usually they would end up making love on the muddy riverbanks, and anyone snooping in the bushes would have beheld the spectacle of a white man whose flesh was puffy and airy like unkneaded biscuit dough writhing sometimes atop, sometimes beneath, a black woman, both of them giving off the wild grunts and passionate outcries of rutting beasts. And even when they rolled off each other, their passion temporarily sated, they still touched with their extended hands and feet like lovers sprawled out on a featherbed.

They should have had little to talk about. But the very opposite turned out to be true. Phibba was something of a chatterbox, and wherever she went, she seemed to be trailing behind her a long kite tail of sentences fluttering about this and that and the other. As for Hartley, he loved to hear her talk, and the sillier he thought her opinions, the more he loved to hear them. He was always asking her what she thought about this and that, as a way of priming the pump of her talkativeness, for once she was started he knew that she would be hard to stop.

Forget that Phibba had the ancestral past of a tumbleweed or that her African surname was Kati and that she had been named Phibba only because she had been born on a Friday (if she had been born on a Monday, she would have been named Juba); or that Hartley was the latest in a line of Fudges whose ancestry extended back to Adam and Eve (so, for that matter, did everyone else's except that the world was too shortsighted to grasp that fact). There was also the difference of language—Phibba knew the patois that Jamaicans spoke but her mother tongue was Coromantee—while Hartley knew English, French, and German in the way a parrot knows how to squawk. He had also acquired at Eton a rote knowledge of Greek and Latin, enough for him to read the original classics. But, of course, he never did. As for Phibba, her world was strictly one-dimensional, her life and daily goings and comings closely regulated by her condition of enslavement. Hartley's outlook, on the other hand, was crammed full of Greek demigods and effigies whose petrified forms haunted the gardens of his family mansion. This all meant that the two lovers were as unalike in their fundamental makeup as it was possible for two people to be who were members of the same species.

Yet they quarreled only occasionally and their little differences were only pinpricks on their relationship. One of the regular arguments they had was over other women. Phibba was jealous of any little flavor or attention Hartley might show another female slave and had to be reassured almost daily that his heart belonged to her and no one else. Years later a scholar would point out that in the plantation society black women produced, brown women served, and white woman consumed. What the writer might have also said was that the competition between all classes of women for the attention of the few white men was constant and unrelenting.

Hartley took Phibba to his own bed, occasionally at first, but then more and more regularly until it was understood that she would sleep at his side every night unless some extraordinary circumstance was prevailing. She was sharing his bed one night, for example, when a new slave went mad and ran amok in the slave quarters, slashing at the air with a machete, sending the slaves fleeing their dingy shacks. The backras woke to the clamor and Mahoney went into the slave quarters; when the man was pointed out to him, without saying a word, the Irishman shot him dead from a distance. He returned wearing a triumphant smirk like he had just destroyed a wild dog and openly boasted to the backras about killing the slave with a single shot. Phibba was angry at the outcome and complained bitterly to Hartley.

"Him shoot de man down like him was a dog. No word o' warning. Nothing. Just bang, bang and de negar dead."

"What else could he do?" Hartley asked. "The fellow had a machete. He chopped a woman earlier. Mahoney couldn't afford to take the chance."

"Chop what? You see him chop anybody?"

"No, but everyone says that's what he did."

"You show me de woman dem say him chop. Him don't chop nobody. Dem just looking for excuse to shoot de man down like a dog."

"I don't particularly like Mahoney," Hartley said stubbornly. "But I think he had every right to do what he did. I would have done exactly the same."

"Dat's because you's a backra. Dat why you say so."

"Now, look here, Phibba, I could say the same thing about you."

"Say what? Dat me is a backra?"

"No, that you believe as you do because you're a slave. I'm not saying that," he added quickly, "I'm just saying that I *could* say that."

"You better not say it," Phibba scowled.

"We are what we are, we say what we are, and we do what we are. That's how life is," sighed Hartley, and as soon as he had finished this sentence, he felt proud of himself for being so philosophical, so Etonian.

Phibba, who was not philosophical, said airily, "You better shut up about it if you ever want me to drain dat donkey hood again."

Love is as wild and as profligate as a weed. It grows where it will grow. It brooks no opposition. It makes men and women behave in ways that are alien and outlandish to their ordinary natures. It suffuses everything, every act and every deed, with the glow of plausibility. And to a thinking man like Hartley, it made life seem like an enigma.

Most mornings he awoke feeling entirely philosophical. He would lie in bed pondering some eternal and inscrutable paradox, feeling like a pilgrim staggering on the plain of ignorance where cruelty abounded and godlessness was the norm. Beside him Phibba would snuggle while his every heartbeat throbbed with a pulse of love for her. He would sigh with longing and marvel that he loved a woman who could neither read nor write and knew how to write and spell only the word *Stop*, which she often used in her prayers.

One morning she awoke to find Hartley staring at the ceiling because he could not sleep. She lay beside him, curled up cozily against his naked body.

"What you look at?" she murmured.

"I'm thinking about a problem," he said huskily.

"What you think about?"

"I am wondering if we do what we are or are what we do."

"What kind o' trash is dat, donkey hood?"

"You know I don't like that name."

"Nobody in de room but me. And nobody know better dan me dat you have a donkey hood. Maybe you have a donkey brain, too, dat make you think foolishness."

"It's not foolishness. It's philosophy."

She began playing with his genitals. "What name philosophy?"

"It's thinking about what we are and who we are."

"I know de answer to dat. You a man name Hartley. You come from London. Me a woman name Phibba. Me come from Africa. What else you want know?"

"How did I get here?"

"By ship. Same way as me."

"But why am I here?"

"Because you ride on a ship dat bring you here. Oh oh. Donkey hood growing big again."

"You'd never make a good philosopher," Hartley said with a sigh as she mounted him, making the bed springs creak hideously, setting his teeth on edge.

One morning Hartley and Meredith ended up alone at the breakfast table. It was shortly after Christmas and the shreds of jollity were still clinging to the plantation even though the annual outburst of festivity had disappeared like yesterday's fog. Gone from Meredith's mood was his usual sunny and optimistic outlook.

"Do you know what's happening right next door?" Meredith asked bluntly.

"What next door?"

"In Hispaniola, the French side."

"I get no news up here," Hartley said as he took a bite out of a slice of bread.

"They're slaughtering white people. Men, women, and children. Eyewitnesses say that some of the killing crews are carrying around with them the heads of white babies to remind the beasts to show no mercy."

The two men ate in thoughtful silence.

"They say that some ten thousand white people have already been butchered. Men, women, and children. Hacked to death in public. Children ripped from their mothers' arms and put to the sword. Awful. Reprehensible."

"I don't think it's likely to happen here, do you?"

"We've come close. But the one thing that stops them is fear. Fear of what we'd do to them. I think it's time to hang another head."

The two backras ate in silence for a few minutes.

"That's what I'll do. I'll hang a head today," Meredith said with decision, daintily wiping the corner of his mouth with a napkin. "I'll have it put where everyone going to the fields can see it."

"But how do you know anyone will do anything that deserves the death penalty?"

"Here the death penalty is not deserved, it's applied. And I'm the one who applies it."

Hartley was turning over the idea in his mind, trying to grasp the philosophical difference between "deserved" and "applied," when Meredith abruptly changed the subject.

"I know you've been taking your woman to your bed

every night. There was a chap some years ago who did that on another plantation. One night they had a quarrel before they went to sleep. Know what she did?"

Hartley shook his head and stared hard at the older man.

"She cut his throat as he slept."

"Phibba would never do that to me," Hartley said sharply.

"That's what this fellow used to think. Now he knows better, doesn't he?"

"I don't know," Hartley answered. "Does he?"

On that disagreeable note, the two men parted. Hartley headed for the stables, his footfalls crunching against the stony road that coiled around the great house and flowed like a dried-up riverbed across the pastures and cane fields to lance into the thick, green woodlands and disappear into the foliage. It was such a still morning that a man could not help but ask himself what he was doing here and other philosophical questions about the meaning of life and where everything seemed to be headed.

That was the sort of heavy thinking Hartley was doing as he strolled toward the stables where his horse should be saddled and waiting for him. No one who saw him that morning could guess how deeply he was thinking. Most likely they would think he was looking around him like an inquisitive cat, that the beautiful prospect he saw spread out against the skyline did not arouse him to a secret profundity. But that was where the ordinary onlooker who could see no deeper than the vest a man wore on his way to a soiree would be utterly mistaken. For inside the heart of a man like Hartley was intricacy and a bottomlessness of understanding—or so he believed.

Really, a man of depth and substance was like an iceberg, showing only a frivolous white tip to the world while the vastness of his being and character lurked underneath unappreciated, unacknowledged, and known only to himself.

By the time he reached the stables, he was feeling profoundly philosophical.

That evening as he cantered home he passed a recently severed head impaled on a pole at the beginning of the trail the slaves used to reach the fields of the plantation. When he asked Phibba if she knew whose head it was, she said it used to belong to a Coromantee slave named Quamin who was always trying to escape.

As he'd said he would, Meredith had applied the death penalty.

CHAPTER 14

Two years flew past.

Although still a young man, Hartley Fudges had already learned that the years do not pass at a uniform pace, that some creep past like sickly turtles while others come and go with the thundering gallop of racehorses. But since his love affair began with Phibba, the time Hartley spent in Jamaica took wing like a bird. It was Phibba who made the difference. Nothing else had changed in his life. There was the usual turmoil in the breeze, and all throughout the passing years the same fretfulness of spirit and edginess of temper that Hartley found when he first landed in Falmouth was ever present like the smell of salt air from the distant girdling ocean. But his heart felt different. And although he still did not love the island, he no longer hated it.

The years also passed without the abrupt climactic changes that a European such as Hartley expected with the passing of time. The land experienced only subtle changes in the blooming of certain kinds of flowers or fruits, and all throughout the island the days paraded past wearing the same green foliage all year, unglamorous and unchanging like a shopkeeper's apron. There were some mild changes in the rains and in the nighttime temperature because of the altitude of the plantation, but these were so slight that they were hardly noticed.

Then the inevitable happened: Phibba got pregnant. When she first told Hartley, he received the news with dread he tried his best to conceal. He took a long walk by himself the first morning after she told him the news, trying to sort out his true feelings, worrying what his father would say to having a brown grandchild and how such a one would look on the wall of the family mansion where the generations of dead Fudges, wearing the halters of gilt frames, peered out captiously at the living climbing the staircase. He had the oddest feeling that he had befouled the generations of his family. But by the end of the third day he was reconciled, and the love he felt for Phibba overcame the prospect of fathering a changeling child with her that would look absolutely nothing like the previous generations of Fudges.

One night he and Phibba took a stroll through the grounds of the plantation and had a long talk about their feelings. It was an oddly uncomfortable moment between them and required him to say things he was not used to saying to a woman. He was beset by a feeling of utter absurdity as though he was reading lines belonging to a character in a bad play.

At one point in the walk, she turned to him and asked bluntly, "You don't want Phibba to have de baby?"

Hartley was so taken aback by her directness that for a few seconds he had no answer and could only stare at a distant mountain as if he saw some expression on its inscrutable green face that mesmerized him.

"Now, Phibba," he said soothingly, "I didn't say that. I didn't even think that. What I said is that any child you have for me will look quite different from anyone else in my family."

"So you think our baby going look like monkey? A so you think?"

"I think nothing of the sort! Stop trying to put words into my mouth."

Night fluttered over the fields and mountains that loomed in the distance. In this oceanic darkness, the only light visible was the phosphorescent wakes of swarming fireflies.

"You always say dat. But dat make no sense. How can man stuff words into anyone's mouth? Tell de truth. You wish dis baby never come."

"I never said that!"

Phibba began to quietly weep, her chest heaving as if she were drowning. Leaning against his shoulder, she wept like her heart was broken. Hartley took her into his arms and rubbed her back, which is something she liked him to do, while she sobbed convulsively, her cries primordial and jumbled and with the inarticulateness found only in fresh grief.

"Phibba," Hartley whispered in her ear, "you don't understand."

"Me understand," she gasped with a shudder of self-revulsion. "Me is a black woman, a slave. You is a English lord, all high and mighty. You come to me like a god. Me come to you like a goat. You don't love me. You say so, but you don't mean it."

"I do mean it, Phibba," Hartley said earnestly. "I wish I could prove it to you."

It was an ugly, emotional scene, and all throughout the melodrama, Hartley Fudges felt like he was floating disembodied and removed from himself even as he held her and whispered regrets and consolations. Eventually, she quieted down and the two of them embraced in the darkness as a puffy yellow moon glided over the mountains without a sound and dusted the fields with the color of saffron. Then the two of them, arm in arm as if trying to prop each other up, made their way in the soft moonlight, towing fuzzy intermingled moon shadows behind them as they headed toward the great house.

The baby did not last very long. Phibba miscarried in her ninth week and passed a bobble of blood presumed to be the child. The Scottish doctor said that the commingling of white and black blood was never healthy, and even if the child had come into the world, it would probably not have survived infancy.

"It look to me dat all blood is red," Phibba said waspishly.

"That's because you have no medical training," the doctor snapped.

"It looks red to my eyes too," Hartley said.

"I think I'm through with both of you," the doctor said petulantly, standing up and opening the door for them to leave.

In the third year of his exile, a letter from England appeared on Hartley's doorstep. It had taken three months to reach Jamaica and it seemed to Hartley a nearly miraculous artifact from another planet. He seized it like a starving man who hasn't seen food in weeks and hurried to his room to read it in peace. Phibba was there, cleaning.

"What dat?" she asked as Hartley tore open the envelope and extracted the letter.

"A letter from England," Hartley said.

Taking it from him after a token resistance, she examined the letter upside down and sniffed the stylish copperplate hand in which it was written. Hartley took back the letter from her and stroked it as he would a kitten.

"Who write it?" she asked.

"My father."

"So read it so me can hear him talk too."

She settled on the bed and made herself comfortable while Hartley read the letter from the foreign paterfamilias. This was what it said:

My dear Hartley,

By now you know that the man to whom I gave you a letter of introduction has been killed and his place taken by another. No doubt this unfortunate succession has been of some inconvenience to you that I pray might have been made bearable by the high esteem in which the world holds the family name of Fudges. Confident in this belief, I hope to one day receive a letter from you confirming that you are settled in some office worthy of your ample talents and energetic temperament.

However, that is not the purpose of this letter, which has far more somber news that I know you will deeply regret as much as many people do here in England.

Your brother Alexander is dead, carried away by typhoid fever, leaving his young wife a widow whose immense grief is scarcely made tolerable by the family condition in which she now finds herself. Our physician estimates that she is in the third month of her pregnancy but calculates her prospects of delivering a live child to be excellent. Since the outcome of this issue affects your own family position so far as inheritance of title and holdings are concerned, I have been advised by our lawyer to notify you promptly of what has occurred and what, given the uncertain outcome of childbirth even in robust women, is likely to occur should some unforeseen consequence be visited upon the child and its mother. If perchance the issue of the birth is female or stillborn, your position in the succession of this family would rank you as my heir and your replacement of me upon my death be legally assured. However, that is an eventuality, which in spite of the advantage to you, I can only hope, for my benefit, is still many years distant. Of course, if the child is male, as the issue of your brother, he would be entitled to inherit everything I own and you and your possible future offspring would have no claim upon my estate.

I do not know what to advise you to do or even how I would proceed if I were in your shoes. If I were settled well in Jamaica, I would continue in that position until I saw how matters turn out. Be assured that as soon as anything occurs that would affect your succession to my title and inheritance of my estate, I will immediately advise you. In the meantime, may God love and protect you and return you safely one day to England.

"Me no understand," Phibba complained. "What 'im say?"

"He says my brother is dead."

"Me sorry. Who kill him?"

"Nobody. He died of a fever."

Hartley felt a momentary urge to confess to her the truth about the duel he had arranged in a scheme to kill Alexander, but he thought better of it and said nothing.

"What de last part of de letter mean?"

"It means that perhaps I should consider returning to England," Hartley said softly.

Phibba looked at him with a flash of terror in her eyes. But she hung her head and said nothing.

* * *

It was a time of uncertainty and wild talk, the first few years that Hartley spent in Jamaica. Manumission was in the breeze, and from serving meals to the white man, the slaves picked up scraps of news at the dinner table and began to suspect that they had already been set free by the white man's king but that Massa was keeping the truth from them. The talk among the white men openly at mealtime was of the agitators for emancipation in England who were clamoring for the abolition of slavery, and the slaves misunderstood the fragments of information carelessly scattered by their masters. Out of the discontent blew a murderous wind.

Periodically, there were outbreaks of violence throughout the island, some noticeable enough to be a footnote in a history book, others involving incidental murders that warranted only local news among a people whose sensibilities had been hardened over the years to rampant cruelties. But every now and again would come an eruption of anger and brutality that would fizzle out but leave behind a terrible scar on the humanity of onlookers.

In this troubled time, for example, there was the murder of a dray cart owner who delivered shipments from overseas that landed at Falmouth.

Hartley and Meredith were riding the plantation grounds when a strange slave came rushing up to them crying murder. The two backras rode to the scene of the crime to see what the commotion was about and found the dray cart operator slumped on the ground in a widening pool of blood. His throat had been cut. Whatever goods he had been transporting were gone and the cart was empty except for splotches of blood splattered everywhere over its wooden seat.

"Don't you recognize him?" Meredith said. "It's the chap you bought your slave from."

Hartley stared at the man, unable to wrench his focus from the lurid wound in the man's throat which had been sliced open from ear to ear, giving the bizarre appearance of a clown's painted mouth gaudily opening up in his neck.

The two backras walked around the stranded dray cart, their hands on the pistols tucked into their waistbands, starting at every suspicious sound, while the man remained slumped on the ground where death had left him and the two mules munched on overhanging bushes with the abstracted air of library browsers.

"Untie the mules," Meredith said. "We'll take them to the plantation."

"What about him?" Hartley asked, pointing to the dead man.

"He's beyond help. But we can always use good mules."

The two men bustled around the cart and soon had the mules tied to their horses and were trotting down the rugged hillside trail that trickled into the plantation property.

"What'll happen to his body?" asked Hartley.

"If he has family, they'll come and collect it. Otherwise nature will eventually swallow him up. Look, she's already gone to work."

He pointed to the sky where the turkey vultures, known in Jamaica as John Crows, had begun the ceremonious circling waltz of death, dropping closer and closer to the ground where a fresh meal lay soaked in a gravy of blood.

"That's why it's against the law to shoot John Crows," Meredith explained. "They're Jamaica's undertakers. In a week, only bone will be left of the poor chap. The rest will be devoured by insects, rats, John Crows."

They rode on in silence.

"This is a hard land," Hartley finally murmured.

"People die in Europe too," Meredith said, "not only in Jamaica."

"They do die," agreed Hartley, "but they die differently. And their dead bodies aren't left lying on trails."

"Sometimes after a big battle, the corpses lie untended for weeks," Meredith said.

They rode back to the plantation, leading the mules behind them. As they dropped off the mules at the stable, Hartley wondered aloud to Meredith, "Do you think Cuffy is behind this?"

Meredith reacted with surprise: "Your former slave? Why on earth would you think that?"

"He hated that man. He threatened to kill him."

"People are always threatening to kill someone here. It's part of the island's heritage."

They walked toward the great house, chatting amiably about how things were different in Jamaica and England.

Over time, Hartley Fudges became keenly aware that his relationship with Phibba appeared to others in the plantation society as a grotesquerie. Occasionally he would see himself and Phibba together as others did and he would wonder what on earth ever possessed him to dote so extravagantly on a woman who was obviously very different from him in every conceivable sense. What on earth was the Earl of Fudges doing with Phibba from West Africa? It was the variant of the baffling question that the French writer Marcel Proust would have one of his lovelorn characters ask himself in his lamentation at the end of a tumultuous love affair—how could he have become so passionately involved with a woman who was not even his style?

It is an unanswerable question. The roots of love lie buried deep inside the psyche. True, Phibba was a statuesque woman with a compelling beauty and a lively manner that was captivating. But Hartley had met such women before and they had not affected him like Phibba. She had him in such a thrall that he simply could not stay away from her. Once or twice he tried to insert a wedge of time between his visits to the slave quarters or Phibba's to his room on the second floor of the great house, but inevitably he would find some reason for hurrying to her side. And when he was with her, he wanted to be nowhere else.

Meredith took Hartley aside one day and told him in a not unkindly way that women like Phibba were sometimes known to alter a man's judgment with bush teas and herbs.

"Has she been feeding you anything that tastes odd?" Meredith inquired. "Any liquids, soups with a bitter aftertaste?"

Hartley bristled at the suggestion that Phibba had captured his senses with the witchcraft the slaves called *obeah*. "How can you ask me a question like that?" an indignant Hartley replied.

"It was just a thought," Meredith answered gruffly, walking away.

"I haven't been obeahed!" Hartley yelled at the retreating backra.

Without looking back, Meredith gave an absentminded wave before he disappeared around a corner.

Hartley could not figure out why he was so drawn to Phibba. He simply could not explain it, but she tugged at his heart with a physical force such as gravity or magnetism. He remembered a dialogue of Plato where the philosopher theorized that a man used to be a creature of two parts before the gods separated the halves at birth. Since that calamitous day, the two halves have roamed the world looking for the missing part to whom they crave to be rejoined. It was one explanation the Greeks had for homosexuality, but to Hartley's mind it was even more applicable to the desires of men and women. Phibba was part of him, and he of Phibba, and only when connected by the isthmus of donkey hood were they once again conjoined into an undivided continent. It was a frivolous carnal geography, but it was the only explanation that made any sense.

Phibba knew nothing about this bizarre theory that Hartley had constructed to explain their odd relationship, nor did she hold the equivalent in the private chambers of her heart. She lived in a world where capriciousness and unexplainable strands of destiny governed the fate of all, and she had learned to accept anomaly, coincidence, and even miracle as part of the world's everyday bounty. On the day she was captured, she had taken the right fork of a jungle trail and had stumbled into the ambush of slave traders, a misstep that would prove ruinous to the rest of her life. Now that a backra loved her and she him, she had no reason to ask why. If a brick fell on her head, there was no reason. If a rose petal fluttered into her lap, there was even less. In a world of chance and uncertainty, blessings and blights will come and go like summer rain and should not be questioned.

That was how Phibba saw her love affair with Hartley.

CHAPTER 15

The year 1808, which came and went like any other, had the distinction of being the year after slavery was officially abolished in England by an act of Parliament. This cataclysmic change in the mother country seemed to have no impact on the peculiar institution in Jamaica. The plantation society dug in its heels and deployed its formidable lobby to defend to the death its way of life.

One evening as a grainy twilight grudgingly gave way to darkness that spilled like bottled ink over the Jamaican countryside, a ragtag group of six men squatted in a rough clearing. Most of the men were barefoot, clad in ill-fitting rags, and armed with machetes or crude clubs. One toted a makeshift *assegai* or spear made with a knife blade wedged into a shaft of wood. The men did not speak, but only waited as still as stone.

The terrain around them was clumpy and overgrown with shrubs and bushes covering a countryside of egg-shaped hummocks. The land appeared impenetrable, the bushes were so thick, but here and there dribbling through the vegetation were the faint imprints of footpaths that the men knew by heart and could follow to the glow of starlight and the waxy light of the half-moon.

The men were all young and black and in the nearly impenetrable darkness they were so still they might have been mistaken for rock formations or tree stumps. One of the men stirred and clambered to his feet. In his right hand he held a spear whose blade had been polished so brightly against a river stone that its cutting edge seemed to be cocked in a sinister grin.

"Ready?" the man who had just stood murmured.

The other men got to their feet without a sound and with the spear carrier leading the way, they melted into the dark background of the bushes and disappeared down the throat of the night.

They padded through the thick underbrush like a pack of wolves. Soon they came to a cut-stone wall some unknown slaves had laboriously erected over the years. At the wall, the spear carrier halted until the men were huddled close enough to hear his whispering.

"Walk where me walk," the man urged. "When we reach inside, show no mercy."

"No mercy," the men intoned like priests at a liturgy.

The leader picked the time well, and on his signal, the six men scampered across the trail, climbed over the cut-stone wall, and darted on the side of the main road to the plantation using as cover the hedges and bushes lining it. Ahead of them loomed an enormous wave of darkness that marked the presence of the great house.

They slipped inside the house through a door an inside henchman had left unlatched. The house dog, a massive big-chested brute, had been fed some sleeping herbs by another conspirator in the household and was snoring raucously as the men stepped carefully past him. One of the men chopped the dog viciously on the head with a machete, killing it as it slept without drawing even a yelp. Then the men climbed the stairway stealthily, pausing every now and again when the floorboards popped or the stairs squeaked. Soon they were on the second floor, where the backras slept.

The assassins fanned out down the hallway and, at a signal, slipped inside the dark doorways as noiselessly as the shadows of swooping birds of prey.

After a breathtaking moment, from the different bedrooms came the splattering sounds of hollow whacks as the sleeping backras were savagely chopped with machetes. Anyone standing in the hallway could hear the distinctive skull-cracking sound made by these murderous blows. The flash and thunderclap of a pistol shot and the sound of shouting erupted from a room. A breathless moment later, Hartley Fudges, still clad in pajamas, was hurled violently out of his room, and dragged down the hallway with a rope tied around his neck. Outside, the night rang with a noisy clamor as dogs and watchmen came running to the great house, their shadows dancing erratically on its masonry walls from blazing torches.

The killers, with Hartley in tow, raced downstairs to the first floor of the great house and escaped through an open window, barely evading the milling watch. Hartley, the rope around his neck nearly suffocating him, trotted meekly behind his captors and was led toward a dark slab of dense woodland.

Without hesitating, the assassins plunged into the woods, following a trail only they could see. They did not talk but every now and again the entire party would stop and listen to the night to hear if they were being followed. As he was dragged along and stumbled over roots and bushes, Hartley was thankful that Phibba had been assigned to work the mill for the night by Mahoney, as an act of spite, for the intruders would surely have killed her if they had found her in a white man's bed.

They traveled the whole night, slipping through seemingly impenetrable underbrush until they came to a switchback trail that zigzagged across the face of a thickly wooded mountain and emptied into a grassy plateau on which several shacks and huts had been cleverly built in a pocket of trees and bushes so as to be virtually invisible from afar. The layout of the shelters was roughly circular, and in the middle of the compound were the ashes and charred wood that were evidently the remains of a communal bonfire. After their wearying trek from the plantation to their hideout, the band of men settled down on the grassy plateau with exhaustion. One of the men tied the rope around Hartley's neck to a tree. Some of the men fell into an immediate sleep; others who had been splattered with the blood of their victims tried to clean themselves off with leaves they ripped off bushes.

Hartley could not imagine why he had been spared and not slaughtered like the others. As the sun beat down on top of the mountain and the day dragged past, he was left sitting by himself tied to the trunk of a tree and mainly ignored except for the occasional grim flicker of a look he got from passing men. When he tried to question any passerby about why he had been brought here, he was warned to shut up if he valued his life.

As he got used to his surroundings, Hartley began to notice that for such a slipshod hideout, which had the disheveled look of a slum, there was a surprising discipline and military preparedness to the camp. He observed a regular changing of the watch that was carried on throughout the day. Without being prompted, someone would collect a weapon and disappear into the bush, and a few minutes after he had gone, the lookout he had relieved would slink out of the thick shrubbery, find a vacant spot in the shade, curl up, and immediately fall asleep. Everything was surprisingly military even though Hartley got the impression that the people were simply sauntering around with little to do. A few hungry dogs, their ribs chiseled on their bellies by starvation, stalked around the campground desperately sniffing the ground for something to eat.

The sun, meanwhile, was scorching and in spite of the rope around his neck and the discomfort of the heat, Hartley had just dozed off when someone woke him up by kicking him in his rib cage, untied him from the tree, and, leading him to one of the sagging huts, shoved him roughly through the doorway. As his eyes grew used to the interior dimness, Hartley looked around and saw a figure on the ground staring up at him: it was his former slave, Cuffy.

The boy had grown into a man. He had gotten taller and more muscular, and all the baby fat had melted from his face. Hartley was stunned at first, and he could only stare with bewilderment.

"Massa, how you do?" Cuffy greeted him sarcastically.

"What're you doing here?" Hartley sputtered.

"Dat's not what you should ask. You should ask how come you still alive."

Hartley was at a loss for words, so he said nothing. Cuffy stood up, approached him, and said in a sinister, taunting tone, "Ask me why you still alive."

Hartley scuffed at the dirt floor of the shack with his big toe. He'd left his room so suddenly that he hadn't had time to put on his shoes and had been barefoot since his abduction. The soles of his feet were sore from a long night of walking. He was miserable from a lack of sleep. To argue with Cuffy seemed futile.

"All right, then," Hartley said softly. "Why am I still alive?"

"Good question! Why you still alive? You still alive because I want it. Dat's de only reason you still draw breath." Cuffy moved closer and glared hard at his former owner. "What else you want ask?" he sneered.

"I have to ask, I suppose," said Hartley, "why you want me alive."

"Very good, Massa. Very, very good," Cuffy mocked.

He took an exuberant turn, imparting a shiver to the floor and walls of the wattle-and-daub shack. Before either man could say another word, someone appeared at the doorway and spoke in a strange language to Cuffy, who snapped at him and made an impatient gesture for him to go away.

Hartley glanced out the window, which had no glass but was merely an opening in the wall, and noticed for the first time that there were one or two women scattered among the men in the rough-and-ready campground. He spotted a bamboo lean-to against an outcropping of rock from which drifted the smell of smoke that identified it as a makeshift kitchen. The slopes of the surrounding hillside were planted in yam and other ground produce, and all the inhabitants of the camp were besmirched with dirt and clad in tattered clothing, giving them the scruffy look that came from outdoor living.

Cuffy yelled out the window in his African tongue, and two women fanned the fire coming from the kitchen to dissipate the smoke that was coiling off into the sky.

Turning back to Hartley, Cuffy said abruptly, "Me keep you alive because we have one question to ask you."

Hartley blinked rapidly, like a man suddenly dazzled by sunlight.

"You may ask me any question you like," he said softly.

"Why won't a gentleman fight a duel with anyone but another gentleman?"

Hartley was stunned. Squirming uneasily, he struggled to regain his composure. "What kind of question is that?"

"Answer it!"

After a moment's thought, Hartley said, "Well, he can't very well duel with a fishmonger, can he?"

"What name fishmonger?"

"Someone who sells fish."

"So why won't a gentleman fight a duel with him? Because de man sell fish?"

Hartley sighed with exasperation. "Because gentlemen only kill other gentlemen unless there's war declared. Then they kill anybody who wears the uniform of the enemy—even a fishmonger. That's just the way gentlemen are raised."

Cuffy seemed agitated to hear this pronouncement. He paced to the window and peered out moodily at the slumbering camp. "I want you to learn me how to be a gentleman," he said abruptly.

"But why?"

"So you and me can fight a duel."

"Fight a duel? Over what? And why would you want to fight me of all people?"

"Because you de enemy. And you think you better than me. So, first me become a gentleman. Then you and me fight a duel and prove who is de better man."

Hartley pretended to be thinking seriously about this preposterous scenario, while Cuffy stared at him intently.

"But why?" Hartley asked. "What did I ever do to you?"

Cuffy's face suddenly hardened. Standing by the window, he beckoned to Hartley to come over. "You see dat chicken?" he asked, pointing to one scratching near the ashes of the bonfire. "Dat is not de perfect chicken. Dat is de imitation chicken, no so?"

Hartley was mystified. "Yes," he said carefully. "At least, according to Plato."

"Because of you, I'll never get de opportunity to be de perfect slave."

"But why?"

"Because you set me free—you and you damn freedom."

A thin silence intruded between them. Finally Hartley said, "I thought I was being generous with you."

"To cheat me of de chance to be perfect is not doing me favor."

Hartley felt suddenly peeved and blurted out, "No matter whom you ask, everyone will tell you that what I did for you was kind and merciful. You can bend and twist that any way you like, but what I did was good."

Cuffy was staring at him intensely. "You learn me to be gentleman or me kill you right now."

Hartley stared at him with astonishment. "But how do I do that?"

"You must know," Cuffy snapped impatiently.

"This makes no sense," Hartley said feverishly.

"Dere's an old saying in Africa, *If you want to understand de lion, become a lion*."

Hartley's head was spinning as he tried desperately to think. He could tell from the look on his face that Cuffy was on the verge of exploding. What he needed to do, thought Hartley, was to humor his former slave until he could sway him with reason. There was a madcap logic behind Cuffy's rage. Obviously, he didn't grasp Plato but misunderstood him just enough to be befuddled and confused. If Hartley proceeded cautiously and tactfully, he might be able to turn the silly argument on its head and come to an entirely different conclusion.

Hartley gave a loud sigh as if he were being forced to do something against his better judgment. He sagged visibly as he spoke. "All right," he said quietly. "I'll teach you to be a gentleman."

Cuffy nodded curtly. "And when me is a gentleman, we fight a duel on de fields of honor to de death."

"If you say so," Hartley mumbled.

"I say so," Cuffy snapped. "Begin right now. What me must do?"

Hartley stared at Cuffy, his mind racing. Cuffy was looking back at him with a murderous intensity.

"Well," Hartley said, "to begin with, you don't stand right."

"What wrong wid how me stand?"

"You slouch. Gentlemen never slouch. Here, look at me."

As Cuffy watched him suspiciously, Hartley stood erect like a soldier on parade and did a stiff-legged turn around the small shack. He felt like a fool as he demonstrated the correct posture of a gentleman, drawing on exercises he and his brother Alexander used to perform as children when they played army using wooden guns. He was also remembering some lead toy soldiers he'd collected as a child and how they were always molded in a straight-back posture. With limited room inside the shack, Hartley suggested that they move outside for practice.

As the sun rose higher in the sky and the warm exhale of the tropics blew over them like a damp breath, Hartley and Cuffy stomped around on the occasional level stretch of ground, practicing walking straight without a strut or a braggadocio hop. The camp began to wake up and here and there people watched them as they posed in place or strode from tree to tree. Cuffy, becoming aware of the attention he was drawing, started to ham it up like a bad actor rehearsing his stage movements. But while the people might whisper about the two men, no one laughed openly at them, and the one person who looked like he might break into an uncontrollable guffaw hurried back inside his shack and stayed there until the two men had stopped the practicing.

Aside from feeling like a fool, Hartley also felt put upon and resentful and several times he was tempted to call off the whole ridiculous game no matter what the consequences. But when he thought that this meant never seeing Phibba again, he quickly changed his mind and fell back into the game.

Cuffy was dead serious about learning to be an English gentleman and was quite prepared to kill Hartley over it. This point was driven home that morning when Hartley, angry over being part of a humiliating spectacle, muttered *sotto voce*, "Acting like a bird still won't make you fly."

Cuffy, who had been sitting nearby on the ground, stood up slowly, uncoiling like a poisonous snake until he was upright and within murderous range of his former owner. In his left hand he gripped the assegai, his fingers flexing restlessly around the shaft.

"What you say?"

Hartley, looking into Cuffy's eyes and seeing that death lurked only a heartbeat away, hastily backed down. "I didn't say anything," he replied disarmingly.

"You say something," Cuffy hissed.

"No, I didn't," Hartley blurted out cravenly. "I was just talking to myself."

"I hear you say something," Cuffy insisted.

Hartley quickly tried to change the subject by saying, "You're still strutting too much. A gentleman carries himself with pride, but does not strut."

"Me don't know what you mean by *strut*," Cuffy complained.

Hartley demonstrated by putting a boastful bounce to his step and striding back and forth in front of the shack as Cuffy looked on suspiciously. In a flash, the moment of peril had passed.

When the two had repeatedly practiced the walk of a gentleman until the strut was gone from Cuffy's gait, they took a break from the lessons. Hartley asked for some paper and a pencil to make a list of the traits of a true gentleman, claiming they were too many for anyone to remember.

"I also need some proper clothes instead of these pajamas," Hartley said, indicating the garment that hung over him like a shift.

"You can wear dat," Cuffy proclaimed. "You a prisoner of war. You must look different. Watch me now—is so de walk go?"

And he strolled from tree to tree glancing over his shoulder intently at his tutor for approval.

After the morning's lesson was finished, Hartley was tied

again to the tree and left sitting right in the middle of the handful of shacks with the scorching sun mercilessly raking the land. He tried to wriggle himself into the shadow of the tree but the rope around his neck was too short. People trotted by him back and forth, paying him no more mind than they would one of the dogs.

Left to himself, Hartley began thinking about his troubles. How could he make someone into a modern English gentleman? What did Cuffy think, that Hartley was God? Without doubt there was a protocol to being a gentleman. The problem was, it was a protocol so deeply etched in Hartley's consciousness that it lay beyond words or glib formulation. He knew it as well or as badly as he knew how to breathe. But if anyone had asked him to express in plain terms the act of breathing, he would have similarly stumbled. What Hartley instinctively knew but couldn't put into words was—to paraphrase an observation a Shavian flower girl named Eliza Doolittle would make some hundred years later—the difference between a man and a gentleman is not how he behaves, but how he is treated.

And how can one control that? What Cuffy was doing was treating life as if it was a masquerade, as if one could assume by playacting the aspects of a genuine gentleman just like that! But this was an absurd notion. Look at him, an ancestral member of the upper class by birth—it had taken the world twenty-three hectic years to make Hartley Fudges an exemplar of his class with all its accoutrements and niceties. If only he'd kept his mouth shut instead of bragging about his life as a *bon vivant* in London, about his imaginary heroics on the fields of honor and all the other glamorous cock-and-bull stories he'd fed Cuffy. Now here he was, about to be butchered if he couldn't make Cuffy into a gentleman. Using Hartley's own words, the former slave now occupied a universe that seemed a nightmarish mishmash of nonsense. For God's sake, look at what the brute had done to the teachings of poor Plato. Perfect chicken, my foot! Hartley laughed sardonically to himself at the profound ignorance of the bumpkin. He really was a fool.

Anyone noticing him bound to the tree would think that he was slumped over on the ground in the deepest despair. That's because no one else could see or feel the cataract of thoughts and impulses in which his whole being was aswirl. How could he make a social dunce like Cuffy understand the subtlety of pedigree and ancestry? How could such a one understand what upbringing contributed to a gentleman's life? He wouldn't understand the philosophers Hartley had read in their original tongue—Aristotle, Plato, Heraclitus, and so forth (Hartley himself had not understood them). He wouldn't understand the toilets of Eton much less its playing fields. And finally, he would never understand that vast conspiracy of subordinates and classes including maids, garden boys, stable hands, tradesmen, and shop helpers of every type and scope who, by genuflecting to the concept of the English aristocracy, were directly or indirectly the creators of Hartley Fudges and other pampered aristocrats.

Hartley was convinced that he was doomed.

During these days and nights he had plenty of time to think about his predicament and about what he could do to escape. The problem with escaping was that he didn't know where he was or how to find his way back to the plantation. With their knowledge of the terrain, the renegades would quickly track him down. Yet what choice or chance did Hartley have? He had none. He could only pretend that he was teaching Cuffy how to become a gentleman when, in fact, he was merely marking time while he tried to devise a plan of escape.

CHAPTER 16

What Cuffy wanted him to do was simply impossible: Hartley Fudges quickly came to that conclusion. Creating an English gentleman required years of upbringing and careful nurturing by a cabal of nannies, teachers, butlers that Cuffy would never have. Cuffy would have to be taught to speak in the posh accent of received pronunciation. He would have to be taught table manners and etiquette; for example, to not burp out loud in public; to give up farting, and if that required a sphincter discipline beyond his gifts, to acquire the art of passing wind noiselessly. He would have to master dressing like an English gentleman.

Hartley was at first in utter despair and just couldn't even imagine how such a thing would be possible. In fact, the very thought of it, the very idea, was too preposterous to even contemplate, especially under the decrepit and shabby conditions of the camp. But then it occurred to him that if he couldn't change Cuffy into an English gentleman of the nineteenth century, he would never have to fight a duel in which he might possibly be killed by his former slave.

And he had every reason to think that the boy would kill him. The encampment was no parliamentary democracy where decisions were reached after civilized, logical debate. A leader here got his way not by the force of persuasion but by being stronger, tougher, and braver than the other men. From his observations of the camp and the men who lived in it, Hartley concluded that Cuffy was their leader because, of all among them, he was the fiercest.

The only way Hartley would survive would be to outthink the man who held him captive.

Hartley had never been philosophical enough to wonder whether the world he lived in was sane or mad. It had a backbone of sense enough to make one accept life's anomalies. But now that he found himself held prisoner by renegade slaves, the leader of whom thought he could transfigure himself into an English gentleman simply by adopting the manners and outward appearances, he found himself on the brink of thinking the world quite mad. What he was faced with, Hartley decided, was a dilemma that would require superior thinking and strategy.

First, he would tell Cuffy that a person could not be a gentleman unless he looked the part, which meant dressing like a gentleman, not a ragamuffin. So while Hartley would pretend to be trying his best to turn Cuffy into a gentleman by changing the boy's speech, he would also be making the transformation as difficult as he could by insisting on picky details. Second, he would emphasize that a true gentleman spoke English flawlessly and always with received pronunciation. He knew that Jamaicans had trouble with the initial "h" and with the "th" combination—for example, they said "tree" when they meant "three." Hartley devised an exercise that consisted of common "th" words such as "the," "they," and "that," which Jamaicans typically pronounced "de," "dey," and "dat." Yet as simple as this islandwide miscue should be to fix, Hartley discovered that he could not instruct Cuffy to repeat these words a hundred times per day because Cuffy could not count to a hundred; in fact, he could not count at all.

Then there was a shortage of books. In all the camp not a single book was to be found. The camp was home to escaped slaves, most of whom could not read or write and had no use for books. Hartley pointed out to Cuffy that without books he would never overcome his illiteracy.

Two days later, after the men had returned from a night raid on a plantation, they brought back several books, including among them *Clarissa* by Samuel Richardson (1689–1761), the most bloated novel in the history of the English language. Its first edition contained 969,000 words tamped down into 1,536 pages, and tells its story in an epistolary narrative.

On the morning the book arrived, Hartley was summoned to Cuffy's shack and presented with it along with a book on etiquette. *Clarissa* had a single drop of blood on the cardboard cover but was none the worse for wear.

"You read dis book," Cuffy ordered.

"*This*," Hartley corrected.

"Dat's what I said."

"*That's* what I said."

"Don't repeat what I say."

Hartley sighed. He was still dressed in the pajama smock that he had been wearing since being abducted, and he spotted a small pile of clothing that the raiding party had just captured and deposited in a corner of the shack.

"I say," Hartley asked, "do you much mind if I try on some of those clothes to see if they fit me?"

"You have clothes already," Cuffy growled suspiciously. "Dese are my gentleman's clothes."

"These are pajamas!" Hartley said patiently. "I can't be wearing pajamas all day long. Pajamas are what a gentleman sleeps in."

"How come I don't sleep in pajamas?"

"Because you're not . . ." Hartley began, but caught himself just in time. "Because you're not quite ready for them just yet. You have to work up to pajamas. They come later. Please let me have some proper clothes."

Cuffy looked at him like a tailor measuring a customer for a suit. "Take some clothes," he said, gesturing at the pile.

But after Hartley had carefully selected a shirt and a pair of pants, Cuffy took them away and said he would wear them himself.

"But what about me?" Hartley wailed.

"You already a gentleman," Cuffy observed wryly. "You don't need to look like one."

That night Hartley began reading *Clarissa* by firelight to the band of escaped slaves. Hartley thought the book wretched and sanctimonious, filled with bogus pieties assembled in a holier-than-thou gruel, and did not want to read it. But Cuffy insisted that the whole camp be entertained by the captured backra, so Hartley had no choice but to read the book with as much enthusiasm as he could muster. At first, the group gathered around the bonfire seemed interested in the reading, and in the roseate glow of the fire the black faces were raptly focused on Hartley's words.

The first letter was dated January 10th and was from a Miss Anna Howe to Miss Clarissa Harlowe, the eponymous character of the novel. It began:

I am extremely concerned, my dearest friend, for the disturbances that have happened in your family . . . I long to have the particulars from yourself; and of the usage I am told you receive upon an accident you could not help; and in which, as far as I can learn, the sufferer was the aggressor.

Mr. Diggs the surgeon . . . told me that there was no danger from the wound, if there were none from the fever . . .

Mr. Wyerley drank tea with us yesterday; and though he is far from being partial to Mr. Lovelace . . . yet both he and Mrs. Symmes blame your family for the treatment they gave him when he went in person to inquire after your brother's health, and to express his concern what had happened.

Another couple paragraphs of this kind and the listeners had become restive with much yawning breaking out among them. Only Cuffy understood what the book was saying.

"A duel!" exclaimed Cuffy. "Dem fighting a duel."

"Yes," confirmed Hartley. "They were."

"But dey using swords instead of pistols," observed Cuffy.

"That's correct," Hartley said, yawning.

"But when we fight our duel, we'll use pistols."

"*If* we fight our duel," Hartley said crisply.

"Who say we not going to fight our duel?" Cuffy demanded.

"You know the rules."

"Cuffy must become gentleman," Cuffy said, hazarding his best received pronunciation. "Must learn to talk like a gentleman."

"Wha'?" contemptuously dissented a slave named Quashie. "You going talk like him?"

"Me going talk anyway me want," Cuffy shot back.

Quashie muttered under his breath.

"You don't like it?" Cuffy challenged.

Scowling, the man lumbered to his feet, his eyes fixed on Cuffy. The moment grew taut like a drawn bowstring. But then just as quickly the tension dissipated, and while the fire licked the hardened features of the men's faces with a playful glow, Quashie lowered his eyes and shuffled away into the night. With a baleful eye, Cuffy watched him until he disappeared into the darkness.

"Read more," Cuffy growled, sitting cross-legged before the fire.

Hartley read some more.

Over the course of the next few weeks, the attempt to transform an African slave into an English gentleman continued. Every day Hartley and Cuffy worked on received pronunciation, saying "tree" and "three" over and over again like men possessed. For the first few days, Hartley felt like he was involved in pointless labor and was overwhelmed by the futility of what they were trying to accomplish. He would finish the session disgusted at the results and feeling like a complete fool. Sometimes he would try to talk Cuffy out of the fool's errand they had embarked on and the argument would go around in circles to no avail. Hartley would say, with exasperation, "Why do we have to do this? What's the point?"

Usually Cuffy would reply offhandedly, "We have to fight a duel. Only another gentleman can fight a duel with a gentleman."

"But that's just the point! Why do we have to fight a duel?"

"When de time is right, I will insult you. I'll box your face before witnesses."

"But why?"

"Because dat's what gentlemen do."

"*That's* what gentlemen do, not *dat's*."

"I didn't say *dat's*. I said *that's*."

Another contentious pause intruded between them. Finally, Hartley broke it.

"What I mean is, what injury have I done you that requires bloodshed?"

"You made me look small before my people."

"I didn't mean to. It was all a misunderstanding."

"I could have been the perfect slave. I could have been Plato's slave."

"There's no such thing."

"Dere is too."

"*There* is too."

"My point, exactly."

Hartley sighed.

"Dat was pretty good, wasn't it?"

"*That*, not *dat*."

"Who's saying *dat*? Not me, I assure you."

Hartley had to admit to himself that Cuffy's use of such words and phrases as "exactly" and "I assure you" was a definite sign of progress. But they were making no headway on the issue of the duel, and it seemed to Hartley that he was doomed to suffer the ignominy of being killed in a duel by his former slave.

The night after he began reading by firelight to the escaped slaves he was unable to sleep. Nights in this mountainous countryside were moist with dew and generally cool from a sporadic breeze as light as the stroke of a feather duster, but Hartley was in great discomfort because of the rope tied around his neck that attached him to the tree. He lay awake many nights trying to think up ways of humoring Cuffy and his twisted obsession to become an English gentleman and fight a duel with his former owner.

The instruction continued, day in and day out. Sometimes Cuffy was eager to tackle a perplexing subject such as the conjugation of irregular verbs. But just as often he would become impatient and testy with Hartley for insisting on pinpoint accuracy in the use of grammar. One day Hartley was going over the forms of the verb "to be," drilling Cuffy in the positive and negative variations, when the boy exploded, "*I was, I wasn't, you were, you weren't*"—what kind of shit is dis?"

"It's not shit. It's English grammar."

"I can't stand it anymore. You drive me crazy."

"Nobody said it was easy to become an English gentleman."

"It's stupid."

"Personally, I'd never fight a duel with anyone who used *ain't* as a negative form of the verb *to be*."

"Why do people talk in de first place?"

Hartley did a turn inside the small shack. "I know a man who rejected a challenge from a bogus English gentleman who used the word *them* as a demonstrative adjective."

Cuffy looked worried, for he didn't have a clue what Hartley was talking about; in his imagination he thought that his former owner had an incalculably rich storehouse of expressions that were right and wrong and that a slave such as he would never even come close to matching. In this estimation, Cuffy was quite wrong. Hartley could not tell an adjective from an adverb and knew no more about demonstrative adjectives than did the man in the moon. But this particular construction had so baffled him when he was a boy at Eton that it had been seared into his memory by an unforgettable number of canings. Now he flaunted it, giving Cuffy the impression that many more esoteric admonitions stocked his mental shelves and he just happened to pluck this one from among many.

"Look at them big ground lizards," Hartley said coolly.

"Where?" asked Cuffy, who was not particularly fond of reptiles.

"Oh, I'm merely giving you an example of the use of *them* as a demonstrative adjective. It's awful."

And Hartley shuddered as a wave of revulsion washed over him like a ocean breaker. Cuffy watched, impressed. For the first time he almost gave up the attempt to become a gentleman.

"Maybe me can't do it," Cuffy muttered.

"Can't do what?"

"Learn received pronunciation."

"Are you finally coming to your senses?"

"I might as well kill you now and be done wid it."

"I wouldn't be so hasty, if I were you," Hartley said cagily. "You're making progress. Good progress, indeed. And if you kill me before I've finished the job, who will teach you what you need to know to speak and act like a gentleman?"

Cuffy turned grave. He sat down heavily on the dirt floor and looked morose. "All I wanted was a whipping every now and again. Why didn't you just oblige me?"

"Listen, Cuffy," Hartley encouraged him, "did you hear what you just said? *Oblige*, now there's a word you wouldn't have used a month ago. But now you use it off the cuff. You're learning to be a gentleman. Your vocabulary has grown immensely."

"I know," Cuffy said. "Some people say they can't understand me sometimes."

"They're just jealous."

The lesson being over, Hartley tried to leave, but Cuffy stopped him with the motion of his hand.

"I know that you don't intend to ever say, *Cuffy is now a gentleman. The time has come to fight the duel*."

Hartley moved to protest but Cuffy silenced him.

"I know that is what you intend to do. But it won't work. I have made up my mind. When I think I'm ready, we'll capture an Englishman. I will speak to him. He will tell me whether or not I'm a gentleman. If he says yes, we fight. If he says no, we work some more."

"But what if he doesn't know?" Hartley protested. "He could be from Ireland. He could be a Scotchman. They're both ignorant of the English. It's not a fair test."

"It's fairer than waiting on you to say if I'm ready."

The whole world had become a lunatic asylum, Hartley thought as he was led back to the tree where, his smock now grimy and soiled from continuous wear, he was tied up again like a trespassing goat.

CHAPTER 17

Life in the camp was hardscrabble and grim. There was little to eat—one starchy meal a day—and nothing to do. The renegade slaves, which was how Hartley regarded everyone in the camp, lived in a constant state of tension and jumpiness. Occasionally a sentry would sound a false alarm by blowing the *abeng*, a traditional instrument made from the horn of a cow and used by Maroons to warn of an approaching enemy. When that happened, with a brisk scurrying the campground would empty in a heartbeat as everyone would melt into the surrounding woodlands, leaving Hartley tied up at his tree, peering around with stupefaction. Even the dogs would disappear into the thick foliage.

The first time it happened, Hartley thought he was saved, but since he could hear nothing but the soughing of the wind in the trees, he glanced around wildly, hoping to spot someone coming to his rescue. But no soldiers came and the occupants poured back into the camp chattering excitedly, making jokes about the stupidity of the watchmen who could not tell the difference between the footfalls of stalking soldiers and the scampering of wild boar.

Cuffy himself came and examined Hartley at the tree. He walked around his former owner, looking him up and down carefully, and said, "You did not cry out for help. Dat's what saved your life."

And to demonstrate his seriousness, he hurled his makeshift spear with a savage blur of his arm, sending the weapon flying across the campground and burying the blade into the trunk of a fringing tree, where it quivered on impact with a hollow thunk.

Cuffy retrieved the weapon and walked over to where Hartley sat on the ground begrimed almost beyond recognition, his pajamas wrinkled and dirty and splattered with mud, making him resemble an animal that lived in a burrow. After another long searching look, Cuffy ambled off, turning to say over his shoulder, "This morning we work on *th* as in *three*." And a little later on, one of the warriors came and took Hartley to teach Cuffy another lesson in the art of speaking like an English gentleman.

As the days of ridiculous lessons passed, Hartley became impressed by Cuffy's ear. He picked up the nasal pronunciations of a posh English accent easily, and after three weeks of intensive practice, the former slave began to sound like a stuck-up English gentleman. Among the camp word spread about Cuffy's new accent and everyone marveled at how different the former slave sounded. He still did not look like an English gentleman, mainly because he was not dandified enough, having neither the proper clothes nor the accoutrements. Moreover, wig wearing was the hot style of the day, but Cuffy had no wig. And later, when a raiding party returned with a wig, it looked preposterous when perched on his head.

Yet with all the refinements he attempted, Cuffy still seemed a sham Englishman. If one could not see him, he sounded—or had begun to sound—vaguely English. But when he showed himself, his clothes seemed slipshod and patchy, like the garb of an out-of-season John Canoe dancer.

Meanwhile, the change that had come slowly over their leader made an impression on others in the camp, who began sounding English themselves by aping his speech. Phrases like "Jolly good," "I beg your pardon," "You don't say," "Old chap," "Old bean," and "I say" began spreading infectiously around the camp like hoof-and-mouth disease among cattle. Most of these Johnny-come-lately speakers sounded like caricatures of an Englishman. Only Cuffy sounded authentic.

This daily tutelage between Hartley and Cuffy would begin with an exchange such as:

Hartley would enter the shack after knocking on the frail door, and say, "Good morning, old bean. Are you quite ready to begin?"

"Yes, I do believe I am. What shall we do today?"

"I thought we ought to make a fresh run at the subjunctive."

"Capital idea. I simply haven't quite gotten it yet, have I?"

"It is one of the most difficult constructions to master. Even the experts have quibbles among themselves about it."

"By Jove! Do they really?"

"Use of the subjunctive correctly is a critical measure of class in England. The common man doesn't use it properly because he doesn't understand it."

"Poor benighted chaps."

"Of course, speaking good English doesn't help you be a better butcher or tradesman."

"Nor a better fishmonger."

"Exactly. Now, shall we get cracking?"

"Yes, let's."

Anyone eavesdropping outside the shack would have

wondered if the source of this chitchat was a pair of lunatics. Anyone actually seeing the tatterdemalion white man and the curiously dressed black one, whose britches were overly snug and who wore no shoes, would have been convinced of it.

The better at sounding English that Cuffy became, the nearer drew the duel he was determined to fight with Hartley. It occurred to Hartley that he still had only one defense—finding fault with Cuffy's mimicry of an English gentleman. No matter how much miscellaneous loot raiding parties brought back from the plantations they attacked, no matter how many pants and shirts for men, wigs and various pieces of jewelry, Hartley was always of the stated opinion that Cuffy looked ridiculous. Nothing Cuffy tried on, Hartley would insist, looked good on him or made him appear to be a realistic gentleman. The exchanges on the subject that they had went like this:

"Now, how do I look? Like a proper gentleman?" Cuffy would ask, parading around in some of the latest clothes brought back from a plantation that the rebels had burned down last night.

Hartley would smirk with obvious contempt and chuckle to himself loud enough for Cuffy to hear, which would cause the other to swell with anger.

"What're you trying to say now? That I don't look real?"

"No, you don't. You look ridiculous."

"I don't like to be told that I look ridiculous. I hate looking ridiculous. Find another word, because I don't like that one."

"Preposterous, then. Outlandish."

"I don't like those words either."

Hartley would stroll around the freshly bedecked Cuffy, like an art connoisseur appraising a new painting.

"It's just not right. You just look . . ."

"Don't let me hear you say that word."

"What word?"

"The word you were about to say. I don't like them word."

"You mean, I don't like *that* word. Remember the lesson about using *them* as a demonstrative adjective?"

"What's wrong with how I look? I look like an English gentleman."

"Not to me, you don't."

"But you can't say what's wrong. All you say is that I look ridiculous. What you need to say is why I look ridiculous."

Hartley sighed.

"And I don't like that sound either."

And then Cuffy would pout as they continued to bandy words and opinions back and forth about how authentic or inauthentic he looked.

One day the truth came out. They had gone through the usual preliminary sparring about how Cuffy looked when the conversation took a new turn.

"It's because I'm black, isn't it?" Cuffy asked angrily.

"I've never seen a black gentleman," Hartley said quietly. "And my family is hundreds of years old."

"In all of England there are no black gentlemen?"

"None that I know about."

"How can that be? In all of England?"

"I don't know. I just know that there are no black gentlemen in all of England, Scotland, and Ireland."

Cuffy paced up and down. They were outside his small

house. Everywhere around them the day's work was being done. Some men sat around in the shade of trees, cleaning their weapons. Some others were preparing the meal for the day. Others were laboring in the ground provisions field, building the mounds for growing yam. Suddenly, Cuffy stopped and stared at Hartley as though it was the first time he was actually seeing the Englishman.

"There's nothing wrong with Cuffy," he declared. "There's something wrong with England."

"It's you who are black."

"England is blacker than me."

"Than *I*," corrected Hartley. "Remember, the unstated part of the sentence is *than I am black*."

"Go back to your tree," Cuffy said contemptuously. And he waved for a guard to come and take Hartley away.

As he tied Hartley to the tree in the middle of the camp, the man, who had been picking up the new way of talking, declared in a phony English accent, "What what? How are we now?"

"Oh, shut up," said Hartley.

"A bit rude today, aren't we?" the fellow said genially. He was humming "Rule, Britannia!" written by James Thomson and set to music in 1740 by Thomas Arne. Its chorus was:

Rule, Britannia! Britannia, rule the waves:
Britons never shall be slaves.

It was a jingoistic jingle known to almost every Englishman in 1808. When he was bored, Hartley would occasionally hum it or sing the chorus. He didn't know exactly why, but even in his pitiful condition, singing that chorus about the global hegemony of the English never failed to make him feel better. In his present predicament, the thought that he belonged to a nation that ruled the world bucked up his spirits. It was another of his habits that the escaped slaves around him picked up. And now, with no idea what the words meant, the slave tying this Englishman to a tree was humming the chorus of that chauvinistic song.

Hartley squatted on the ground, resting against the trunk of the tree. It was only a matter of time before he would have to face Cuffy in a duel. But he was comforted by the thought that surely an Eton old boy, a university graduate, could figure out how to get out of his present fix. His best chance to slip away would be late at night when the camp was sleeping, with only posted guards dispersed around the perimeter against the rare possibility of a night attack. The English, like certain tribes of American Indians, did not usually fight at night. They preferred, in the European style, to line up in their dressy splendid uniforms and, during broad daylight, march within range to exchange volleys of lethal gunfire with the enemy.

One day, after another lesson, Hartley again asked Cuffy why they had to go through the stupid experience of a duel.

"It's the principle of the thing," Cuffy said airily, as if he could hardly believe his ears.

"*Principle*? You got that from me. Even now, you can't tell principle from a kangaroo."

"What's a kangaroo?"

"Precisely my point."

Cuffy did not get the point. The truth was that he didn't exactly know why he wanted to fight a duel with Hartley.

Men often want things without knowing why. All he knew was that he had been deprived of respect because of Hartley. If his master had been different and more understanding, Cuffy, the perfect slave, could have been the talk of the plantation. Generations would have remembered his name and perfection. But all that fame and applause had been ruined by Hartley and his heartlessness. Now no one could say that once there had lived an unmatched slave named Cuffy who was so perfect no model of him existed in Plato's afterlife.

The white man had ways of immortalizing his own. The books that talked if you knew how to read them, the scraps of paper that brought news from across the sea—these were the instruments that made the white man live forever, long after the memory of his deeds had been laid waste by the passing of the generations. What did Cuffy's people have to preserve their own stories? The best they had were *griots*—whose songs about spectacular deeds and heroic men and women preserved the lore of the ages. But any memory that depended on one who breathed was frail and corruptible. When the griot stopped breathing, his song died. Books did not breathe; paper did not breathe. The white man lived forever on an endless plain of eternity; the black man appeared, lived, and vanished like an insect. What was fair about that, when the black man was more than equal to the white man?

These were the ideas that Cuffy was pondering. Hartley, meanwhile, hadn't a clue what the other was thinking.

"I asked you," Cuffy said sharply, "what's a kangaroo?"

"It's an animal that lives in Australia."

"Where's that?"

"You don't know where Australia is?"

"Dat's why I asked."

"It's a country far away on the other side of the earth. Actually, it's at the bottom of the earth."

"How can that be?"

"The world is like this," said Hartley, picking up an orange off the ground. "We're here." He pointed to the top of the fruit. "Australia is here."

"The people hang upside down? Why don't they drop off?"

Hartley sighed. "I don't know why they don't drop off. I imagine some do."

Hartley had decided to cut his losses. There was no way he could explain to Cuffy why Australians didn't fall off the upside-down earth like overripe mangoes. To tell the truth, it was one of the axioms of modern living that often puzzled Hartley too but which he simply accepted.

He returned to the lesson with a disingenuous vigor that belied his confusion.

All these contentious exchanges had done was to convince Cuffy that he needed to come up with some other measure of whether or not he had become enough of a gentleman to be worthy of being killed by one. What he lacked in formal education, he more than made up for in imaginative thinking. And over the course of the next few weeks, he came up with a scheme for verifying that he sounded sufficiently like a gentleman to pass for one.

It occurred to Cuffy that a true test of how he sounded would be if a stranger who could not see him mistook him for English because of how he talked. He shared his thinking with no one. But what he had in mind was to capture a white man and have him listen to Cuffy and Hartley talk without being able to see either one. If he thought that both voices belonged to Englishmen, then Hartley would be forced to treat Cuffy as an equal and face him in a duel.

Cuffy did not know it, but many years later Alan Turing (1912–1954), a gay English technology wizard, would propose a similar test to gauge the intelligence of a computer. The Turing test was based on an old parlor game called "Imitation" in which a man and a woman were locked in separate rooms and fed questions by guests to whom they gave typewritten replies. The object of the game was for the guests to tell the gender of a respondent by the answers. (In 1950, the Turing variation to this test placed a computer and a human in separate rooms. Guests were then prompted to ask questions and try to tell human and machine apart by their replies. If the questioners could not tell from the answers which was the computer and which the human, the machine was approximating human intelligence.)

All Cuffy needed to put his plan into effect was a white man who could unknowingly be used as a judge. It took a raiding party three attempts to return with a suitable candidate. The escaped slaves were used to killing white people, not capturing them, and on the first two tries their prisoners died on the way to the camp from wounds they suffered in being abducted. The third time the party was returning from a raid empty-handed when like a godsend they came across an indentured servant, a white man newly arrived on the island. He was a coarse little man and reminded some of the slaves of a rodent, perhaps a two-legged coney, an animal resembling a rabbit and one that has been extinct on the island for years.

No class other than the slaves in the plantation society

was as wretched as the indentured servant, who was usually white. In exchange for free transportation to the foreign land where he would work, the indentured servant pledged his labor for a period of around seven or eight years. At the end of his servitude, he was usually given a lump sum of money or a piece of arable land on which he was encouraged to settle. The few who did could count on little more than a grubby subsistence from their small holdings.

This particular indentured servant was a common man from Newcastle, who had little family in the world. If he had remained in England, he would have worked as a day laborer for the rest of his life, doing backbreaking work for a pittance. He was as far removed from being a gentleman as he was from being a brontosaurus.

On the morning of his abduction, he had just landed in Falmouth the day before and had spent the night sleeping in the outdoors. This morning he intended to find out where his indentured master resided and to report for service. All this was on his mind when he had been wandering down a rutted marl road hoping to encounter someone from whom he could beg directions, his future master not having met him at the landing wharf as they had agreed many months ago. Instead of obtaining directions, he was abruptly seized and tied up and led toward the camp in the cockpit country.

The captured man, who said his name was Eugene Price, did not know that he had landed by bad luck in what was an unacknowledged no-man's-land in the undeclared war between the slaves and plantation owners. So when he was surrounded by an armed party of twelve warriors looking for white people, he felt a mixture of terror and astonishment. And when he was taken roughly into the makeshift camp of shanties and huts that provided an outpost of refuge for the escaped slaves to wage guerrilla warfare against the English, he could hardly be blamed for thinking that he had blundered into an outlandish game whose rules he didn't understand.

The strange ritual this Englishman was put through mystified him. He was blindfolded and taken to a section of the camp in which there were two houses side by side. He was curtly asked to listen to the way each man talked and say which one was English. After he listened for a few minutes, Eugene Price scratched his head and mumbled, "I dunno, governor, they sound a bit alike to me."

"You mean we sound the same," one of the English voices cried ecstatically.

Price figured from the reaction that he'd said the right thing. He asked to listen again, and after hearing several more sentences spoken by both voices, he confirmed that there were two lords, one in each house.

"I bet I can tell you where they went to school too," said Price loftily. "I'm not exactly sure about this, but I think they both went to Eton, and afterward, to one of those high-and-mighty universities such as Oxford."

Both men emerged from the houses and Price saw with a sinking heart he had been wrong: one of the men was a savage African, the other was a proper aristocratic bugger. He was about to begin a litany of apologies for his mistake when he inferred from the situation and the chatting men that the black one, who was obviously the guv, was very pleased with the answers he had given.

Then the oddest of all things happened: the black man slapped the white one across the face and snapped, "Choose your weapons, sir!"

"It doesn't matter how you sound," the white bloke squirmed. "I told you before, there are no black gentlemen."

"There most certainly are!" insisted the black chap. Turning to Price, he asked in a friendly voice, "Aren't there, sir?"

And the whole argument seemed to crash to a halt with everyone staring hard at Price.

For a long indecisive moment, Price had a creepy feeling that everything was hanging in the balance, that his next few words would make the difference between life and death. He looked from one face to the other, fumbling for a clue to the antecedents of this quarrel. Then he took the plunge.

"Why," Price squealed ingratiatingly, "there certainly are black gentlemen. I never met one meself, mark you, but my cousin's wife's sister said her 'usband, poor chap now dead and gone, used to work for a black pooh-bah by the name of Lord 'igginson as his equerry—that's the name they give the man that takes care of a lord's 'orses, and this 'igginson was one of those big muckety-mucks and black as the ace of spades."

"See!" the black lord cried triumphantly.

Hartley looked at Cuffy and said evenly, "You don't understand, do you? A man is not a gentleman because he tells the world that he's a gentleman. He's a gentleman because the world tells him that he's a gentleman."

A look of anger ignited Cuffy's face. "Tomorrow," he said venomously, "you either meet me on the field of honor or I'll shoot you down like a dog."

Hartley shrugged and muttered defiantly, "I'll meet you. But you still don't sound English." He sat on the ground, still tied to the tree, as the evening thickened over the land, and wrote letters of the alphabet with his finger in the dirt.

Price did not know it then and never did afterward, but he had unwittingly made the right guess. By saying what he did, he saved his own life while dooming Hartley. That same night as the raiding party departed in the twilight, Cuffy ordered them to drop off Price in some impenetrable woodland and spare his life. Before they left, Price came over to where Hartley was tied.

"Sorry, guv," he whispered. "I think I might have said the wrong thing. Did I?"

"You certainly did. What could you have been thinking?"

"I wasn't thinking anything in particular," Price squealed. "They always told us at the agency we should give the savages what they want. That's what I was doing."

The raiding party beckoned to Price and he scurried after them, throwing a furtive wave to Hartley and whispering, "God bless you, sir. Good luck!"

Then he was gone and the gaping silence swallowed the camp whole.

The communal fire that was lit every night burned down to a sputter of glowing embers, losing more and more of the people who usually came and warmed themselves. No one paid Hartley any mind, no one asked him to read from *Clarissa*. Occasionally someone stumbled without talking past the tree to which he was tied. Hartley would not even look up to see who it was.

The new moon made its appearance late and cast only a faint pearly glow over the matted countryside. Hartley would periodically snap awake and rise up off the ground to peer around him. He was doing this for the third time when he suddenly heard a voice whispering from behind a nearby bush.

"Donkey hood, can you walk?"

CHAPTER 18

When Hartley heard the voice of Phibba calling his nickname from behind a bush, he nearly went mad with joy. The camp was desolate and dark, dimly lit by a single ship's lantern on the ground whose serpent's tongue of flickering light made love to the enormous darkness. Everyone and everything was so still it was as if the world had been turned into stone.

Phibba, her dark figure moving like an animated lump of night, darted from behind the bush and cut the rope tied around Hartley's neck.

"Phibba!" he cried.

She put her finger to her lips and cautioned him to be quiet. Then taking him by the hand, she led him into the woods, pausing to allow their eyes to become accustomed to the darkness. He stumbled after her but they did not speak.

Eventually the woods seemed to thin out and soon they were slipping through the darkness as stealthily as two snakes, their breath coming in short gasps from the excitement and tension.

"How did you find me?" Hartley asked at one point.

Phibba put her finger to her lips and shushed him again. "Dere's a watchman here someplace. We don't have time to talk. Just follow me."

And with that she slunk through the woodland, still clutching his hand as he followed behind her.

He did not know how long they walked. All he knew was that the exhaustion he felt and the lack of exercise over the period of his captivity made him noisily gasp for breath. Phibba squeezed his hand, warning him to be quiet. After what seemed like hours, they came to a section of the woods where the trail was more clearly tamped down by footsteps and their progress was easier. By then his breathing sounded like he was being strangled, and Phibba stopped while they both sat down in a clearing that branched off the trail. She warned him not to talk louder than a whisper. The night around them rang with the cries of insects and the gargling intestinal sounds of croaking lizards. Fireflies threaded the branches of trees and bushes with strings of lights, and overhead they could barely make out the lidded cyclopean eye of the new moon.

The days and nights of his captivity had come and gone and left no footprints, so he asked Phibba how long he'd been there. She told him that she had been looking for him for over six weeks. When he asked how she'd found him, she replied hastily that she had some friends who'd helped her and had taken an oath to not say who they were.

"Dey say Cuffy want you to fight a duel," she said innocently.

"How did you know about that?" Hartley cried.

"Slaves know more dan you know dey know," was all she would or could say.

She suddenly stiffened and put her hand across his mouth and drew him down onto the ground until they were both clothed in the thickest sheets of night. Then he heard it, the distinct sounds of footsteps approaching, and a few heartbeats later a group of shadows flowed past them on the trail, no more than a few feet away. The raiders passed so close to where Phibba and Hartley were hiding that he could hear the belly of one man rumbling from hunger. Within a moment or two, the gang had ghosted past and disappeared into the woods.

Phibba immediately leapt to her feet, took Hartley's hand, and started off in the opposite direction down the trail. They walked steadily for the rest of the night, and daybreak found them on the edge of the area marked on maps as *The Land of Look Behind* and headed toward the distant high country of the plantation property. Soon Phibba stopped, and leading Hartley in the dawn light, she settled the two of them down in the shade of a flowering bush, where they made breathless love on the ground.

"Me miss me donkey hood," she whispered during lovemaking. Hartley was about to repeat his usual rejoinder, "Don't call me that," but restraining himself, he declared with a touch of bashfulness, "Me miss it too."

Phibba chuckled and they hugged one another. Within a blink, the two fell fast asleep, their bodies a tangle of black and white limbs that from a distance resembled a sleeping zebra.

Although the ground made an uncomfortable bed, the two slept through the hot belly of the day when the sun burns fauna and flora without mercy, slows down bees and speeds up flies and the only creature likely to be seen moving around the torrid countryside is the sly mongoose. But in 1808 there was no mongoose in Jamaica; this soon-to-become pest would not appear in Jamaica until 1872 when a man by the name of W. B. Espeut, in a stupid ecological miscalculation, introduced four males and three females to Spring Garden, Portland, intending the newcomers to check the growing population of brown rats. What Espeut apparently did not know was that the mongoose hunts by day while the brown rat prowls by night. The two consequently seldom crossed each other's paths and today compete, along with the mosquito, for the unique distinction of being the worst national pest.

They woke up as the sun was setting, and as soon as the darkness had regained its grip on the countryside, they set out again on their journey. On the way, Phibba whispered news about the plantation. Three of the Irish overseers had been killed in the attack, one had been badly wounded, and one had since fled the country. Meredith had survived and had killed one of the intruders with a pistol shot; after that, he crawled under the large canopy bed with a sagging mattress and into a great pocket of darkness underneath that hid him from the attackers.

At first Phibba thought that she would find Hartley dead on the property, but when daybreak brought no sight of him, she assumed that he had been taken prisoner—why, she did not know. The operation of the plantation had suffered a crippling hit with the killing of Mahoney, O'Hara, and Yates. Years of experience in sugar plantation management had died with them.

The couple trudged through the night, stopping only once to rest. Then morning broke and they settled down under a tree to sleep through another hot day. It was then that Phibba dug into her dress pocket and handed him a crumpled letter that she said had come for him.

Meredith, she explained, had given it to her for safekeeping in case Hartley should return alive. The handwriting on the envelope told him the letter was from his father, and sitting under the shiny limbs of a guava tree, Hartley read it in a whisper. It was a short and blunt letter, obviously written and posted in haste.

My dear Hartley,

I have some somber news to give you. Your nephew-to-be has been stillborn, leaving you the sole and true heir of all my property, possessions, and titles. I can add nothing to this revelation except to say, as many others in this vale of tears have previously noticed, that Providence works in mysterious ways. Come home quickly, I beg you.

When Hartley was finished reading, he and Phibba sat under the tree without talking while the dawn light oozed over the woodlands like egg white. Finally, Phibba asked, "What dat letter mean?"

"It means I must go home, and quickly."

"But what about Phibba?"

At first he did not know what about Phibba. As he sat there with the runny dawn breaking all around them, he was momentarily stunned and confused. Everything had happened so quickly. The whole world seemed to him to be topsy-turvy, untrustworthy, unreliable, and capricious. Phibba was sitting no more than two feet away from him, glancing around anxiously.

"Phibba will be all right. You don't need to worry 'bout her," she eventually said.

And she lay down nearby, squirming to get herself comfortable, when he came to a sudden decision.

"You can come with me," he declared bravely.

"Phibba live wid lords and ladies?"

"It'd be a constant war," he muttered, lying beside

her. "But we'll fight it to the bitter end. And we'll fight it together."

"If you say so," she said sleepily with no conviction.

"I do say so," he replied firmly.

The plantation and its sloping grounds looked the same as always and seemed to Hartley to be unchanged when they emerged from the final stretch of woodlands, climbed over the cut-stone wall, and stepped onto the property. In the great house Hartley surprised Meredith, who was in his office doing some paperwork.

"You're alive!" Meredith exclaimed, jumping out of his chair and rushing over to greet Hartley.

The cantankerous cook beamed at him with a toothless smile and fed him the first good meal he'd had in weeks. As he shoveled down the food, Hartley described his captivity and the way he was treated while Meredith listened studiously, interrupting every now and again to ask a question. Hovering near the table, the cook was pretending to be fussing around with dishes.

Hartley was immediately assailed by an overwhelming feeling of revulsion and hatred for the great house, the plantation, himself and everyone who played a part in it, and wanted nothing more than to get away from this incomprehensibly heartless and ghastly dungeon of hell. He saw everything to do with slavery and manufacturing sugar as evil and wicked beyond measure, and the sight of the walls of the banquet room crowded with ornately framed and stilted portraits of the detestable generations of absentee owners peering out at the phantom birdie of portraiture with an unconscionable smugness gave him the urge to set fire to the house and burn it to the ground.

He shuddered with a feeling of loathing that had no equivalent in words or expression, and Meredith, who was sitting across from him, seemed to be reading his mind because he said quietly, "It is what it is, no more, no less."

"It is what we've made it," Hartley countered. "God will call us to account."

"David Hume says there's no God. There's only us."

"*Someone* will call us to account, then."

"Wha' 'appen, Massa Hartley," the old cook intruded, "you don't love we food anymore?"

Hartley looked at her for such a long tenuous moment that she turned away with embarrassment. He had no reply to make, so he simply said nothing.

"Things are bad right now because we are shorthanded. But we'll come back, you'll see. Don't abandon ship. We need you."

"Yes, Massa Hartley," the cook intoned. "Don't dash we away."

Then she shuffled off into the kitchen, muttering to herself about the ingratitude of this new generation of backras.

"I have to go back to England," Hartley said. "I'm the new Duke of Fudges."

Meredith seemed genuinely pleased. He leaned over the table and shook hands with Hartley. "Congratulations, my boy," he said warmly. "I'm sure you'll bring honor to the title. I've always thought that if I weren't in charge of a Jamaican plantation, I'd like to be an English duke."

Hartley digested this revelation. "But you'd rather be doing what you're doing."

"I'd hate to be enslaved. But, God forgive me, I rather like being the enslaver."

Hartley finished his breakfast.

"I'm sorry, my boy," Meredith said coolly after a while. "I didn't make this world. I just live in it. I didn't make me, either. I can't help what I like."

"Neither can I," said Hartley.

An awkward pause intruded on their conversation.

"I just think we can do better," Hartley muttered, with a shrug. "I'm not sure what I mean, but that is the way I feel."

"I'm sure we can. But this is a very hard world and a very big one. It's impossible to fight it."

Hartley tilted his head to one side like a man deep in thought. Finally he said, "I'd like to take Phibba with me."

"You can have her for fifty pounds. We can settle up accounts if you really want to leave."

"I have to leave."

"I know, I know. You want to claim your throne while you can. And I don't blame you a bit. Let's settle up accounts."

The account ledger told a bare-bones story of the life of Hartley Fudges as an overseer on a Jamaican plantation. He had been in the employ of the plantation for a little over three years, during which time he'd earned close to £400. Altogether, by the time he paid for Phibba and for what he owed the plantation for miscellaneous services, he had about £200 left, just enough to buy him and Phibba a passage to England.

When he emerged from Meredith's office, Hartley was in a jubilant mood, feeling the exhilaration of a young man on the verge of overthrowing the circumstantial drabness of his life. Already his heart was softening not only toward Jamaica and the plantation, but toward the whole rogue world at large where people often ran amok over bagatelles and skin color was the overwhelming determinant of a person's future. He was in this lighthearted mood as he headed for the slave quarters to find Phibba. Night was falling like a feather and he could feel and taste the windblown tang of the distant sea.

He found Phibba sitting on the small wooden veranda of the board shack she shared with her father, staring into space as though she was trying to divine the future. The shack had no veranda chairs so she sat on the floor, her back propped up against the front wall of the house. Hartley sat beside her to the amused glances of slaves who gathered in small groups and were characteristically chatty at the end of another day.

"You packed and ready to go?" Hartley asked her.

"Phibba can't go to England with you, donkey hood," she said with a sorrowful sigh.

He handed her the bill of sale that Meredith had just given him. "I've bought you. You're now a free woman."

She fingered the piece of paper with wonderment and looked hard at the cursive scribbling Meredith had just written in ink, announcing to the world that for a payment of fifty pounds she belonged to Hartley Fudges who had now set her free. Being unable to read, she could only marvel at the power of what could've been the tracks of carpenter ants marching across the paper and accomplishing wondrous feats of magic.

"That paper," he said, "tells the world that you're free."

They had an argument about what it meant to be free and what she would do in England. Who would she know there but him? She would look like no one else. She would stand out everywhere she went and feel like a monster.

They paced around the room while the night bled dark over the countryside and they spoke about what he would do and what she would do, and sometime around midnight the two of them fell entwined on the bed where he slept fitfully with two loaded pistols at his bedside table.

CHAPTER 19

There was just one road to Falmouth, but it was a road only in a metaphorical sense. It twisted and coiled over parched hillsides and dreary swamps, lanced through clotted woodlands, and emptied like a placid creek into the occasional valley or pasture. The roadbed was an uneven surface of potholes, jagged fissures, and protuberances like cracked teeth. It was the same road that had brought Hartley to the plantation; now it was carrying him and Phibba away to England.

They began the trek early because even though the metaphorical road was the only way to reach Falmouth from the east, stretches of it were so abandoned and desolate that ambushes by escaped bands of slaves were common. Cartmen therefore preferred to travel this road in groups rather than alone, and when Hartley and Phibba left the plantation they were accompanied by two other carts, each manned by a driver and a sideman and drawn respectively by two mules and two donkeys. The wayfarers pulled out of the plantation premises long before the sun could claw its way above the sheltering mountains and begin to broil the earth with the tropical heat. Phibba rode beside Hartley, who got out frequently and walked when the little procession was climbing a hill and the donkeys or mules were obviously laboring.

It seemed to take forever for the travelers to clear the

premises of the plantation, dray carts being notoriously slow and pokey-pokey, and Hartley found himself urging on the overworked animals and mentally straining at the bit to put distance between him and the great house. Phibba was in a playful mood, and as the cart rattled along, she pointed at one of the donkeys and whispered coquettishly to Hartley, "Donkey hood," to which he replied with a put-on gruffness, "Don't call me that name." She giggled and made a face.

The journey began with the usual bantering among the men. When they started out the morning was still cool, and everyone was rested and in good spirits. But by the time they entered the first stretch of dense woodlands, the men had become quiet and watchful. All the talking and joke telling died out and was replaced by a jumpy alertness.

On an island, every road leads eventually to the sea, and once the little group of drays had emerged from the first woodland and had crossed the crest of the mountains, every eye could see the unwrinkled blue Caribbean ocean stretching like a starched altar cloth toward the horizon. Here the small caravan separated, one cart heading for a great house in the mountains, another for plantations in the valleys. Only the dray that carried Hartley and Phibba continued toward Falmouth. By midday the rugged cart on which the two rode was bobbing over tree roots and fissures and slowly descending the mountains toward the sea where the rutted metaphorical road intersected the main one that skirted the coastline.

The driver was a leery man and had a loaded pistol tucked into the waist of his pants. When his eyes were not fixed on the path ahead, they probed the surrounding thicket for signs of life with the quick stabbing plunges of a knitting needle, and more than once he thought he saw something and grabbed onto the butt of the pistol while his stare remained riveted on the passing shadows. But every time the shadow would turn out to be caused by the breeze or the antics of lizards, birds, or stray livestock.

Hartley was also keeping a constant watch over any bush or shrub that was big enough to conceal a man. He could not believe that he was getting away so easily, that in a few more hours, with Phibba at his side, he would climb aboard a ship bound for England. He was looking forward eagerly to the moment when the tallest mountain in Jamaica would slip beneath the waves and vanish from the horizon, and this detested land of hatred, turmoil, and confusion would be finally behind him. In the meantime, he was highly alert to the impending danger that might be lurking around the next corner or below the crest of the next hill.

They were halfway down the slope of a mountain with a cut-stone wall paralleling the road when a gunshot blasted the peace and the driver slumped forward with a glance of horror and plunged a finger into a pulpy hole that had suddenly opened up in his chest.

"Mary, mother of Jesus!" the man managed to cry just before he toppled off the dray with a death groan. His sideman took off downhill, screaming with terror, and was quickly swallowed up in the thicket. Hartley and Phibba were left alone in the dray cart staring in the direction from which the shot had come. As they gaped, they saw the face of Cuffy solidifying against the background of shrubs and bushes.

Dressed in a grab bag of mismatched clothing his gang

had stolen during plantation raids, Cuffy was a resplendent caricature of a comic book Englishman. He wore a pair of ill-fitting, baggy pantaloons; a shirt so tight that it squeezed a ring of exposed flesh out of his belly; and a purple sash that hung off his waistline like a peeling bandage. Nothing matched; every shred of his apparel clashed in a hideously mute war of rioting colors. Topping off the ensemble was an ugly flat hat with a vulgar cockade, like an overripe tomato, hanging off its brim. In addition, Cuffy had mastered the swagger of a patrolling busha—or so he thought—and with a malevolent expression he closed in on the cart while Hartley and Phibba stared helplessly. Almost without a sound, his band of followers, most dressed in the rags and tatters of the typical slave, seeped out of the woodland and encircled the small cart. Next to Cuffy stood his lieutenant, Quashie.

"Are you ready to fight our duel?" Cuffy asked in a taunting voice, speaking in the clipped nasal accent he'd learned under Hartley's tutelage.

"You know the rules," Hartley mumbled.

"Yes," Cuffy answered, "gentlemen only fight duels with other gentlemen. Well, now I'm a gentleman. And this is what I think of you," and he slapped Hartley hard on the face, snapping his head back.

Hartley stood glaring at his own feet. Phibba moved to his side protectively and held his hand. A light came on in Cuffy's face.

"We either fight a duel right now," he said softly, "or we kill your woman."

Hartley stared at him with disbelief. "I'll fight you," he said evenly. "But if I kill you, what will happen to us?"

Cuffy looked around at his men before gesturing to

Quashie. "If this Englishman kills me, I want you to let him go. Is that understood?"

One man said, "Him nah going kill you. We nuh have fe worry 'bout dat."

The other men nodded and smirked at the preposterous idea of their leader being killed by the Englishman.

"So it's agreed?" pressed Hartley. "If you die, your men will let us go?"

There were murmurs of assent among the group.

Cuffy was afire with excitement and eagerness, like a child at Christmas. He beckoned to one of his men who trotted over carrying a case of dueling pistols recently captured from a plantation. It was an elaborate set of Belgian pistols with geometric designs that looked like runic scribbles all over the barrel and handle, and it came in a box almost big enough to serve as a coffin for a stillborn baby. The inside flap of the cover was inscribed in several languages with calligraphic characters that said the same thing in Spanish, French, German, and English: *Pistolas de Duelo / Pistolets de Duel / Duellenpistollen / Dueling Pistols Set*.

Meanwhile, the other men were treating the duel as if it were a sporting event, and many of them engaged in the back-and-forth raillery of spectators at a football match.

Hartley examined the pistols carefully. The shooting mechanism was a flintlock, an invention that originated in the mid-1550s and was gradually being replaced in 1808 by the percussion cap, which was itself destined to be replaced by the modern bullet. The pistols were almost a foot long, weighed two and half pounds, and fired a lead ball through an unrifled barrel. Gunpowder was wadded into the bottom of the barrel by a rod and the spring-driven hammer (nicknamed the *cock*) tipped with a piece of flint. When the gun was fired, the flint struck a piece of steel known as a *frizzen* and made a spark that ignited the gunpowder. The result was a deafening bang as the lead ball exploded out of the muzzle of the gun at a murderous velocity.

Flintlock pistols were notorious for misfiring. Most were equipped with a hair trigger, and in the usual ready position, the hammer of the pistol was pulled all the way back. But while the pistol was being carried, it was a common practice to pull the hammer halfway back to allow for a quick shot. Often, the hammer set in this position would cause the pistol to prematurely fire—hence the expression "go off half-cocked."

As the two combatants went through the ritual of choosing a pistol and loading it, Phibba paced around anxiously, begging both of them to stop and consider what they were doing. Both men were breathing hard as if they could not get enough air. The onlookers were joshing with each other and placing bets on who would get off the first shot and where it would likely strike.

"What? De whole o' you gone mad?" Phibba shrieked as the two men continued to prepare for their encounter.

Quashie, swollen with pride because of his special role as second in this strange English ritual, was fussing about like a distraught innkeeper whose overbooked rooms were not ready for occupancy. He presided officiously over every particular of the ceremony. He had rehearsed every part of it and now finally his moment had come to show how much he knew about this English game that was shrouded in such complex habits and strange rules. Many of the watching men were openly jealous of Quashie and looked on sullenly. Yet in spite of themselves, all seemed caught up in the spirit of the moment.

"Why are we doing this, Cuffy?" Hartley asked his former slave, hoping to somehow talk him out of the folly he was bent on committing.

Cuffy answered with a venomous intensity: "You set me free! In front of everybody!"

Phibba, who had been hovering near the duelists, butted in: "Him set me free too."

"See dat! Is there no end to your heartlessness?" snapped Cuffy. "Must you destroy everything and everybody? Listen to me. I don't even know how I should sound when I talk. I sound like you, not like me. I think like you, not like me. First you stole my voice. Then you stole my brain."

"Blood don't have to shed here today," Phibba begged. "No reason for blood to spill. Donkey hood, say you sorry and make we go about we business."

"What's that you call him?" Cuffy asked suspiciously.

"Donkey hood."

Cuffy took a brisk, agitated spin around the knot of onlooking men and scolded Phibba, "How can you call an English earl *donkey hood*? Don't you have any respect?"

"Me respect everybody, even you," Phibba said fearlessly.

With some pushing and shoving and jostling, the men rowdily formed two ragged lines to create a shooting lane for the duelists.

Quashie asked, "De shooters ready?"

"Ready," Cuffy declared.

"I'm ready," mumbled Hartley.

"No, no!" Phibba screamed. "Dey not ready."

"Stand back-to-back," ordered Quashie.

Walking stiffly, the two men, their backs rigid and straight, their pistols clasped tightly against their chests, paced off the distance.

Phibba screamed, "Dis is madness! Donkey hood, nuh do dis!"

When the shooters stopped, Quashie blared out, "Turn and face your enemy."

Like windup dolls, the men turned mechanically.

"Take your aim," Quashie commanded.

The men took their aim, and for a second the duelists, the onlookers, and Phibba were frozen in a ludicrous tableau.

As he readied himself to fire, Hartley bitterly regretted sharing with Cuffy so much of the hearsay accounts of duels he had picked up from roaming the streets and bars of London. He tried to remember if he'd told Cuffy what others had impressed upon Hartley as the primary rule of the good duelist: don't be in a rush to get off the first shot. Most likely you'll miss and have to stand rigidly in position while your adversary takes aim to his heart's content. If you flinch or move in any way, your adversary's seconds are empowered by tradition to shoot you down.

As the two men aimed at one another from a distance of roughly thirty feet, Hartley was furiously telling himself to relax, to take his time and aim, to not be hasty, and all the while he was facing the pistol of Cuffy which was steadily pointing right at his head.

Just before Quashie gave the signal to fire, Hartley shuffled his feet, trying to plant himself securely against the kick of the gun, when something ghastly happened: his gun fired with a thunderclap that caromed off the next row of hills and noisily whiplashed over the scene of the duel.

In the ensuing silence that followed, Cuffy was standing erect and still like a garden statue made of stone. He gave no sign of a wound. He did not recoil from the impact of a bullet; no blood gushed out of him. Nor did the gun he pointed at Hartley in the least bit waver. From Hartley's point of view, the muzzle of the pistol gaped at him like a serpent's open mouth.

"Don't kill donkey hood!" Phibba cried in a quavering voice.

"Donkey hood," Quashie said sternly, aiming his own pistol at Hartley, "don't take another step. Stand and receive you shot."

"My gun went off accidentally," Hartley heard himself saying. "I didn't mean to shoot. It wasn't a real shot." Then he added lamely, "Stop calling me that execrable name."

"*Execrable*," Cuffy murmured. "What does that word mean?"

"Shoot, man! For god sakes, shoot!" urged Hartley.

"Hush you mouth, donkey hood," Quashie chided. "De man can take all de time him want."

"My name is the Marquis of Fudges. Now, shoot!"

"Don't shoot donkey hood," Phibba wailed in an anguished pitch.

With a malicious chuckle that sounded like the sadistic purr of a playful cat, Cuffy continued to train the pistol steadily on Hartley. "You ever see a more perfect slave than me?" he taunted.

"Shoot, damn you!"

"Nuh shoot donkey hood!" Phibba screamed at an even higher, shriller pitch.

"Answer me!" Cuffy barked. "Was I not the perfect slave?"

After a tense moment, Hartley replied, "If you say so," staring at his feet, unable to look any longer down the muzzle of the gun that was about to kill him.

"Don't move, donkey hood," Quashie warned.

Cuffy chuckled with triumph and the hand holding the pistol fell to his side. But then, his mood suddenly changing, he said savagely, "So why did you free me, you damn Englishman?"

He abruptly raised the gun and aimed it at Hartley again.

"No!" Phibba shrieked, jumping in front of her English lover. The gun went off and the bullet meant for Hartley pierced her chest, ripping open her heart.

"Phibba!" Hartley screamed.

It took her less than two seconds to hit the ground.

By then she was already dead.

The small ragtag company of men gathered around the fallen woman as Hartley knelt over her sobbing hysterically, as if that could bring her back. It was unnerving to the onlooking slaves to see a white man stricken with such profound grief over the death of a black woman. None of them had ever before witnessed a weeping busha, and to this spectacle some reacted with open scorn.

"Hush up you mouth, man," Quashie said contemptuously. "All de bawling in de world won't bring her back."

Cuffy snapped, "Mek him bawl if him want bawl."

Then he seemed to remember himself and his present condition, for he added in his best accent, "Of course, it's his prerogative to weep if he wishes."

Realizing for the first time what a fool he must sound like, Cuffy closed his mouth, looking gloomy. The other men began a clamoring about what to do with Hartley. Several asked Cuffy if they could kill him. One asked for permission to cut his throat. Another offered to disembowel the Englishman. A third wanted to cut his head off and attach it to a pole just like the backra would do if he had the upper hand. A babble of confusion arose as each man tried to give advice to Cuffy about what to do with him.

Oblivious to the threats buzzing in the air, Hartley remained on the ground bent over dead Phibba. He was still weeping openly, loudly, sucking in noisy globs of breath.

"What a way dis man cry like a woman," Quashie spat contemptuously.

"Shut up," Cuffy snarled, deep in thought. To Hartley, he murmured, "Sorry, Massa. Phibba gone to the land of the perfect chicken."

"Where is dat?" Quashie asked. "What you mean by *de perfect chicken*?"

Hartley stooped down to rearrange Phibba gently on the ground as if she could still feel discomfort from the rocks under her head. He wobbled to his feet and stood there shakily. "Please shoot me," he urged Cuffy.

"Why should I? You wouldn't beat me when I begged you to."

"Please, please shoot me," Hartley pleaded again in a small voice.

"You English people expect black man to do everything for you. Pick up after you, give you grind in the canepiece, polish you shoes, cook you dinner, and now shoot you too. Be a man, Hartley Fudges. Shoot youself!"

"Me will shoot him," Quashie offered.

"No," Cuffy snapped. "The only one here entitled to a shot is me."

"Is I," Hartley mumbled dully.

"Sorry," Cuffy said, red-faced. "The verb *to be* takes no object. I knew that too, damnit!"

Cuffy cast a final lingering glance at the dead woman crumpled on the ground and shook his head with what seemed to the small assemblage like a gesture of regret. With a wave of his right hand toward the woodland, he climbed over the stone wall, followed by his men.

"You dirty black brute!" Hartley exploded. "Come back here and shoot me!"

"You hear what dat man just call you?" Quashie gasped.

"I heard what *that* man called me," Cuffy corrected. "Let him scream. He must suffer too, like I did."

"How you suffer?" Quashie scoffed.

"You wouldn't understand," Cuffy said airily. "You're not a gentleman."

As noiselessly as shadows, the band of renegades slipped after Cuffy into the underbrush, leaving Hartley wailing and hurling insults after them to the empty skies.

CHAPTER 20

After the men had left, Hartley sat on the cut-stone wall and tried to decide what to do. It was a sorry-looking wall that appeared out of nothing and led to nothing. In a more ancient time it might have marked an important boundary of ownership. Now it was a meaningless relic of a forgotten dispute and as enigmatic as the bone of an extinct animal.

Hartley was in an angry and sorrowful frame of mind and every now and again he was racked by a sob. Sometimes he paced down the hillside and then abruptly raced back to touch Phibba all over her face and limbs like he was hoping to coax a flicker of life within her and bring her back. But it was no use; she was stiffening with *rigor mortis*. Her hands and cheeks were cold; her eyes were cemented shut. Sprawled out near Phibba was the dead driver attended by a buzzing cloud of flies.

Returning to the plantation was out of the realm of possibility. There would be too many questions asked; too many of his fellow workers were dead. No one on the plantation would likely mourn for Phibba—her mother being dead and her father half-crazed from rum drinking. She would be missed no more than a mule or cow or horse. Yet he could not leave her body on this desolate hillside for dogs, rats, and John Crows to eat.

Deciding that he had to bury her, he rummaged

through the dray cart for a tool to dig a grave. He found a rusty machete and tried digging with that, but the mountain was stony and the ground unyielding, and he barely made a scratch in the thin layer of topsoil.

Then he had an idea—he would hide her body in a thick grove of trees and cover it with rocks. He found a suitable depression in the ground that was hidden behind a patch of thick bushes, and carrying her there, he laid her out of sight of the metaphorical road and began covering her with rocks.

It took him all afternoon to bury her, and a curtain of darkness began descending on the hillside before he was finished. In building her grave, he was careful not to remove too many stones from the same stretch of wall for fear he would arouse the suspicions of curious passersby. Instead, he walked beside the wall, inconspicuously removing the stones he needed and hauling them back to the grave site. Then as now, a cut-stone wall was built without mortar, each stone carefully facetted by a hammer and hand-fitted. As long as he was careful, no one would notice the missing stones.

When the darkness came, he stood over the crude grave and muttered his last goodbye to Phibba. He wept and moaned in a blubbering way he thought undignified. But he could not help himself and was just thankful that no one was present to overhear his unmanly outbursts.

The moon climbed into the sky, and by its delicate glow he gave the body of the dead driver a push that sent it tumbling down the hill. Climbing into the driver's seat, he started across the bumpy road, the dray cart rumbling and clattering loudly in the emptiness.

He traveled until the moon had slipped behind a

mountain and the terrain became difficult to see. As the road leveled off at the coast, he pulled over, and settling down on a grassy roadside patch, he fell asleep. When he woke up the sun was already clear of the horizon and the moist air was getting sticky from the tropical heat. He started up again and after some few hours he crossed the Martha Brae River and the spires and steeples of Falmouth loomed against the skyline.

Making inquiries at the dockyard, he discovered that three ships were sailing today for England and he was able to buy passage aboard one because of a last-minute cancellation caused by the unexpected death of the passenger. He saw an omen in that—he would be leaving Jamaica in the place of a dead man, and he had many macabre thoughts about this aptness of circumstance.

A few hours later found him standing at the taffrail of a French-built barkentine watching Jamaica sink slowly into the green blue sea as the wind and tide nudged the ship gently toward the horizon. He exchanged no small talk with anyone but was silent and solitary in his grief.

He heard a small child say to its mother, "Mummy, why is that gentleman crying?" and the mother reply, "That is no gentleman. Gentlemen never cry in public."

The voyage back to England was plagued by stormy weather and took a little over three months. But the Hartley Fudges who landed in England was not the same as the one who had left three years ago. His heart had a dark and mournful side filled with thoughts and images and glimpses of Phibba. He spent one night in London before hurrying to the family mansion where he was reunited with his father. He passed the next few weeks presiding over the family's affairs as the heir apparent to the family dukedom. He fired a butler who had once been aloof to him, and he made unmistakably sure that all the staff knew who was destined to be absolute ruler over the family mansion.

Some few months after Hartley's return to England, his father was considerate enough to drop dead of apoplexy, leaving the dukedom and its riches to Hartley, his only surviving heir, while he was still young enough to enjoy them. A year later, Hartley married a woman of the old school who had many "not" virtues. She was not a fanatical churchgoer, not a conniving spendthrift, not a vain clotheshorse, and not a chatterbox. Altogether, she was not a bad woman, not rich but not poor, and not quarrelsome, being blessed with the contented disposition of a pregnant ewe.

With this woman as his wife, Hartley, now the full-fledged Duke of Fudges, settled down to live the life of an aristocrat and to breed a new generation of Fudges. He fathered five children, two boys and three girls. But the girls all died in childhood and only the two sons survived. His wife made Hartley an agreeable lifelong companion, and together they spent many sociable years burying daughters and raising two sons—one the designated duke, the other a spare. Hartley Fudges felt reasonably confident that his dukedom would survive the ages long after he himself had become a portrait on the wall.

It was a Friday evening in 1848, and Duke Hartley Fudges, now in his sixties, and his two grown sons were in the library of the family mansion drinking port wine and having a heart-to-heart. The Duchess of Not had retreated into her private chamber, for she understood that men gathering in the library around a bottle of port meant that no women were welcome, which was just as well because she had no taste for the braggadocio talk of drinking men.

Hartley had just finished telling a story of his three-year adventure on a plantation in old Jamaica, and although the boys had heard it many times before, they were just as attentive as if it were new. As usual, their father had become nostalgic about the adventures of his youth.

Yet the stories Hartley told were not entirely complete. He said nothing about his capture by the renegade slaves, about his makeshift duel with Cuffy, or his love affair with Phibba; nothing about Phibba rescuing him from Cuffy's stronghold or giving her life for him. Nothing was told about how he had mourned for Phibba by spontaneously bursting into tears several times on the voyage back to England. But he told his sons enough to lend an exotic appeal to his narrative. Yet he did not want to glamorize black people or hint to his sons that sexual affairs with slack black women were acceptable. Moreover, he would have been mortified if any of his family ever found out about Phibba's nickname for him. Duke Donkey Hood would never pass muster in Whitehall.

The two sons, George the firstborn and Richard the dispossessed, were facing radically different futures. George, under the grim rule of primogeniture, would get everything upon Hartley's death; Richard would be at the mercy of fate. The second son had discussed with his father the scant options open to him, but still didn't know what to do with his life. Richard despised the idea of being a clergyman. A military career was not to his taste. That left him with only one useful option: migration. But, unlike his father, he would not go to Jamaica.

By 1848 the plantation system in Jamaica lay in ruins. With abolition, many of the former slaves had fled to the mountains where they established villages far away from the waving seas of cultivated sugarcane. They disdained working on the plantations as paid hands, and the laws on the books meant to compel them to do so were unenforceable without the driver and his whip. In the eyes of the laborers the plantation was a wretched dungeon of hell where their forefathers had been worked to death. They wanted no part of it, no matter what the inducement. With the plantations shutting down, the great houses were abandoned and the fields of cane came under the domination of weeds. Jamaica's influence in parliament plummeted and the phrase "as rich as a Jamaican planter" disappeared from polite speech.

Hartley as a man in his sixties was quite different from the man he had been in his twenties. Aging does harden some men, making them crotchety and more set in their ways, but for the great majority the effect is just the opposite—the heart grows softer, the judgment wiser, the impulse kinder. It was this older, gentler man that Hartley, and men of his age, would have their own sons emulate.

The aristocratic Englishman is an oddity. His heart, soul, and sensibilities are covered by an armor plating of manners that makes it difficult to predict what he will do. He will have dinner with you and be most convivial and entertaining and afterward go to his room and shoot himself as if his suicide was simply late like an overdue bus. He fills his head with the litter and scraps of ancient cultures and knows many words without understanding.

His feelings are cocooned behind fortifications and every transaction he has with the world is ritualistic and bristling with hedges and provisos like a promissory note. He is at war with carnality and bodily functions. Form and style are as important to him as outcome and content, and this craving for perfection finds its fulfillment in his meticulous toilet training. Such was the architecture of Hartley Fudges's soul.

When Hartley first returned to England, he missed Phibba with a benumbing intensity. He thought about her every hour of the waking day; when he slept he dreamt about her. They had shared a ravenous appetite for each other's body. Sometimes he could smell Phibba, and taste Phibba and hear Phibba and see Phibba in all the vividness of a recurring dream. Over and over he replayed in his mind burying her in the bush.

He never shared this feeling of profound loss with anyone—not his wife, not his sons, not his drinking companions. No one who knew him had the faintest inkling that his mind was a museum in which Phibba and Jamaica and the plantation and Cuffy were stored and kept in a state of suspended animation.

In his old age, Hartley Fudges loved to stroll alone through the ornamental garden with its statuary frozen in the dynamic but motionless acts of hunting or leaping or gamboling behind bushes, every figure forever captured in the lifelessness of stone. In the solitude of his walks, Hartley secretly treasured being the thirty-first Duke of Fudges, one bead in a long necklace of dukes gone and yet to come. And when the new generations of dukes arrived, waiting to receive them like an old faithful nanny would be the family mansion.

To the English world, the family mansion was the ancestral home of an old, respected aristocratic line of men. To the colonial world it was the breeder of claim-jumpers, invaders, and glib usurpers. Under the doctrine of primogeniture, the mansion had hatched many generations of second sons who were blown abroad like airborne spores to infest foreign islands, archipelagoes, and continents. Already Richard was considering going to India, formerly the crown jewel of the far-flung British Empire.

Nearly everyone Richard knew who understood his circumstances urged him to go. If he was lucky, he would return to the mother country with a head full of memories to share with the emerging pupae of English second sons. If he wasn't, he would fall in battle trying to subdue rampaging natives and be memorialized, to paraphrase Rudyard Kipling (1865–1936), in an ironic observation like this: *Ten thousand pounds falls to ten rupees*.

It would be bad enough to be killed. But a fate worse than death would also befall him if he should perish at the hand of a Calcutta coolie.

He would look ridiculous, in a platonic way.

Perfectly ridiculous.